Lorali

LAURA
DOCKRILL

HOT
KEY
BOOKS

First published in Great Britain in 2015 by Hot Key Books
Northburgh House, 10 Northburgh Street, London EC1V 0AT

A CIP catalogue record for this book is available from the British Library.

ISBN: 978-1-4714-0422-1

1

This book is typeset in 10.5 Berling LT Std using Atomik ePublisher

Printed and bound by Clays Ltd, St Ives Plc

www.hotkeybooks.com

Hot Key Books is part of the Bonnier Publishing Group
www.bonnierpublishing.com

For my mum, Jaine, and my dad, Kerry.
Thanks for teaching me to imagine.
Love, Laura Lee (Chicken Monkey).

Lorali

PROLOGUE

There was a storm in my heart.
There was a war in my heart.

They had promised me everything on my tapestry. I would wear it forever. I was going to change. Transfer. From the white – translucent – slip I wore now: the tail that looked as though it belonged to any nameless fish in the underbelly. And I was going to *realise*. Become. I was going to *resolve*. I was to be cleansed as *something*. For real. I would have an identity. A form. And not just any. They said. It would be beautiful. *Beautiful*. They said. The best of any kind. I was royal. My tapestry would reflect that. They said. They said. In the development. During the resolution. That the colours and textures would be so vibrant that they would shine through the surface and project on to the clouds of the sky. The *sky*. That's how beautiful they would be. *That's* how *special* I was. It would be royal. Shine. Glow.

Illuminate. Violet. Purple. Green and sprawling like sea moss. Sea ivy. Rose. Like the coral. Silver. Like the chipped seashell that spirals up when I dance. Pearl. Oyster. Gold. Ink. And I would wear it. They said. And everybody would know about it.

Everybody.

There was a storm in my heart.

There was a war in my heart.

Because they had lied.

New air. For the first time. Rummaging. Like hands. In my lungs. It feels. Tugging. This new air. Overwhelming. Burning. Freezing. Fresh. On flesh. Stinging. Ripping. Muscles. Tearing. Scratching. I am dead. I am dead. I have to be dead. I have to be dead. From this pain. I am – not dead. No. Too much feeling to be dead. Filling. Instead. New. Oxygen. Heat. More burning. Lots. Blowing. Expanding. Gulping. Swallow. Do I swallow? I am exploding. I am exploding. My eyes. They are drying. This can't be right. This can't be. Can it? They didn't tell me about the eyes. They are drying out. Regret. Too fast. What have I done? Take me back down. Can't I? Blink. Blink. Stinging. New. Ripping. Blink. It's dry. This air. Like knives. Cutting. Salt. I feel the salt. I taste it. Now. My nose. Is it broken? Hydrate? I can't. Raw. Raw. Blister. STILL BURNING. My chest. Throb. My heart. Beating. Cold. Cold. Hot. I don't – I – my nose. I can't. Swallow. My mouth. My tongue. It's dry. It's . . . HAVE I MADE IT? WAIT, DID I MAKE IT? DID I MAKE IT? I DON'T KNOW. HELP. I DON'T KNOW. Swallow. Air. Tight. Tight. My – ears. The noise. Cracking. Cracking. Get out. All loud. Big. Churn. New noise. Deep. Big. My brain. The sea. The sea. Squashing. I can feel it. Every move. Crashing. Smashing. Freezing. Big

2

heavy head and skull. So heavy. My lungs. Still. In. Out. In. Out. Calm. Calm. Calm. *You can't go back. You know you can't.* Be still. New bones now. And every bone. Dragging. Heavy. Bold. Lift. Shhhhh. I can't. Struggle. Considerable. Wait. Are they? Mine? Legs. Oh. Oh. It's happened. The wave. The wave. I am not forever now Lorali. I have to swim. Or I'll drown. Swim like a Walker. Swim like I can walk. Walk. Heavy. Move. I can't. Move. Bulky. Drag. Like metal. Let go. Let go. I look down. I have . . . I do. I've got them. Two of them. Legs too. Legs. Feet. And toes. Toes. Toes. Feet. And heels. And ankles. Bone. Bone. Skin. Like they said. Forbidden. Mother. New. Skin. Veins. Blue lines. Purple. Red. Blood. Flowing through. Squeeze. Stretch. Flex. Step. Out of the wave. Out of the Whirl. Away.

I have made it.

I have made it. And then I fall.

PART I

RORY

THE EDGE

It's my birthday today. My chest faces the sea, my back against Hastings. My home. My dad and I started this tradition. Every year, on my birthday, even if it was raining, he'd skip off work early and we'd get a massive bag of fish and chips. My mum can't cook. She can bake, but can't *cook*, so we'd go, just us, and sit right on the cliff side looking over the water, right here where I stand now, watching the sea hitting the rocks. It was our thing. He would get himself a bottle of Carlsberg and me a can of lemonade and we'd say cheers and eat the chips and talk a bit. Sometimes we didn't say anything at all. That's how you know you're comfortable with a person. On my twelfth birthday he got two bottles of Carlsberg and one can of lemonade and he mixed the beer with the lemonade to make me a shandy. On my thirteenth birthday he didn't buy the lemonade at all. That night Mum smelt beer on my breath but she didn't moan because she knew I'd been with my dad. That was before he left for Spain. When he was still with my mum. When he was still being my dad.

I still like to do this on my birthday. I even get the Carlsberg too if Susan is working at the offy but if her dad's there I don't because I don't have fake ID. I don't buy a beer for him, like how people do sometimes when somebody's dead. Because my dad's not dead; he just doesn't give a shit.

For some reason, the air feels tight. The clouds feel like they have joined up to make a pillow, which is now suffocating our tiny town. Summer is over but there is still this trapped atmosphere. It's like the sky is holding its breath, waiting to blow its guts on us. The edge is the best place to sit because if you look straight ahead and if the weather is right, the sea and the sky merge perfectly together, seamlessly, so you can't see where the sky ends and the sea stops. Right now it's just a blotchy thick mass.

The seagulls are right knobheads round here too, but proper jokes if you've got the patience to mess about with them. You can throw the black ends of your chips to the sea as fast as you can and watch a seagull swoop it up seconds before it hits the water. A moment later and the chip would belong to the fish. Not the bird. Just like the view of the sea and sky, the line of separation is almost invisible.

Flynn and Elvis, my two best mates, had jobs lined up for them when they turned sixteen but that's because they are not expected to go to college like me. I'm the youngest by a few months and it felt weird them both being sixteen and me not. It was like they were in some private club that I wasn't invited to. But I didn't say that obviously. I'm meant to be starting college in two days' time and I am dreading it. I don't want to go. It's not that I want to start earning for myself or that I don't want to learn – I want to get out of Hastings altogether. Move to London. Or *anywhere*. I feel like the world has so much more to offer.

This can't just be *it*.

Can it?

Course, I never say that to the boys about wanting to get out. Elvis's parents, who are casino and Elvis Presley fans obviously, own the arcades down on the seafront and the big one on George Street, so Elvis has been stuffing the teddy bears in the glass boxes for a bit now and it suits him. He also earns extra cash at the weekends at the market, spraying the smell of 'leather' onto plastic fake-leather handbags, wallets and belts. 'Cow in a can' is what he calls it.

Elvis is a hustler. An alternative kind of smart. Street-smart. He never passed an exam in school but he could pick up a dead car off the roadside and fix it up. He always finds the little glitches in life and hacks his way in, like outsmarting the staff in every shop into somehow giving him a free pair of trainers, headphones, vouchers. I can't remember the last time I paid for a cinema ticket when I've been with Elvis. He has this town wound round his little finger, so why would he ever want it to unwind? Mum calls him a 'mover and shaker' because he has his fingers rammed in loads of pies but I think that's Mum's gentle way of saying she thinks he's a wrong 'un. Them two have never really seen eye to eye exactly, but that's only because she thinks he introduced me to *everything* that she doesn't want me to meet. Like fags and alcohol and, well . . . life in general. He will end up owning the arcades himself one day. We've grown up together. Since school. And no matter how cocky he is, for all the hustling and scheming he does, he always has my back.

Flynn, like me, is smart enough to go to college, but he just doesn't want to. Flynn lives in a converted lighthouse on the seafront with his nutty old granddad Iris. They turned the bottom of it into a wild little shop where they deal in antiques. Iris is as old as Hastings; everybody says he is mad but I don't mind him. Flynn does what he does. He feels much more comfortable around objects than people anyway, and although I sometimes worry about the idea of Iris influencing Flynn 24/7, I kind of don't blame him for keeping his head down and working at the shop. Chairs can't piss you off like people can.

They both finish work around six and then we're going to go out for my birthday. I say 'out', I mean, 'see how many sips of beer we can drink before we get thrown out of The Blue Anchor'. Or 'how much J. D. we can smuggle into The Serpent before grumpy Barry kicks us in the balls' – when really I think he should promote our mischief. Hastings got its bloody name thanks to smuggling. He should be supporting us keeping the tradition alive!

It's a wonky town, Hastings, built on cobblestone and disfigured brick. Sometimes it feels so sleepy but you know it's sitting on these secrets like roots under paving slabs. The weeds will soon start shooting through the cracks in the pavements like little worms of sprouting truth.

George Street is the main shopping street in the Old Town. People say it's *charming* but that's just a blanket word for *crappy* and *small* and *falling apart*. Mum says I don't appreciate it properly. The road is cobbled together with misfitting odd ends of stone; the shops are dinky and twee with old-fashioned fronts, beams and wavy glass windows. Other than the antique shops, teahouses and pubs, which seem to make up the majority of Hastings, there really isn't much on the strip for a teenager. If you walk up, which is the only way other than the sea, there are winding weirdo alleys, all bent like crooked teeth, and steps and houses shoved next to each other – too close, like overstuffed bookshelves. Slanted roofs, pokey chimneys, crumbling brickwork and windows and doors all weather-beaten and nibbled on by the hungry mouth of the sea air.

I live at the top of the hill and that hill, I swear to god, is so steep, it feels like you could kiss your shoes when you are walking up it.

But that's Hastings all over. Where I live is a curveball. It reminds you that the globe is round.

But it feels like the only place that exists on it.

I am throwing the black chip-ends to the gulls when Elvis texts me *Jack's coming*, which means he's managed to get the whisky, probably nicked from his nan's cupboard. Still, I'm not complaining. It's my birthday and I'm looking to get drunk; I collect the vinegar-and-oil-drenched wrapping paper of my bag of chips and walk along the stones back to the front.

And then, out of nowhere, as my mum would say, the heavens open up. Big swirling, rolling clouds, so grey and dense and heavy, and it's mad, like the sky is about to explode, and then thick marbles of rain begin to pelt from the sky. I start to run but running on pebbles is like running on porridge. My face is getting ripped off by the wind, my eyes are gushing with tears and the air has basically sucked all moisture out of my mouth and left me with a tongue like a lizard tail.

Just when I think it can't get any worse it begins to thunder. Hailstones now. The size of dice. *What?* My hair is a complete state already and I look like a bedraggled tramp. I pull my Nike jacket over my head and run under the legs of the dead pier for protection. It's got hazard tape all around it but I ignore it and duck underneath. I need a moment. I can text the boys, save my skin from being separated from my body, and stop myself from being turned into a human kite.

Under the pier it's wet too, but a lot drier than being out in *that*. I sit down on the pebbles and catch my breath, panting. I don't like it under here though, none of us do. Somebody burnt the pier down a few years ago and so now it just stands ancient and charcoaled like the skeleton of a giant mosquito. It's also not safe. It could crumble down on my head at any second – I can hear the creaking cries of its old aching, rotting body groaning in the wind. *Imagine if I died here*. Like this. All alone. Then again, I think I nearly had my heart vacuumed out of my chest in that weather, so it beats that.

There's something so weird about the ghostly memories that linger round the dead pier. I try not to think about it and reach for my phone. No signal and my battery is low. Stupid weather and stupid shit phone.

I can see the sea going crazy, the water slamming against the brittle legs of the pier, foaming and fizzing and spitting like a rabid dog. This is nuts. Where has this come from?

I decide to wait for the storm to pass. I start to read the graffiti on the worn wall behind me. I recognise some of the handwriting because I've grown up with these adolescent tags my whole life, the same anarchic angry scrawls that now mean nothing. I keep getting distracted by the angry sound of the sea though. It's rioting, wrecking itself like how a child hits itself in the face when it's upset. That is when I notice what looks like an elbow.

It has to be an elbow. Pointy and fleshy and human. It can't be anything else . . . a knee maybe? No, it can't be – why would a person be here? I start to frighten myself; I am not up for finding some dead person here today. Then again the pier is desolate . . . it would be a perfect place to commit suicide. Or it could be someone who went too far out alone and got scooped up by the tide?

I think I'll leave it: go now, face the weather and pretend I never saw it. But what if it's a *person* person? With a family. Or worse still, a child. *What if it's a kid?* I take a closer look: it is a small elbow. Shit. Poor thing. I don't want to find some dead *kid*. Not here. Not like this. Drop me out. I'm leaving. I'm going,

Arrrrrrr, but what if it's *not* a suicide but a *murder*? Nope, can't deal with this. It could be *anything*. Say somebody's missing? Then what? I'll have to live with knowing what I saw and not saying anything for the rest of my life. Like a coward. I am proper paranoid now. Oh please let me get some phone signal so I can call somebody and ask for help!

But then the elbow moves. It's *alive*. I am scared now, trembling. I gulp. Decide to move closer. I take my time, stepping carefully and cautiously. I slowly pick up a wedge of driftwood and hold on to it. I've practised this before, self-defence, with my baseball bat at home – hold the wood high, take a step, and then another and another and then another and –

It's a girl, about my age, completely naked. I drop the wood and let her eyes carry me towards her.

THE SEA

THE FLOATING HOUSE

Liberty is tired now. Old. This is the worst state I have seen her in. She needs painting, mending and improving but she never threatens to sink, or fails to glide on the floor of my wrecking waves. It seems, at times, like the whole of the ocean and everything inside it loves *Liberty* – or respects her, at least. Although she has been thrashed about and teased she has never capsized, never gone under. Her nickname is 'The Floating House' because she looks exactly like a vast Tudor mansion stuck onto a cabin and hull. Some think she looks ridiculous, bobbing about like a grand house that has slid off the edge of a cliff and manages to stay afloat; others find her appearance comforting or reassuring. But she makes everybody smile, no matter what they think of her. Even I know that no matter how much *Liberty* is done up, she will always slide back to her own ways; she is a creature of habit, a beast of comfort and won't change for anybody. Not even her boys: for all their effort, she remains a scruffy girl.

Despite *Liberty*'s magnificent size – her walls that seem to go on forever, her billowing sails that look like ladies' bloomers drying on a washing line – she has a certain familiar charm to her, a sense of detail and fragility that makes her feel cottage-like.

But like all mothers, though she appears harmless, when it comes to her boys, she is a weapon. She is a strong ship and the boys, her crew, they belong to her and she to them. Her anchor, an umbilical cord that reins them in like smooth maternal wisdom. We have a lot in common; her love, just like the ocean, is uncontrollable, never ceasing. It is wild and true. If I do say so myself.

Otto, a year before twenty, is eldest of the Ablegares and so naturally, by default, the captain. A warrior with a simple heart, he is looked up to and respected for his kindness, yet liked little. It seems the Ablegare boys will go to great measures to get any glimmer of attention or praise from Otto, but when he does reward them with this side of his personality it is heart-rending and powerful. Otto loves nothing more than to play. He lives his life like a child. Everything is a game, a match, a competition. For a pirate, he rarely shows his sword – he is much more interested in mind games. But once the knife is out, the games are over, usually in his favour.

Otto lives for two reasons: to laugh and to protect his younger twin brothers, Oska and Jasper. Oska looks up to his big brother. He is loyal, enchanted and impressionable. Would do anything for his brother. But Jasper, although he does as he is told, has an inky, wild rebellious streak that will occasionally strike. Jasper is electrifying, like a fork in a power socket. He has dark hollow bullet-black eyes. There are no two ways about it: Jasper is unpredictable, cold and mad, and it is no secret that he is also dangerous – loved very much, but dangerous. If these words fail to convince you of his untameable inner monster, you only have to know of the shiny snake-like scar cut like a gutter down his spine to understand what makes a mad man *that* mad. Perhaps you'll hear about that in good time.

Liberty watches her boys pawing through their newly stolen loot, stripping and dissecting the guts of the treasure-filled potato sacks; this is the Ablegares' favourite reason to exist.

'We have to hide all this before the yats board.' Giacomo smiles as he raids the last sack of treasure, pulling it out onto the chest of *Liberty*, her torso now splattered in clunking, shining findings. 'They will lose their shit if they see this.'

Oska skins up on his knee. The tobacco leaves stir in the breeze like a mini autumn scene on his lap. 'We all know that *someone* will lose their shit when they see *you*.'

Egor grins dirtily. 'She's blusky for Momo.' He is stitching a fix into one of *Liberty*'s sails. For such a rogue rhinoceros of a young man he has the tiniest and most delicate fingertips that can see to the most fragile of work; he is a truly refined artist in that respect.

Giacomo waves the boys' comments off, although his brow arches. It is true. One of the Sirens has become a little *too* taken with him.

'No, it's just a wax every now and then.' He sighs, scratching his neck. The mottled purple flower of an ageing love bite sprays up under the collar of his crisp white shirt. He had told her not to.

Oska snorts. 'That's not what she thinks. You always forget the rules – press and duck, press and duck – but it's your own fault . . . you keep her hooked with the compliments and presents.'

'I didn't give her any presents!'

'You gave her the pearls.'

'They weren't worth much.'

'To her they were. How many presents do you think a skank like her gets? *None*. So to her it meant something.'

Egor empathises. 'Man's a romantic. He's a gentleman. He can't help it.'

'Yeah, and now she's *on* you, bruv.' Oska pats his pockets for a flume.

'Pussy-whipped!' Egor snickers through the thread in his teeth.

'No! It's her that's whipped. You're like nicotine, Mo. She's addicted to you; can't get enough of the stuff!' Oska licks the Rizla paper of his roll-up, keeping the tobacco inside with his fingertips, the roach in the corner of his mouth making him mumble. 'She's on you. Hard. You give her too much affection, then once you try to take it away – *OUCH*. Cold turkey.' He laughs affectionately, lighting, inhaling, blowing smoke.

Giacomo shrugs. 'The rejection is the *connection*. What can I say?' He can't help but smile, pulling on the roll-up. A largish part of him loves the attention from females, even if it is unrequited. Even if it is from a wild Siren.

'You gonna wifey off that yat?' Egor asks, already knowing the answer.

'Are you dizzy? Momo wouldn't wifey off a smatty jezebel like that. She's grimy,' Oska answers.

'Maybe my man Momo has an *acquired* taste.'

Giacomo cracks his neck. 'Nah, she's just a bang. It's not a thing. She doesn't care.'

'She will care if you break her heart.' Egor pierces the sewing needle back into the deep black flesh on his arm. Egor is fed up with losing his needles and the boys like to look fresh so he keeps a whole sewing kit of various pins and spikes in the soft flesh of his upper arms.

These boys are proud. They always, even – no, *especially* – at sea, dress in immaculate sharp-collared shirts with starched, pressed suit trousers, braces and polished winkle-pickers or laced boots. Egor manages the grooming of the boys. Egor is Caribbean and keeps a dense afro himself but works hard to maintain the swag of the others' hair, which is trimmed, oil slicked or clean shaven, with the exception of Oska, who wears pigtails but somehow manages to make them look like the best hairstyle in the world. Their faces are smooth and defined with not even a sign of shaving spots or the shading of new hair roots, apart from Giacomo, who wears a humble well-kept pirate beard, which, for his age of eighteen, says a lot about him. Egor plucks their brows, trims their nasal tunnels and keeps their hands and nails manicured, clean enough to feed new babies grapes. 'Don't slip. You gotta look good,' he grins, his tongue forcing its way through the hippo-like gap in his teeth, 'always.'

Some wear more jewellery, but all the boys wear a small silver hoop or cross in their left ear. All also wear a silver chain holding an anchor, but most keep this under their shirts, as close to their hearts as possible.

Oska inks the boys when the days are smooth, but nearly all the boys keep their tattoos to their arms, legs, lower neck and torsos; nothing that would make them look like a bad sort, nothing that would tarnish their impeccable, flawless shine, hinder that chance of a pocketing hand delving into a handbag and getting away with it too.

The boys have prepared a lunch of octopus spaghetti and vodka. They like to dine *big*. And there is reason to celebrate: the steeple of stolen Rolexes, wallets, gold, silver and precious-stone jewellery from careless holidaymakers glistens by their table. Otto sits at the top of the spread, his sword at his side and a new Rolex on his wrist; the mother-of-pearl face judges its new owner. His seat is a wooden throne made from odd ends of crate with one of Egor's own hand-stitched velvet cushions for comfort. He holds his knife and fork upright, like a cartoon imitation of a hungry person, ready and king-like.

'Fam.' He grins. 'We have hit the belly with our booty this afternoon. After we fill, let us laugh at the loot. Salute.' Otto raises a glass to the roof of the clear sky and all the boys bury their glasses into one another's. 'Let us eat! And be wavey!' Otto announces, and the boys don't need telling twice as their faces meet the food, as they swirl eel-like ribbons of pasta on silver forks, chink mismatched glass tumblers made from recycled jam jars and stolen crystal, and get drunker and happier under the soft glow of late summer.

Liberty kisses the rocky shore of Savage Qualm. A little island. It is a clustered mangle of rock and cluttered, clattered sandstone and salt. It is home to the Sirens. The birds of the sea. These *chicks* are a unique and rare breed. At first glance they are all woman. Tangly, knotty, unwashed hair, harshly rotten but equally striking features. They are attractive in their own way, if you like that sort of thing. They wear feathered scraps that could be described as dresses, skirts, bodices, which they stitch together themselves with the help of Egor. Their skin is thatched in tiny pricks, pimpled like a plucked goose, although olive from their outdoor habitat. They are covered in bruises, cuts and grazes, as they are usually drunk. To me, they are no different from the drunken Walkers – humans, if you like – who sit in front of me in the summer, drinking and smoking and howling until the moon comes. Just more dangerous. They have wings. Huge feathered wings that span across the rock. The wings are splattered in earthy natural colours: greys, greens, blacks, reds, speckles too. They can fly. If they want. But it is dangerous for them. And they are lazy. They prefer their prey to come to them.

There is another feature that makes them different: instead of feet they have claws. Like a bird. The same almost-dinosaur scaled legs, ankles and feet that birds of prey have, and then huge sharp black claws that they use for attacking. Some of the chicks wear holey fishnet tights too, which makes the entire look even more bizarre. Red lipstick, even. Push-up bras. Suspenders. Cheap browning hoop earrings.

The Sirens are infamous for their appetite. They lure lost sailors and fishermen to their island with their song, their charming personalities, their eccentric style and flare; some of the Sirens like to stuff their bird feet into Dr Marten boots to appear the real deal. It always works for a gullible, bedraggled, sex-deprived sailor.

The Sirens are welcome aboard *Liberty* as they aren't interested in the Ablegares' lunch. The Sirens like the delicacy of spoilt, rotten human flesh. Human flesh that they have preferably just had sex with: they like to taste themselves in the blood. The older the flesh, the better. The acrid tangly entrails. The bitter taste of chewy, stringy, decomposed muscle as it knots around their teeth. Hacking at bones with their claws and hands. The Ablegares aren't at risk of being eaten by the wild Sirens because the Ablegares are useful to them. Powerful. They know my waters well and, besides, they make for a good mate, or at least look like it. And besides, the Ablegares are too skinny. Apart from Egor – but then they would lose their tailor. And no Siren who likes a frock of feathers wants that.

The Sirens clamber aboard the boat. They are already intoxicated from their own supply of heady whisky. The seven Sirens flock the large table. Help themselves to vodka. Smoke. Some sit on the table: legs open and scraggy hair so greasy and heavy with salt that it doesn't even blow in the wind. Tanning, giggling, picking old rancid skin from their teeth, they fester the table. They reek of dirty bed. Of nests. Of ripe, warm blood. Cleo, the one that has a soft spot for Giacomo, curls round the back of his chair, hugging his chest close. Her new pearls press against him. Her grubby nails claw into his hair, inhaling him; if she could snort him up her nose she would.

She giggles, nibbling his ear. 'I don't know whether to kiss you or eat you,' she growls.

Giacomo laughs politely, batting her off and then pauses. (I am thinking I might have to call Giacomo by his informal sobriquet 'Momo' as the others do or else you will end up terribly confused. It never ceases to stun me how a nickname can often knock out a birth name completely . . . Then again, I've had so many myself . . . the sea, the ocean, the water, the blue, the deep. I could go on. Shall we stick with Momo? Very well. The rest is such a hullabaloo it's nice to have some simplicity.)

'Wait.' Momo holds the table with his palms. 'Do you feel that?'

'What?' Egor slurps a tentacle, his other hand slung round the shoulders of a Siren.

'Listen,' Momo instructs.

'Chill, bruv,' Otto reassures him, his hand stroking the legs of another Siren. The Siren giggles back dramatically.

'Yes, Momo, my love, *relax*,' Cleo says, trying to massage Momo.

He wriggles out of her desperate tug and stops chewing his lunch. 'Be quiet! Listen . . .'

Cleo smacks his hand. 'Stop dicking about. If you don't like me, just say so.'

Momo ignores her fishing for compliments and asks the table, 'Don't you hear it?'

'Mo. Mo,' Jasper says snakily. He likes to break names up when he is cross at somebody, as if verbally demonstrating the physical pain he could cause. He doesn't like his mealtimes interrupted, even the Siren combing her hand through his hair is beginning to severely irritate him. 'You're doing my head in,' he barks at her. 'I'll bite off those fingers of yours if you do that any more.' She snatches her hand back as though she has just got an electric shock.

23

Momo hushes him, his heavy eyebrow perched at an angle. 'There. Did you hear it?'

The boys simmer down to quiet, the Sirens keep their lipstick-painted mouths shut, and Momo is thankful that they do or else he will have to face Jasper's temper later. He is right. Under the water are vibrations. The deepest, bluest, unmistakable moan of whale song. Which means one thing: they have been summoned, and when they stand to leave the sky opens and the rain, like diamonds, falls on their haircuts.

RORY

HAPPY BIRTHDAY

I have already decided not to tell Mum. Not because I want to keep a secret from her but she's just such a law-abiding citizen; she would go ape-shit. I'm not certain of anything yet and the girl has said nothing, just keeps looking at me with those eyes like she wants something from me. There are some people who have the eyes of babies or animals, not the actual eyes themselves, but the look within them. It's innocence maybe, but she looks wilder than that, almost *untamed*; yes, that's it, *wild*. Feral. This girl, she has that look. Eyes that look *into* you rather than *at* you.

I can't bring my own eyes to her body. Other than on TV and the few porno mags that Elvis has knocking about, the only women I have *seen* seen are my mum (which is a view I wish I could forget) and Bev. And that was just the top half. Sort of. This doesn't count anyway . . . The only thing this girl really looks, if I'm honest, is *chapping*, like, proper cold. Blue lips, hairs on end and pale. It makes me freeze just looking at her.

Without being weird, I can't think for the life of me how I am going to get a naked girl through the Old Town. The town where everybody knows me and everybody asks questions.

She is pretty, I know. But it isn't like that. I find myself more intrigued. Curious. Even more scared of her than anything.

My phone has no signal so I can't make any calls and I can't risk leaving her here alone. Be normal. She's just a person, Rory. She's just a person.

I take my jacket off and hold it out to her. She flinches from my sudden gesture and her eyes get even wider. 'Here,' I say, and shake the jacket. 'Here,' I say again.

She says nothing but lets her teeth chatter freely. I check left and right as if crossing a busy road. I'd die if somebody I know sees me like this. I get closer and wrap the coat over her, trying to not touch my skin on hers; I do it how the barbers do it with those gowns you wear when you get your hair cut – swift and professional and all in one move. I keep my eyes away from her chest and pretend she is a mannequin in the window of a clothes shop. Except with . . . nipples.

Right.

I dart my eyes down.

I can tell she is proper nervous. 'OK?' I ask, as the jacket clings to her small shoulders and then, just as I think she might crack a smile, the jacket slips off with the wind and onto the wet stones with a slap. I have no choice but to put it on her properly.

'I'm NOT going to hurt you, OK? MY name is RORY and I AM FIFTE— no – SIXTEEN.' Great start, she's never going to trust a boy – I mean, man – who doesn't even know how old he is.

I am speaking to her as though she is one of the French kids who came to our school for the exchange and everybody spoke to them like they were dumb old people with hearing problems. 'KEEP WARM,' I say and then I act out the look of freezing, which is really embarrassing. I try again with the coat, closer this time. I take her arm. It's the exact temperature of the air, cool and smooth, and her skin is a new level of softness that I can't even compute. Then I realise I haven't really touched anybody before. I haven't hugged my mum proper proper in years and, well, I don't go round holding hands with the lads or people would start talking. I think about how this is one of those things most blokes look forward to in life, putting their jacket round a girl. I never thought this would be my first experience of it.

She lets me take her wrist, and her fingers gently fall through the sleeve effortlessly, as the coat is too big for her, and then I do the same on the other side.

She smells of all things new.

I bring the coat round her, but don't want to risk it coming off again, so now, face to face, I try to find the zip to do her up, and it is well awkward, as I can't quite grip the little metal bit to slot the zipper bit in and my thumbs are a mess. I'm shaking. I try to focus my eyes on the zip but my pupils keep springing all over her body, a bit wanting to look. I keep telling my brain to stay calm *and just do up the zip*.

Her belly button. Her thighs. Her collarbones. Her hips. Her – I start thinking again about what I'm doing, about how mad this is. *Does this count as kidnapping?*

I stand back to take a look at her. Her bare legs shake; they are creamy but opaque, like tracing paper. I can almost see the blood pumping through the veins like blue juice through a straw. And they have blueing blotches on them. I look at my jeans. I *have* got boxers on . . . I could . . . I can see how on paper this seems like quite an idyllic way for a bloke to spend his sixteenth birthday – dressing a naked girl – but in reality it's hell.

I take my jeans off – I wear them most days so they are loose and slide off my hips easily – and the wind attacks my legs instantly, so cold it's almost boiling hot. All pins and needley. Her hair blows across her face; she doesn't pull it away from her eyes. She looks like art.

'Here.' I hold the jeans out and pull the bottoms of my boxers down as low as they'll go to try to cover as much of my skinny legs as I can. They are dark blue and could possibly pass as shorts; well, that's what I tell myself. I'm not that hairy and am worried she's wondering whether I've done all that puberty business.

She doesn't take the jeans. I panic. I change my mind and step back into them and then she lowers her head, her eyes looking sad. 'You want to wear them? You can. Please, here . . .'

My voice doesn't sound like my own, I seem to have lost my identity and my personality has changed to that of a house brick.

She doesn't move.

'OK,' I say. I check again for passers-by and then quickly for a phone signal. Still nothing. Even in this weather I feel an unusual sweat take over my body. I wipe my brow.

I breathe out. 'OK. How do we do this?'

I shuffle towards her feet. Each toe is perfect and tidy, not like mine or Mum's. I take a foot in my hand and it's like holding a rag, small and floppy and soft. She wobbles when I lift her foot and falls onto my back, her hands on my shoulders. Her near fall breaks the awkwardness slightly and I reassure her. I can be in charge now because she has let me. I then lift the foot into the jeans and wriggle it as far up the leg as I can, being as non-weirdo as possible, and then do the same as before with the other foot. I then wrap her arms round my neck and lift her into the jeans, pulling her weight and the jeans with me as I land her to standing position. I look to the sea and the distance as I do up the zip and button on the jeans. The sweat is pouring into my eyes and there's no excuse for this amount of perspiration.

She is as light to lift as a fairy. She lands back on the stones as silent as stepping on snow. The jeans hang loose and I adjust the belt to the smallest hole but it still bows and I picture us running through the Old Town in the rain and her jeans sliding off, and how much that *can't* happen.

'Hold on,' I say and I find my door keys. I use one to create a new hole in the leather to make the belt wrap round her tighter. Thank god this isn't one of Elvis's pleather belts. 'There,' I say and smile, a bit proud. I look up and she smiles back. It is worth it.

She is wobbling around like a newborn deer on ice skates. I think it is because of the jeans but I don't want to ask. Maybe she is wounded, has broken a bone or something and I didn't notice because of the nerves. Either way, she is here now, *safer* back at ours with me than on her own. But I can't risk bringing her in with me right away, not with Mum there wanting to eat birthday cake. I decide I'll just pop in, be a moment, let Mum know I'm back and then find a way to distract her enough so that I can bring the girl indoors without her noticing.

'STAY HERE, OK?' I say, pulling my Nike jacket round her tighter. The raindrops on her eyelashes quiver, the skin on her tingles. She is like one of those antique paintings, one that's been retrieved from the bottom of the ocean, salvaged from some grand ship. I capture the moment. Her standing there, gazing at me, in the garden with its overgrown weeds and brambles. Even if somebody were to look, they won't see her, least not in the rain.

'I'll be real quick, I promise. Don't move.' And she literally doesn't. Not even a nod to show me that she's understood.

I scramble for my key, need to get inside, distract Mum, and get hold of Elvis and Flynn. Then I've got to get them off my back for a bit because now my phone signal is back to full bars it won't stop pinging about arrangements for tonight. What am I meant to say? *Sorry, lads, but now I'm responsible for a naked girl.* What on earth? I take a final look at her over my shoulder and lift my finger up as if to say 'one sec'; meanwhile I'm thinking, *I need a lifetime.*

I run round the front so Mum isn't suspicious. I see her through the blinds in the living room. She's on the phone and she looks like she's been crying. As I get closer she sees me and quickly rushes off the phone. She has definitely been crying. Again.

I prepare myself but the door bursts open before I can.

'Happy Birthday, Rory!' She beams as though she's genuinely elated and pulls me in; she feels warm and – I know it sounds dumb – really *human*. Maybe it's just familiar.

30

I smile. 'Thanks, Mum.' I don't like that she's been crying; it almost distracts me from the girl wearing my clothes in the garden. Mum always cries on my birthday, since Dad left us anyway. Her tears sometimes make me think she still loves him. I don't know if I still love him any more. You can't love someone once they've left you behind. Once they've forgotten about you as though you never even existed.

'Where have you been, love? I was worried.' She rakes her hands through her hair, her sleepless eyes combing through me as I walk to the kitchen. Her touch annoys me. I feel guilty every time I look at her. As though Dad's betrayal has somehow transferred on to me. I'm forever saying sorry to her because he won't. Wanker.

'Worried?' I cough to try to hide my squeaky voice, knowing my mum can read me like a book, and reach for a glass to fill up with water. The spotless surfaces glimmer under the reflective shine of the splattering rain through the window. Mum's been cleaning. The house smells of bleach, polish, air freshener.

'Did you not hear?' she rattles. Her eyes are watching my every move as if I'm a germ about to upturn every angle of the house she's aligned.

I freeze. Locked, belly up against the sink, the tap water has filled the glass and is spilling over the sides. *Please don't tell me this is to do with this girl. Please. No.*

'Hear what?' I eventually scratch out. Dreading her next mouthful of information I drink quickly, so my lips don't react to her reacting.

'The cliff face, Rory. A big chunk of it fell off today, right into the sea.'

'What?' I shake my head. 'Is that it?'

'What do you mean *is that it?*' Mum stares at me.

My response is stale but I am so relieved that it is to do with the cliff and not with the girl in the garden.

'Don't bits of cliff fall . . . a lot?' I ask innocently when I know the answer is *no, not really, they do not*.

'You live in a bubble sometimes, Ror. The storm, the one that has *drenched* you right through as I can see, it ripped the cliff face off! Done my fence in too.' As if it is trying to hammer home her point, the wind rattles the windows so that they tremble in their frames. She scratches her head and looks down at the floor.

I am getting impatient and itchy too. I look over her head, out of the back window, to see if I can spot the girl in the garden but I can't, not from here. 'Is your head still hurting?'

'I've got some tablets.' She rubs her arms. 'I could really do with them kicking in.' For a moment her face morphs into the one I once knew and then vanishes like a waft of a smell you recognise that triggers a memory. And then disappears before you can fully remember it. I smile shortly back and try not to look concerned and with that her face flowers with guilt and she slips back into the role of birthday boy's mum, which I could really do without.

'Cake!' she squeals, changing the subject, and she begins to fill the kettle. 'I've got balloons and there are your cards, loads this year. It's a big deal turning sixteen, Rory.' I think I prefer her depressive state to her feigned happy state.

'I know, Mum.'

'Just to think, this time *sixteen* years ago you were in my arms as a tiny baby and now look at you: you're taller than me.'

'I know, Mum.' I walk over to the cards and cake, the 'altar' that she's prepared for my celebration.

'You were so beautiful. You still are.'

I grin and bear it as broadly as my cheeks will allow.

'Rory.' She stops me in my tracks in a voice that cuts through me. *Has she looked outside? Has the girl come to the door?*

'Yeah?' I gulp.

'Why haven't you got any trousers on, love?'

'I, errr . . .' I keep my eyes on the cake and the cards. 'Flynn met me for lunch and we, errr . . . had chips and we, errr . . . went for a swim in the sea and, errr . . . got wet.' This is a bad idea; Mum doesn't like me swimming in the sea.

'Rory! How many times –'

I need to end this quickly. 'Sorry, Mum, I shouldn't have swum in the sea. I'm sorry. I'm sorry.'

The sour taste in our mouths is as stagnant as a derelict pond, but we don't want to fight.

'Let's have a nice cuppa and a slice of birthday cake and you can tell me all about your plans for tonight. That sponge has been eyeing me up all day. I love birthday cake, don't you? When the jam smushes into the cream. Where are your jeans? I'll throw them in the washing machine.'

'They don't need washing. I'm wearing them tonight.'

'They'll have seawater and rainwater on them. Where are they?'

'No, honestly, Mum, it's fine. They'll lose their shape.'

'They'll be all crunchy.'

'They aren't crunchy – they're fine.'

'I'll hang them to dry then. Where are they?'

She isn't giving up. 'Flynn borrowed them.' I rush out and start flipping through my stack of birthday cards in case Dad has remembered. You never know. Stranger things have happened.

'So you came home in your pants?' Her eyes unpeel themselves.

'Yes. Fine. Yes. I came home in my pant— *boxers*. They are called boxers, Mum. Can we please just leave it there and have some cake?'

I walk over to the cake with the knife and begin cutting it, so I can get this over with.

'What are you doing?'

'Cutting the cake. What does it look like?'

'But we haven't even sung "Happy Birthday" yet.'

'Fuck sake, Mum.'

'Don't you *dare* swear at me like that!'

'Sorry, Mum, I just want to eat the cake and go out.'

'Well, why not forget the whole cake anyway and go out now, seeing as that's what you do every night?'

'Fine. I will.'

'Good. Go.'

'Fine.'

I open the front door to leave. A fight with Mum isn't really what I want but it means I can get away more quickly and we always make up.

'Rory?' she calls out as I open the door. 'Aren't you going to put some trousers on?' She is right. Of course. Again. Sadness washes over me – the way we fight like a married couple makes me sink. Sometimes it's clear that we are all the other has. I have to give my mum fifteen minutes on my birthday. I go back in and we say sorry and sing 'Happy Birthday' in awkward out-of-tune harmonies and open cards (none from Dad) and eat cake, which is really good, to be fair, and I take a big piece for the girl outside and wrap it up in kitchen roll and she pats my head and before I need to lie and say the cake is for the lads, she says, 'What a good boy you are, taking cake for your pals.' And I nod. 'Take care of those cards, there's money in those for college!' I dutifully nod again. 'Tomorrow's your last day as my little boy.'

I smile. *No, Mum, tomorrow's my last day of freedom.* After then, everything has to matter.

Then she sends me, and a pair of clean jeans, back out into the racing wind and the hammering raindrops kissing my head.

Call you in a bit. With Mum, I text to Flynn and Elvis to hold them off for a bit. If I can just think of what to do with this girl for tonight. It does cross my mind to go back and talk to Mum about her but I *know* she will stress about it and think I've gone and got myself a druggy girlfriend who is also a mute or something.

THE SEA

THE GREAT CAVE

Opal Zeal is sitting in the Great Cave where she has been waiting for two hours. The Great Cave is where Opal takes all of her meetings with her select few Walker contacts. That being the Ablegares and . . . yes, just the Ablegares. The Great Cave is well hidden but also an environment suited for both Mer and the Walkers with a large natural pool for Opal and a ledge of surrounding stone that is well lit, cool and dry. She knows the Walkers will make her wait. The Ablegares like to make others crawl towards them, preferably with their tails between legs.

Opal keeps her mermaid tapestry in the flush of a natural waterfall, whilst her torso lies perched on the sparkling smattering of the cave's belly. It is Opal's job to research the Walker world, keep up with current affairs, liaise with the Ablegares and be ready to communicate with Walkers. It is useful for her species to have sea warriors to protect them and fend off fishermen, poachers and other pirates. Opal, because she is smart, exaggerates the benefits of this arrangement to the Ablegares – the terrors too, if they were ever to let her down. The punishment: cataclysmic, naturally. Over the years she has built a decent relationship with the Ablegares, and trusts the pirate boys to a certain degree. Then again, had she been braver and perhaps made some more connections she would have something to compare it against.

Since the death of the late Queen Netta, this protection for the Mer in the Whirl is necessary. The Whirl is the *sweet* little name the Mer dreamt up for the body of waters within me, which they believe belongs to them. A centre of civilisation, if you like. Populated by Mer as the superior species. Ridiculous to begin with, admittedly I laughed when I heard the news, but hats off to them – they have created a world of their own down there. I try not to get involved with their petty politics.

Opal likes her job. The responsibility. The reliance. She enjoys blending between the two worlds, but there is a cost too: her Mer kin mistrust her. Doubt her. And often outcast her. Which wasn't the initial arrangement. She had hoped for a little more one-on-one Walker interaction from the role. She had always been fascinated by the way of the humans and, if she was honest, she hadn't expected *this* amount of work. And what if it came to it? With a missing princess on her hands, what if she was forced to communicate officially with the rest of the Walkers? With *governments*? Without the Mer behind her? It plays on her mind that inside the Whirl they often forget about her completely. Out of sight, out of mind: flinging her out into the open air like some kind of wartime canary thrust into a trench to test for poison gas. Of course the role had been her suggestion, something to keep her sane, *busy*. But now, with Lorali's disappearance, they need her. And she can deliver. And then she can show her true worth. At last.

Opal is one of the most attractively striking females under and above water – and she knows it. Her complexion is a perfect wet-sand colour. Her hair is long and wavy and a murky seaweed green, and she wears it in two towers on either side of her head, like bull horns. Her dragonfly-coloured eyes pop under each sweeping brow of a row of twinkling studs. Across her face, a gold-hooped chain connects her ear and nostril. As Opal is the Mer's representative to the Walkers, this chain signifies her respect for the link between the two – her ear to her breath.

Opal has adopted features, characteristics and attributes of Walkers. Traits that she has observed and brought into her mannerisms and taste. It is important to her that she be accepted if she were ever to enter the Walker world. Ready to shine. She is also totally dazzled and besotted by the fashion of human beings. Mastering her hair, her make-up, humanising her posture, her gestures. Fascinated with the species she had once been as she studies them from my waters.

She doesn't *mind* the tail. She enjoys the compromise of the two worlds, their collision within her. Her tapestry speaks of her attraction towards the Walkers. The patterns, symbols and colours like stained-glass windows cast terrific shadows of her longing to be human. She often falls asleep dreaming of shoelaces, wedges, kitten heels and stilettos. It sounds so simple and small but a hungry little engine in her mind keeps her ticking over.

She knows she doesn't have the strength within her to actually surface herself. Her location is the closest she could come. Surviving from below. Collecting scraps of magazines to stay on top of the latest fashions. Living through the communication with others. A hunger she has a hold over. And a dark selfish part of Opal hopes, although her mission is to protect Princess Lorali, that the young Mer *has* surfaced. That she has made it. That she has legs and feet and is using them. To walk and run and dance and ... of course, wear shoes. That she is enjoying the wonderfully rich and exotic life of land. In her gut she is rooting for that girl and believes she has the strength to surface successfully.

She never comes here, to the Great Cave, alone. Opal always has her whales for protection, a pod of them circling beneath her. They are here now. She can hear the rain outside. A storm growling. One of Queen Keppel's again. Could the queen at least hold off until Opal has met with the pirates before having a tantrum? Lorali has only been gone a few hours and this rage is already nearly as bad as when Netta . . . No, she doesn't want to think about Netta.

Eventually the ripples of water sneak up Opal's body, lapping at her almost dried skin and – *finally* – announce the arrival of *Liberty* and the Ablegare boys. Opal has prepared herself. She doesn't care *too* much about looking pretty when it comes to the Ablegares, but it helps. She wears human make-up that she doesn't want to smudge.

'Oh, O-P-A-L!' Otto sings in glee from afar. His smugness makes Opal shudder with doubt and want to leave the cave but she knows she has to be patient and endure this. She awaits the recognisable clunk of *Liberty*'s anchor sinking into the depths of the unknown, and it comes and goes with a dribbling splash. The sound of Otto's shoes scuffing on the cave floor makes an effective echo as they clap towards Opal. He leans against the open mouth of the cave, his tongue smoothing his top lip.

'Why do I get the feeling we only meet when you've screwed up?' Otto begins to slowly pace. 'This weather is NOT OK. Have one of you lot got your period or something?'

'*I* didn't *screw up* anything,' Opal snaps. She wishes she *could* get a period.

'So do you want to tell me why it's raining catfish and dogfish, or is god watching a tear-jerker?'

Opal regrets calling this meeting with Otto now and almost fancies making up some brilliant news to fob him off with instead, but it would never wash. Mer only ever need the Ablegares' help in a crisis and the Ablegares know this.

'Spit it out, Opal. I'm here and you need me. My brothers and I are nothing but your little toys to fling round the planet to do your dirty work.'

At that, one of Opal's whales snorts out a spray of water from his blowhole aiming for Otto, but Otto knows it is coming and ducks. Otto giggles because he likes games and being kept on his toes, especially with old friends.

Opal sinks into her tapestry. There are moments when her tapestry makes Opal feel indestructible and times when it makes her feel like the most pathetic waif on the earth; nobody can bring both of these traits out in her in equal measure like

40

Otto can. They either play on her terms, like an out-of-reach fish teasing a cat through glass, or on his, like a flapping fish juggled by a cat's paw.

'*Now let me guess* – that's what you're meant to say, isn't it? When you want to pretend you don't know what somebody's about to say?'

'Only if you're a prick.'

'Which you've never seen, so that's not valid.'

'Wouldn't *you* like to think so?'

'I couldn't give a turbot.'

'Are you going to be nice?'

'Are you going to tell me why your whales interrupted my lunch?'

Otto takes an ivory comb from his inner pocket and begins combing his oiled hair. He uses ivory to remind the Mer that they are bait, that they are now *hunted* just like the elephant, that their bodies are precious. He can be a wind-up like that.

Opal exhales and begins. 'The princess, Lorali, has gone –'

'Expensive,' Otto interrupts, thinking out loud with little empathy, his head cranking as if breaking down a sum. 'I have had no news and I would if poachers had her . . . They would have tried to sell it to me first anyway. She's gone. Lost. Stolen. Dead.'

Opal clenches her teeth. 'She isn't dead.'

'They could have taken her . . . just not patched her yet.' Otto holds the comb to his cheek thoughtfully. 'Even a scale of her tail would go for more than you can imagine. And the poachers, they like to keep their stock very private. A buyer would pay no matter the cost – but I don't have to tell you that.'

Otto begins to potter about Opal, eyeing up her tapestry; he bites his lip, his eyes sharpening. He often thinks about her. How trustingly she swims into his hands like a little shrimp. The way she looks to him as her fountain of knowledge, when the Ablegares are so removed from Walker society – only creeping and shifting in and out like an invisible thread that gradually tugs away at pockets and purses.

Opal sinks into the water, her tapestry glowing pink. Blushing.

'Stop looking at me like that.'

'Like what? A hungry fisherman?'

'Yes.'

'Well, that's exactly what I am. I skipped lunch if you remember. I am a hungry fisherman. A *very* hungry one.'

'Just a disappointing version of –'

'Glorified, I'd like to say.'

'You would.'

'Now, now, sea cow.'

Otto crouches down to the whales below. He begins to clack his tongue, calling them up towards him. Opal watches as her whales gently emerge on the surface. She feels light as she watches Otto tickle the chins of her baby darlings. For a moment, she almost understands the attraction of domesticated bliss that Walkers crave. For a Walker, true love is not loving somebody so obscenely that one could eat them. For a Walker true love is security. A brick house. A little patch of garden to grow vegetables. Somebody to nudge under the table at an awkward gathering. Breakfast. An armful of dirty washing. Her own father, he would scoop her up and flip her over his shoulder. She can still taste the aftershave he used to wear. Or had she invented it? She decides to murder this pirate with kindness if it makes him help her.

'Thank you for coming. I am grateful,' she says with purpose.

'You're welcome,' Otto replies but continues to pet the whales. 'It's nice to see a pretty face anyway. You're much more piff than those wild Sirens.'

Opal is stabbed with nausea. The Sirens are the base of base. They are savages. She hates being compared to them.

Otto then begins to imitate the dialect of a whale, as if in conversation with a baby. Opal can see her whales having fun and it suddenly angers her, the way Otto has wormed his way under every single living thing's skin. Her patience begins to dissolve. 'This is the princess, a loved princess, who is missing. Haven't you got anything useful for me at all?'

'Taxidermists could have her. They know that living scales are precious, better than dead – far more . . . *beautiful*. They could be keeping her in a tank blah blah blah –'

'What do you mean by "blah blah blah"?'

'It's my catchphrase. *Blah blah blah*. Do you like it?'

'Otto, that's not a catchphrase, that's dismissive.'

'Wait a second, babes –'

'Don't *babe* me.'

'Easily done.'

'Don't think of me as easy then.'

'Don't act it then.' Otto smiles, his white teeth shining like the inside of a red apple.

The fidgety child inside Otto makes him pick at the walls of the cave, where dehydrated seawater crystals cling and hair-like weaves of silky moss spread like reaching fingers.

'In detail, Lorali could be being fed and watered in a tank, having patches of her scales removed . . . It's very painful and there's a lot of blood –'

'I've got that bit, thank you.'

'Cutting a long *tale* short . . . Apologies. Pardon le pun.'

Opal glares at Otto. His Dickensian waltz is riling her.

He continues, trying not to laugh. 'Even if just a small square of tail was removed, some yuppie would have still made a nice purse out of it thinking it exotic snake or fish skin. But there are people on the black market. *Disgusting* people, of course, that want what you've got.'

'Otto. Please!' Opal turns on him, her voice ringing through the cave, causing loose rocks to quiver. The whales murmur; her vocal current has electrified them.

'Too far?' Otto acts sincere.

'We are well aware of this *black* market you speak of Otto. We've already lost too many of our Mer from the Whirl. It's been an awful time for everybody . . . It makes me sick to think of the tapestries of our species being worn by Walkers. We can't have Lorali gone too. Keppel thinks she's surfaced.'

'So that's why the weather has been so bloody *marvellous*. She's trying to smoke us out. She's blaming us. This is nothing to do with us – it's not our fault, you know?'

'Oh, Otto, you know what the High Queen is like; *everything* is the Walkers' fault.'

Otto rolls his eyes. No, he does not know the *High Queen*. He sort of wishes he did, rather than being bossed about by her skivvy. And he does not like being referred to as a Walker, but he knows he is caught between a rock and a hard place. When Netta was strung up *Liberty* had refused to move a muscle because of the bad weather. He hates being driven like a slave by the Mer but they have monsters that could take down *Liberty*. Threat of Keppel's temper alone is enough to keep him listening.

'She's not going to give, is she?'

Opal shakes her head. 'Not at this rate. Until we find Lorali your life on water will be made hell.'

Otto cricks his knuckles, pounds his clenched fist into his palm.

Opal takes a breath. 'Assuming I have your attention, a cliff face toppled down today from Keppel's vibrations. It won't be long until they start detecting something's wrong down here and sending out the marines again. They will find out what this is about. Then they will want to find Lorali. They will want to resurface us all or get rid of us. We don't know what Walkers are capable of in a situation like this. But Keppel won't stop either.'

'What do you want us to do?'

'Find her. I just don't want her to fall into the wrong hands. Keppel wants to offer a reward but Walkers will do strange things when there's an incentive. I don't feel ready to expose this to the Walkers yet, not unless we are sure.'

'OK. Where did this cliff face fall then?'

'Somewhere in England, along the Sussex coast.'

Otto rolls up his sleeve. Tattooed on his arm are maps. His forearm is the British Isles in pastels. Opal slices her eyes at the ink. Pretends not to find his gift for navigation attractive.

'The cliff fell on this coast. We can go take a cruise down there; I could do with a trip to the seaside. I've always liked those little towns. Hastings is nice.'

45

'Hastings? I've never heard of it. Not even on my radar.'

'Don't get snobby. Do you want me to go or not?'

'It's a place to start.'

'Wait. Remind me why I'm your little errand boy again?'

But before Opal can reply the sound of thunder speaks instead, crushing the sky. Otto, comb in hair, licks his teeth and leaves the cave in a patter of echoes.

RORY

BODY LANGUAGE

I can't call for her because I don't want to make a scene. I also don't have a name for her. I should never have let her out of my sight. It's too late now. I stand in the garden trying to remember her body language, what it was telling me. We learnt this stuff at school about bullying, about how even if somebody might not actually tell you to stop, their body could be shouting it right in your face by simple things, like folded arms or a frown. I'm trying to remember if she was giving off signs that might read 'GO AWAY' with her elbows or something, but I don't think she was.

I'm still holding the slab of birthday cake, wrapped inside a piece of kitchen roll. I am hoping she will eat something. It feels heavy. I can only see the rain pattering, making tiny drum patterns as it ricochets off the rusty watering cans and forgotten paint tins of our makeshift garden 'features'. A snail trails the wall.

She's gone, hasn't she? Maybe it's for the best anyway; best she leaves now before she ruins my *entire* birthday. Now I won't be responsible for her. I can see the lads and get mashed up, celebrate my birthday and pretend none of this ever happened.

I start to head indoors for a shower. I text the boys without too much thought: *where u at?* – but then something makes me turn round. I notice a new gaping crack in the fence; the storm has bitten a gash into it. An open jaw of splintered wooden teeth making an entrance into the neighbour's garden. Mr Harley won't like that. Pedantic old Mr Harley with his fussy, neat, award-winning yard, with its sprinklers and acid-green freshly cut lawn that always makes Mum jealous. The rows of perfectly planted flowers and plants, the cabbages and strawberries (that now look a bit ropey after the storm), the homemade bird table and the huddle of opinionated gnomes looking on. Today they're the luckiest gnomes who ever lived, because in Mr Harley's pond is the naked girl, swimming in the rain.

Lorali

CAKE

I AM SO HOT. DRY. Bone. It's raining but it isn't enough. It's different. It isn't the same as the seawater. I crave that. My skin isn't drinking. Absorbing. My hair is dry. My eyes are dry. Red. Itchy. My nose aches. When I breathe in. It still hurts. Like ice melting. I can't sit out there. The male was kind. But I was desperate for my air. And when I saw the water. The big pool. I just couldn't help myself. In. In. Down. Relief. I swim. I stretch. It isn't right. Not the same. But I have to submerge. I have to be under. And then I do. Splutter. Choke. In my nose and eyes and mouth. Agh. Choke. Cough. Drown. Splutter. UNDER. PANIC. Wretch. Up. But still afloat. JUST. Gasp. Breathe. Lungs. I try again. Down. Can't breathe. Splutter. Choke. I try again. And then it's OK. Breathe. Normally. Naturally. Hair under. UP FOR BREATH. Head. Eyes. Closed. Heart. Bu-boom. Listen. UP FOR BREATH. Tick. Tock. Legs. Heavy. Sink. Flap. Flap. Flap. In. Out. Calm. Like the frog. Like the frog. Like the –

And then I hear him.

'Hey, hey, hey,' he says.

He is worried for me; I know this. Why does he care when he does not know me? Is this a Walker characteristic?

'Hey, are you OK?' He looks at me, all big eyes. He looks at me. Then looks away. Am I wrong? My body. My new body. And me not knowing what to do with it. He holds his arms out. 'Are you OK?' he says again. Tender.

I don't know.

I am shivering. Cold. New. Then hot. Flush. Sick. Nausea. Vertigo. Dripping. Cold. Rough noises in my ears. Dizzy. He is warm. Wet. Soft. Kind. I have done something bad. Or stupid. I can tell. Instinct. Worry. Panic. Mutter. Oh, I don't know anything. It's all big. And new. I think I fall. In my new legs. Clumsy. Into him. His chest. His arms. All around me. Close. Like a child. I feel protection. I sense. But he doesn't know how to carry me. I am so heavy. I am the heaviest Walker probably that ever existed. With metal bones. He pulls me out. Safe. Safe. Down again. Up. Up. Safe. Clutch. Close. Secure.

'I've got you,' he says.

I can focus. Suddenly. Understand. Male. Sniff. Same male. As before. Same Walker. Safe. Sniff.

'I've got you,' he says.

Blur. Blank. Blank.

Cake? What is *cake*? '*Cake*,' he keeps saying. 'Have some *cake*.' I'm only used to eating weeds and fish. Plants. Plankton. The odd bit that floated down. Sometimes fallen bird. But feathers were for our hair. The only bird I ever saw until today was dead and now they fly over my head. But cake? *What if it kills me?*

I try to think back to when I surfaced. How the fear meant nothing to me. How I didn't really care if I even made it or not. And then I did. Then I came through. Then I emerged. Then I tasted air. So bright. My legs. I saw those and those other big flat things. With skin all wrapped round them. Individual were the feet. Different but the same. Like fishes. From a distance they look the same but up close they are unique and not alike at all. Legs. *Like arms but longer*. With flat things on the end. *Like hands but bigger*. Feet. Of course. I have feet. And the little things on the end too. Just like they'd said. *Like fingers but shorter*. Less useful. *Toes*. These were toes. I remember saying: Why are they there then? Why do humans have toes if they aren't useful? *For balance. For balance. For balance*. Wait . . . where is my balance?

After everything I have been through, why am I now scared of this fluffy white blob of food?

'Please eat,' he says again. Holding the cake towards me.

He has been so kind. I still haven't spoken. I don't know what to say. Where to start. I don't want to confuse him. Or encourage him to ask questions about me. Or who I am. Or what I am doing here. I don't want him to turn me in to the government. That is my fear. They all went on about it. I have heard this from Opal too. About what the government would do to us. They would do tests on me. Probe me. Use me for science. I know the horror stories they all spoke of in the Whirl. To scare us.

I want to find *him*. I was so naive to think I could get to him without being noticed. Without being found. And now I am here, with this one, cursing him with my surfacing. Maybe he

51

can help me find who I am looking for. Yes. Yes. But . . . what if he becomes frightened of me? How could I explain? Where do I begin? How can I trust him? I wish I had prepared better for this moment. Opal might have told me more.

'All right, forget it,' he says. He goes to crumple the cake up. To throw it away.

I have to eat.

'Wait.'

Suddenly it comes out. My first word. *Wait*. Like a bubble of thunder it explodes right there. My voice sounds different from before. From what I knew. From what I expected. Clear. Loud. Sharp. Strong. Its vibration judders my nose and jaw. I pierce the air. He raises his brows.

'I want the . . . ca—' I say. I am hungry. And curious. And eager now. I am shivering.

'Cake. Sorry. *Cake*. Of course.' He hands me the white squish in the napkin. We are sitting in a little wooden hut. I have seen something like this before. Just with less torture equipment and weapons inside. Although they are off-putting I can tell that he isn't interested in hunting me.

'This is Mr Harley's shed. I live next door.'

'Is he a hunter?' I ask. Afraid.

'A hunter?' he asks. 'Why?'

'Or a sorcerer? Or a king?'

'What? No!' He shakes his head. Laughing but then confused. 'He's just normal Mr Harley. Why?'

'All of these weapons.' I point around us. Blades. Tridents. Strange forks. Spades. Bottles. Jars. Tins, probably full of potions. I make the boy laugh . . . I think. I remember his name. Rory.

Yes that is it. *Rory*. I make him laugh. Rory. I like the 'orrr' sound of his name.

'These are gardening tools. To keep the garden nice and tidy.' He smiles. 'That's his garden . . .' Rory points at the water. 'Or your own private swimming pool by the looks of things.' Rory laughs again. Then I begin to laugh at him laughing. I don't know why but it feels like the right thing to do. Laugh.

What's a swimming pool? Opal has never told me that. I smell the cake. It smells of what cloud smells like to me. I look at him. He nods. I am worried that this substance will churn my insides out. But I bite into it just the same. I've come this far.

'It's birthday cake. It's cream and jam.' He smiles again. But I have already gone to another place. My eyes widen. Is this some weird drug like the seaweed Mum takes?

'Whoa, are you OK?' he asks.

I think about what terrible grimaces I must be pulling to get that reaction. What's a birthday?

'Good,' I say. The white stuff is all around my cheeks and all over my hands and in my hair. It is the best thing I have ever tasted. Blood rushing. Head hot.

'Have you never had cake before?' he asks me.

I get nervous. Is cake a really *human* thing? Does everybody eat it? Would it show me up as a stranger if I say no?

But I don't need to. Our eyes lock. It feels like all of my life underwater has spiralled down a hole. Gone. And then we hear voices.

RORY

ELVIS

The girl is wearing my clothes and a BBQ cover sheet wrapped round her shoulders. She is shivering. It is only now that I have a proper chance to look at her: her hair is soaking and off her face.

She isn't from round here. No. She has these big sunken eyes that are blue . . . green with gold and purple flashes . . . almost petals . . . like tie-dye splashed through them. And long lashes. You can see the shades of colour on every strand. The same on her eyebrows, which aren't like plucked or anything, but they don't look scruffy or rank. They are natural, spread out, and suit her face. Her lips are plump but dry. Not sore. But she looks thirsty. They are red. Swollen. Like they've been stung.

Her skin is even. Equal. Pure. Smooth. Creamy. Like a piece of furniture: a banister you want to slide down. It is no use shouting at her, asking her why she ran off. I don't want to frighten her. I am still struggling to get the image of her naked out of my head. Her eyes when they watched me watching her.

'Good?' I ask her, laughing. I've never seen anyone enjoy cake like that before. I am sure she must be homeless. Or running away. I feel bad for her.

'Very.' She licks her lips and looks around the shed. I think she is scared of Mr Harley's tools.

'These are tools, to keep the garden nice and tidy.'

'Tools,' she says, nodding, licking her thumb of any remaining icing.

'My mum reckons he uses toenail scissors to trim his grass, so I'm quite happy to see some *actual* tools, to be honest,' I joke. She doesn't laugh. I am terrible with girls.

'Are you the government?' she asks me suddenly.

'Gover— No!' I am shocked. 'What are you on about?' *Keep your cool, Rory. You don't want to intimidate her.* I relax, 'No. Why?'

'The government don't like us. That's why they don't want me here.'

She's crazy, isn't she? No wonder I've not seen her knocking about. No wonder she was bloody naked on the beach. Oh, drop me out. I've landed a protestor. Or worse – a hippy.

Or maybe she is just *different*, unusual. I drive my eyes into hers, trying to understand her. She is looking back at me, not faltering for even a second. My heart begins to thump. Hard.

But then I hear a voice. Elvis. It feels like my whole life has suddenly spiralled down the plughole of the kitchen sink.

How did he get past Mum? Then again, if anybody gets what they want it is bloody Elvis. The girl is looking at me with these eyes, like a child, looking for me to decide what to do next. I am responsible and she is reliant. I don't want to hide her; I want her to feel safe.

It also doesn't seem like the boys are going to leave me alone today, Elvis in particular. Why did I have to be such a dick and send that text?

'Stay here, OK? I'll be back. I promise.' I touch her shoulder. It feels right to make contact with her, familiar and exciting at the same time. Crouching, I sneak out of Mr Harley's shed and slip back through the crack in the fence. Elvis is right there.

'Mate!' He grins like a TV presenter pretending to be your best friend – well, he is my best mate, so technically he isn't *pretending*, so why does it feel so . . . forced? 'Mate, I got your text. You've been quiet. What *is* going on?'

This is the negative side of having people know you inside out. It's great when you're having a laugh but a nightmare when you're sitting on a secret.

'I'm sorry, El. I've had a mad day, my mum . . .' I'm instantly annoyed at myself for bringing Mum into it; everybody knows that you're only waking the devil when you lie about people's health. Doesn't stop me though, and Elvis needs convincing. 'She's not been great. She's not sleeping, and she's on these tablets and they are making her proper emotional so, you know, I've just been looking after her.' I hope he buys this. It's not a complete lie. To nail the coffin in I rub my eyes in exhaustion.

'Ah, mate, on your birthday too?' Elvis cocks his brow. 'That's tough. Well, let's go out now, eh? Have a few jars?' I can tell by Elvis's smile that he doesn't mean a *few* of anything. He is looking to get wasted. Like I had been.

'I dunno, El. My mum, she's –'

'What? Your mum's the one who bloody rang me!'

'She did?'

'Yeah, she called me to say you were on your way to meet us and that she would put twenty quid behind the bar for us. Isn't that sweet as?' Elvis's eyes flicker as if he is already intoxicated, but that is just him, the wildness in him. 'Course I was going to just not tell you and then collect the score off her later . . .' He winks and elbows me in the ribs cheekily. 'Then when you didn't turn up I thought maybe you were up crying in your room. Can picture the scene, lights off, poor Rory, the rain coming down outside. I can see it all now! The plot thickens!'

'Why would I be *crying*?'

'*Joking*, mate. What is *wrong* with you?' Elvis's face falls. It is this girl. I was OK before she came along.

'Oh. Sorry. I'm just feeling . . . I dunno.'

'You're getting well dry in your old age! How long have you been banging on about turning sixteen? Come on, baby boy, it's your day!' Elvis unzips his jacket and flashes me a full bottle of Jack Daniel's. He looks like a dirty salesman but he does make me smile. 'Yeah?'

'I don't know. I don't want to leave Mum really.'

'So why you coming out of your neighbour's shed then, mate?'

'I was . . . erm . . . telling Mr Harley to . . .'

'To?' Elvis looks at me as though he can't quite hear me properly and wants the volume turned up.

'To . . .'

Elvis sighs, rubbing my arm in a manly way. 'Is this about your dad? Did he forget again?'

This makes me feel angry. Not at Elvis but the solid true fact that Dad doesn't care about me enough to even drop me a card on my birthday. It fills me with rage. I realise there is only one way out of this today.

'One.' I force a laugh out. 'I'll have one.'

'There we go! Bev might even be there!'

'I don't want to see Bev!' I don't want to see anyone.

We leave for George Street; I pretend I can see the girl inside the shed, watching me leave. I told her to stay and this time I think – I *hope* – that she will wait. I have to move forward. The clench of worry has already bitten me. Mum watches us walk past the house, smiling that smile that parents and teachers do, that patronising, *I know you better than you know yourself* sort of face, when really you know that they think they know that and the circle never ends.

The moment we begin to walk down the hill I regret leaving the girl in the shed. I've already risked losing her once today. At least the rain seems to have stopped. For the moment.

The guilt goes a little as Elvis brings out the whisky and we take turns to sip and wince as we head for the night, soundtracked to the memories that Elvis is reeling off of other nights like this. When really there has never been a night like this. Ever.

THE SEA

THE ABLEGARES

On a sea of carrier bags, used condoms and plastic bottles, *Liberty* gently rocks up onto the bay, a slush of grey bubbles welcoming her. She has landed. Momo drops her anchor and it hits the pebbles of Hastings with a horrid clunk. The rain has stopped. The clouds tear into scraps.

This is the coast. This is where the cliff face has fallen. There are clumps of rock here. The big miserable face of land looms over me. The tremors pound. Lorali could be here. The town is hot. Warmer. Warmer. Warmer, boys.

The boys step off one by one. *Liberty* waves them off like a proud mum waiting in the car for her sons to go off for a night on the town.

Oska lights a cigarette; Otto fixes his hair with his ivory comb. The air is tight. Egor has a compass-like heart for instinct; he shakes his head. The seagulls overhead drift purposelessly, scrounging for grey odd ends of forgotten chips that don't exist. The dreary, tinny nostalgic musical swoons from the arcades, groaning something miserable along the parade, the ripe heavy smell of hot fat frying hangs in the air. Sweet donuts overpower the smell of fresh golden fish. That and the melancholy plastic-pink mist of candyfloss. The boys stretch their young bones and, boots pattering, head to George Street. There will be a pub somewhere.

RORY

THE SERPENT

In The Serpent our age goes unnoticed by the stoned Australian backpacker of a bartender. His little friendship bracelets and aged festival bands are a greying muddy colour and keep nearly dipping in our pints. Maybe I am jealous. That he was brave enough to just up and leave home and start a life somewhere new. I always wonder how people who live abroad hear about Hastings anyway. Is it even on the map? And her. In the shed. Why did she come here? Of all places. Guilt fills up my throat. I shake her out of my head.

Flynn enters the moment we text him to say we've been served. Flynn gets embarrassed easily and would rather stand round the corner, freezing his arse off and waiting for a text to give him the all-clear, than sit alone in a pub waiting for us *or* be turned away at the bar. Although it's fair enough. Everybody knows he is underage – and if they don't, they would be able to tell by his geekiness and the weird shy little way he carries himself.

Already tipsy from the whisky, the beer floats on top. I sail. My head bobs about, light and loose. Elvis is budgeting the score that Mum put behind the bar, planning when we should switch to just Coke so we can add the J. D. to it ourselves, and although the girl is like a foghorn in my ear, time hypnotically sails away.

The doors to The Serpent open. This time it feels as though they really *open*.

There are five of them.

'What the hell?' Elvis widens his mouth but he's too cool to act shocked, so he pours beer into it instead, like stuffing too many clothes in a drawer, and quickly shuts it.

I can't quite work out their age as they bounce past us, because three of them are completely clean-shaven, so they look really young, but they walk with such confidence – it's as if they've rehearsed this entrance a million times. Then there's this massive black dude hanging towards the back but his face looks youthful too and he has these proper kind eyes like a child, but he's so big you'd think he was a fully grown dad. But he walks with such swag. The last of the five has a beard. I guess that gives something away. *MAN*. I would *love* a beard but I can't grow one. Every time I try, these weak little hairs squeeze out and it looks like the grass did after the woman across the road found out her wife was having an affair and poured hot bleach on the front garden. As if people weren't talking about them enough because they were gay. The grass singed. It died. That's how my 'beard hairs' look. Like dead grass.

It sounds proper mad but I can *feel* these blokes in the pub. Like, you know, when you get goose pimples and a sudden

shudder. The three clean-shaven ones look almost identical –
triplets, maybe? But certainly brothers. I've never seen triplets
before. That's a rare thing in itself.

They look *sick*. Like, you know in those Westerns? Those
films when a certain cowboy, the main one, walks into a bar
and the saloon doors bash open and everybody stares, gawping,
figuring out their next move. Well, it feels like that. The music
in The Serpent is still playing but the sound drowns in my
drunkenness and the madness of the moment, and my first
thought is panic. And then the girl. In the shed.

'I've got to go,' I say and drag myself up from the table.

Flynn throws me a look like *don't*, because I know he doesn't
want to be left alone with El, and I frown because I can't think
what else to do. I'm full from the beer and am swaying.

Elvis nods at the huddle of newbies standing by the bar.
'What? You're not *actually* interested in watching these
nutters?' He laughs all big as if their presence is a joke to him.

'Don't draw attention,' Flynn mumbles into his drink.

I find myself looking at their clothes for labels or brands to
help me figure them out, but I can't seem to find anything.
Not a stitch that would give away who they are. They've got
these insane haircuts – I mean, we get all kinds in Hastings
but seeing them all together like this . . . it's like some kind
of weird cult. Crisp white shirts and suit jackets thrown over
their shoulders with the one finger like a hook. Proper bossy.
Dressed in immaculate sharp granddad shirts with starched,
pressed suit trousers and braces. The works. Their boots are
polished. Proper. I'd never get away with wearing them. I'd
look like a right prick. I peer at their shoes again. So dapper.

I briefly glance down at my trainers and sink into my chair; I feel young and a fraud. Like a sore thumb. Out of my depth.

'Rory. Rory. Mate? You there?' Elvis flicks me in the face. 'You got a crush?'

I throw his hand out of my face. 'Shut up, El, what's your problem?'

'You zoned out there, mate.' Elvis's teeth seem to have grown too big for his mouth.

'Huh?' I blink and hold my head. 'Did I?'

'Proper. Like a zombie. They your type then?'

I pull a face. I can't be arsed with his nonsense.

'You're in a strange mood today. It's shit in here anyway,' Elvis grunts, trying to act like he's not intimidated by them. I'm not falling for it.

I watch the five of them; they still haven't said a word, just quietly going over the wine list uninterrupted, like they understand every posh and confusing word written on it. I would *never* know what wine to order. The one time I took Bev to a restaurant (she would call it a date) she ordered a BOTTLE (who did she think I was, bloody Jay-Z?) of 'house white' and the waiter invited her to taste it and she sipped it like she knew what she was doing, but her taste buds must have been as dead as her conversation because it tasted like rat piss. Eighteen quid that bloody bottle of horseshit cost me. I would have rather had water but I had to drink it otherwise the waiter would have guessed we were underage.

Flynn is glancing at the last mouthful of beer at the bottom of his glass; he has sunk that one fast. Fast for Flynn. He still hasn't looked up. It's like he doesn't want to be recognised.

'You all right, Flynn?' I gently kick him under the table. He looks up briefly at me and then points to the wall, trying to distract us.

'Can you see these marks?' Flynn asks me.

'What?' Elvis says.

'These marks here?' Flynn touches a small row of inky marks on the wall next to him.

'How drunk *are* you, Flynn?' Elvis rolls his eyes and shakes his head but I can see what Flynn's on about. Little engravings in the wall: racked up, like the measurements of a kid getting taller and taller.

'Never noticed them before. What are they?' I ask him. When Flynn notices something that's it. He's gone. His head is off doing some mental cosmic brainy shit that I can't compute.

'These are lines to record the sea, when the tide comes in. This is all the times the pub has flooded – these marks here show how high the water rose.'

Elvis cackles, half of his head peering over to see what the boys at the bar are doing. He leans back in his chair to look like he doesn't give a toss. 'The sea is all the way down there. How's it going to get up George Street and into The Serpent?' Elvis tuts. 'I mean, what does the sea want from in here? Half a pint and a packet of cheese and onion? You're crackers, mate!'

'Floods. He just said that, Elvis,' I argue.

'Whatever. Flynn, you're just pissed. Why don't you go and hang out with your gypsy chums over there by the bar?'

Elvis always pushes things too far. Like now.

Flynn finishes his beer. Stands up, grabs his coat, looks at Elvis and says, 'They're not gypsies. They're pirates.' And he walks out, leaving his glass rattling on the table.

RORY

HOME

After all of the rain, the sky is clear but moving, like the inside of a crystal ball. Like smoke drifting out of the end of a cig. *Why did I leave her? What is wrong with me?* How could I be so dumb as to risk her going missing again? I feel so immature and out of my depth.

I race up the hill but my legs still feel a bit jelly-ish from the alcohol. What an idiot. I'm so angry with myself.

I think about the blokes in the pub. What does Flynn know about pirates anyway?

I sneak under the window. Mum has the TV on and squares of silver and blue are leaping across the patio from the flickers. Next I find the gap in the fence through to Mr Harley's. The shed can't be a hiding place forever. Mr Harley is an early riser, so I am sure he'll be indoors but there are neighbours who love peeking into each other's gardens from their own windows. And they'll nosily be taking great pleasure in seeing what damage the storm has done. Wedging my way through,

I begin to panic. Taking deep breaths I start to fear what I might find once I reach the shed. Maybe she will be cold and frightened . . .? Or maybe I was being ambitious . . . maybe I will find a dead girl . . . Or maybe she won't be there at all.

Moving like a shadow, I take another breath and give a little knock on the door to let her know I am there. I feel guilt. Like *you might have just accidently kidnapped a person* kind of guilt. I shake it off and unlatch the door. I put the torch of my phone on and light up the shed.

'I'm back,' I whisper. I can smell the alcohol on my breath as I look down and see she's asleep on the floor.

It's the only way I can tell if Mum's awake or not: if she doesn't call my name when she hears the latch, she's asleep. I don't dare get too close in case I wake her; I gently tiptoe past – I can see her worn, expired wedding ring, it somehow still seems to sparkle, even after all these years, as though it is punishing her. Reminding her of what she has lost. Or maybe she is secretly taking care of it. I don't know why she still wears that stupid bloody thing.

The TV is nattering away. I turn round to the girl and usher her to follow me. She freezes when she sees the TV. Her eyes ping-pong about, dilating and thinking little ideas. She looks to me as if to say *Are you NOT seeing this?* Weird.

Before I know it, I'm holding her small hand and squeezing it and together, somehow, in my drunkenness and her drowsy newness, we make it upstairs and into my room.

'Phew.' I sigh with relief and turn my lamp on. My room. Simple. A single bed. White walls. A small TV. A few books and DVDs. A laptop. A chest of drawers, some weights that I never use and a football. That's about it. It looks depressing, until I see her inside it. Suddenly it feels as though she was meant to be here, made for *my* room. It feels so weird to have this . . . girl in my house . . . And now . . . Her eyes. *Wow*. They are . . . *splashing*. I shake my head and rub my eyes. 'Sorry,' I whisper. 'We have to whisper.'

She laughs. 'Why do you always say sorry so much?'

'Oh, sorry, do I? I mean – sorry.' And then we both laugh again. 'I was about to say sorry for leaving you. But I'll wait until later. I'll try spreading them out a bit more.'

'I didn't notice you were gone for so long. I fell asleep. I was so tired. And that cake was so good. But it gave me a bit of bang in my head.'

'A bang in the – ha ha. That will be the sugar. It was pretty sweet.'

'I don't know what that is.'

'Sug— You don't know what *sugar* is?' I say like a pisshead. I slur on my words a bit. *Fix up, Ror.*

'No. But I liked it. And I want more.' She says that in a dead serious tone.

'I'm sure I can get you more. Hold on.'

Trying not to rattle about in the kitchen and wake Mum, I scoop up what I can: crackers, cheese, jam, bread. An apple, bit brown but OK. Butter. Crisps. Chocolate. A bottle of water. And another big slice of cake. I haul the bundle upstairs in my arms.

'What's all this?' She begins rustling through the night picnic. I don't tell her to be quiet because I don't want her to be. Her voice makes everything OK. She reaches for the butter first, unwrapping it from its shiny gold-foil paper like treasure. I go to pass her a cracker but she is licking it off the knife on its own. Her eyes roll to the back of her head as though she is having a fit, but this seems to just be her general reaction to food. I am stunned by her and forget to speak for a second.

'No, don't eat butter on its own!' I say, trying to give her a cracker.

'Why? This is the best thing I've ever eaten!'

'Better than the cake? There's more cake here.'

'But this butter is so good.'

'Really? OK. Sorry, we don't have much, it's all I could f—' *Agh!* 'I said sorry again, didn't I?'

'Yeah.' She picks up the whole block of butter and bites into the wall of it. Chewing and squashing the yellow block with her tongue; it smushes out of her teeth. She grins a dirty smile. 'I'm Lorali.'

'You're what?' I slice up the apple.

'Lorali. That's what they call me.' Oh. I stop and take her in. Her freckles. Her eyelashes. Her cheekbones, her tongue melting the butter down, working it to smooth liquid.

'Lorali? Your name is *Lorali?*' On my tongue, when I say it, it feels like sherbet is dissolving into every hole. That is just *such* a fit name. Lorali. *Lorali.* I am a bit in love. A bit in love with this weird girl wearing my clothes, stuffing butter into her mouth off a knife. 'It's a really nice name.'

'Thank you. It's water?' She is pointing at the bottle.

'Nah, it's vodka . . .' I joke. A joke that goes down like an old lady on an icy step. 'Yeah. Do you want some?'

'I think so. Is that OK?'

'Yes, of course. It's for you.' I smile and hand Lorali the bottle.

She drinks and drinks and drinks and drinks and drinks and drinks and *drinks*. I mean, I have never in my life seen anybody drink like this before. She doesn't even look pained or breathless; the drinking just goes on and on until the whole bottle is sunk. I need to take her to a house party – she would *floor* the boys.

'Thanks.' She wipes her mouth. 'It's not salty. It's like spring water, river water.'

I try not to stare. What a thing to say. But she is going to need a wee after that. I hadn't even thought. 'Shall I show you where the bathroom is?'

'Sure.' She gets up to follow me.

'We have to be quiet,' I whisper.

'OK,' she whispers back, following me out onto the landing. She looks confused when I show her the bathroom.

'You OK?'

'What is this bathroom?'

'Well, I know it's not all posh and whatnot, but feel free to use whatever you want. Do you want a shower or –'

Her attention span is short. Already distracted she begins looking at the products lined up by the bath, the shampoos and conditioners and bubble baths – opening them and touching the liquids and smelling the perfumed scents, reacting dramatically to each one. *Lavender. Coconut. Verbena.* I watch her open a tube of face wash and put it to her tongue.

'No!' I say. 'That's for washing . . . your face. Not for eating.'

'It smells like kelp.' She looks worried; I take the tube from her and read the back.

'That's because it's made from kelp.' I don't know much about beauty products. To be honest, I didn't even know I knew the term *beauty products*. Sometimes with Lorali I feel a bit like I am talking to a teacher or one of my mum's friends. Like I have to impress them.

'How strange.' She looks disgusted. She can bloody talk about *strange*.

Then suddenly. Out of nowhere. She wees. Right there. On the floor. Into my jeans. Onto the tiles. And then she looks up, laughs and says, 'Oh . . .' She curls her hair behind her ears and looks embarrassed.

I close my eyes to pretend this isn't happening and reach for the bleach.

Back in my room, I lay out a new clean T-shirt and a clean pair of boxers. Dim the lamp. We are talking quietly and the warm yeasty smell on my breath from the beer is beginning to go away.

'Do you want to change into these?' I smooth the T-shirt out. My drunken clumsiness is wanting to be close to her. I can smell the washing powder. She looks at the clothes she is wearing and nods and begins stripping. Shit. *Whoa. Whoa. Whoa.*

'OK. OK. You can do that. Do you want to go to the bathroom? Or . . . how about . . . I'll stand here. I won't look, I promise.' I go to the corner of the room, against the window so I can't see her. Elvis would have peeked but not me. And even when I see the soft folds of her body arcing and bending reflected in the window, I close my eyes because I promised I would.

* * *

She is in my bed and I am on the floor.

'Rory?' she asks, piercing the moment.

'Yeah?'

'Thank you.'

I wasn't expecting that. I shuffle around, thinking of what to say, until I just say like an IDIOT, 'Don't mention it.' I think I get away with it though.

I try to control the jittery fireworks that are shooting around my belly and act normal. Even though I'm proper *gassed*. Gas mark 500! JurGASic Park! GASSED GASSED GASSED GASSED GASSED! THERE IS A GIRL IN MY BED! A PRETTY GIRL IN MY BED.

I click off the lamp and darkness floods the room. My eyes adjust. My heart is thudding. We soak in the darkness. I think about how maybe I managed to play it a bit cool today and I am quite pleased with myself; other than the drunkenness and nakedness, I think I did all right.

That is, until the bright green glow-in-the-dark stars stuck to my ceiling think it's their time to show their adolescent faces. I have had them up since I was little and always wondered why I never took them down, but now I know it was for them to go ahead and ruin my life right at this moment.

But –

'Wow,' she says, almost breathless. 'How beautiful.'

Lorali

STARS

I have never seen stars before. I know these are not *real* stars because we are inside a house. And I know of houses because Opal told us. She told us about grass. And roads. And shops. It's not all about telling. Some is about reminding. Some of the Mer remember scraps here and there but Opal knows the most. Opal taught us about animals. And religion (which is so confusing. You cannot hold religion.) And dreams. And insects. All those legs. Why does anything need so many legs? She told us about graveyards. And clouds. And nightclubs. And the cinema. But not the swimming pool. Strangely. But of all these things, the stars were the one thing I wanted to see the most. The one thing I couldn't get my head around. Some of the others were allowed to go up. But I wasn't. I was *too precious*. Too *treasured*. They said. When really I think I was just *sheltered*. They didn't want me to know the truth.

The sky and space were too far away for me to imagine. That's why I think Walkers have the best life. Because they are in the middle of the sea and the sky. They get a bit of both. Sail a ship. Fly an aeroplane. Deep-sea dive. Be an astronaut. They are free.

I think about the boy on the floor. Every breath he makes is even. Even and loud. Everything is loud. The air is sharp. It could stab me with its edge. But I know I am safe. Even without the security of what I had before. But my mother. What will she be doing now? She surely won't let me slip away so easily? She will be *mad* and full of sadness. Inhaling herself to a sponge. And Zar. He will be tending to the gardens to busy himself. Wandering the roots of the petrified forest without me. Without his little girl shadowing his every move. Replaying what happened at my resolution. How badly it went. He will walk the whole way round the wood. Hoping to find me hiding behind a trunk as I used to. He will be searching for my colours on the walls of the trees. In the coral and caves. And they won't be there. He will only want to explain. To say he did the best he could. It wasn't his fault. But I had acted so fast. And it was too late. I was the first one to ever surface. They said I'd never make it. And look how I've made it.

THE SEA

THE *CETUS*

Now it is dark. The moon, a skinned onion, white and mighty, with reluctance I'm sure, helps to guide the *Cetus* through my calm.

I can't be biased, though I can tell you that the *Cetus* is the most feared pirate ship in the world. A villainous, wicked ship, with its crew, the Cavities, even worse. To call your ship such a name only certifies that the pirates aboard are bloodless and nasty; that they fear nothing and have little respect for the water and all that inhabits it. Any right-minded sailor or pirate with a regard for superstition knows that just saying 'Cetus' on board is a terrible omen, so you can imagine the statement these women and men are making. With charcoal-black sails, masts like cindered kindling and an engine that pollutes a vile sludgy smoke into my bodies, they hum over my surface. Other than the purr of the engine, the pirates' snorts and the vile spitting, the only other sound is the clanging knell that hangs round the neck of the mermaid skeleton roped to the mast of the ship. The brittle, dry salt-drenched bones. And not just any mermaid skeleton; this is the carcass of Netta, Lorali's grandmother.

RORY

A BRAND-NEW DAY

I can't keep Lorali here. Not with Mum's behaviour, her pills and the cleaning and uptightness. Besides . . . I don't know where Lorali has come from . . . or *run* from. I have to move Lorali. *But where to?*

Mr Harley's shed is no good. It's cold and he uses it too often. I'm just about to flick through the contacts list on my phone when a text comes through from Flynn.

Granddad going nuts today. Doing my head in! Am around if you are – need some company!

Flynn. Of course. His granddad owns some properties in Hastings. One is bound to be empty. It is worth a try, and a risk that I just have to take.

RORY

THE LIGHTHOUSE

I arrange to meet Flynn at his granddad's lighthouse.

I trust Flynn. He isn't one to ask questions. But getting Lorali to the lighthouse is taking longer than expected as she wants to stop and look at just about everything. She wants to touch the bricks of houses, lie in the grass, hold the postboxes, stroke the cars. No girl gets that hyped up over a cashpoint.

I never cry. Not even when my dad left. The last time I remember crying was once at a programme where this dude of a gorilla had to have his arm amputated. The gorilla sanctuary person was worried because even though it was the best thing to do for the gorilla's health, gorilla life is all about survival of the fittest, about strength and being king of the jungle and all that. The keeper was worried that the amputation would make the gorilla an outcast. That the other gorillas would turn on him for his disadvantage. But they didn't. It only made them protect him more. They carried him on their backs proudly and helped him find food and climb trees. It was proper touching. It reminded me of me, Flynn and El a bit.

I'm lucky to have them. Friends that I can trust.

Does Lorali have anybody that she can trust?

We can already hear the screeching of Iris's violin from outside the lighthouse. It sounds like a seagull having its throat slit. The antique shop is open but you wouldn't know it. There are no customers; there rarely are. We step inside.

'He's lost the plot,' Flynn says under his breath, briefly noticing that I have a girl with me who is wearing my clothes but, as expected, asking no questions. Flynn is wired differently from me. Sometimes – no, *often* – Flynn's shyness is mistaken for rudeness. Luckily his unusual behaviour makes no difference to Lorali. But there is something. Isn't there? About her that makes her not like anybody else, something that I can't quite make sense of. I was drunk last night but her way seemed alien to me. She was foreign. Outlandish. A species of her own.

We follow the squawks of the violin. The shop has its lights on, bringing life to every old brass lantern, freaky china doll and strange Moroccan lamp; all the silver spoons are lit up under the warm amber glow, the crumbling chipped vases and pots stacked one on top of the other like disfigured dinosaur spines. Brown crinkled books and faded damp newspapers, sleepy vintage handbags and ghostly Victorian prams. Rusty coins, necklaces, bent-back maps, stained moth-eaten Persian rugs, odd dead gloopy mysterious things in jars – and then that *smell*. That rank, foggy smell of oldness and dryness and forgetfulness. That warm, sweet reek that Flynn's jumpers always smell of. Of cedar wood and cobwebs and muggy sea air. A smell I know. Lorali is fascinated by the shop and gently touches the scaled teapots, coal buckets and shields hanging from the ceiling, her eyes widening.

Iris is standing in the centre of his study in the converted lighthouse. He is by the big open window opposite where the cliff face has fallen. I can't believe the sight of it, how it has fallen like a mound of crumbled sugar. It looks like something from Roman times.

Iris is scratching something terrible out of that violin and I want to bash it over his head. Flynn and I hold our ears and go over to him. He is a massive wreck of man. At six feet seven he stands proper tall, and is only fat around the middle, like on his tummy and back and that. He isn't bent over either, like how some old people become. He is strong, like a stuffed bear. His hair is white like cotton wool.

'Granddad. GRANDDAD!' Flynn shouts to compete with the violin, and pats him on the shoulder. 'Rory's here!'

'Eh?' Iris suddenly stops playing and puts his bow down. Lorali immediately bursts into applause. Has she never heard a bad violin before? My god. Iris blushes from the claps; he smiles and his cheeks redden in a glad shyness. I've never seen him do that before. Then he completely ignores Flynn and me, and his smile stops dead in its tracks as he looks Lorali right in the eyes, and with a straight face, his jaw wobbling, he says in a voice I haven't heard before: 'Your mother's worried sick.'

THE SEA

THE PALACE OF QUEEN KEPPEL

There is a giant petrol-blue octopus. I can't tell you his exact size as he is thousands of years old and very antisocial. But his head alone is bigger than any ballroom that any Walker ever danced in. Eight tentacles, each reaching for miles, trail my ocean floor in the search for the missing Princess Lorali. The suckers shoot beams of light through the water. And the lantern on his head casts distorted patterns on my bed. The search is slow but thorough, and no rock goes unturned.

Queen Keppel's palace, deep in my blue, is a tall stone castle. Built from sandstone but not that chalky yellow colour – it is a coral blush rose and carved in the most fascinating natural grooves and lines in the walls from my waves, fossilising my movement. The palace has gill slits in the walls, and is constantly breathing, circulating fresh water in and out. The windows are gaping mouths and the roof is a mosaic of broken shell, fallen glass and chipped odd ends of worn plastic that shine like scales, spitting speckled light everywhere.

The palace is secure; it has to be for the royalty inside. Marcia, Keppel's oversized sea snake, guards it loyally. Her head, which fills the entire hallway of the house, greets you (or not) upon entry and if you are allowed inside you follow Marcia's ridged spine of a banister upwards. Her body coils to create an inviting staircase and as the house is tall and Marcia long, she manages to bend through the entirety of Keppel's palace, wrapping effortlessly round Her Majesty's many levels and corridors.

Marcia does not suffer fools or nosiness, and if you attempt to climb a level that you are not invited to, you will know about it. The walls are studded with feelers: canary yellow and turquoise oddities with feather-like wispy claws that don't *look* much more than decoration, but each tendril is punctuated with a tiny beady eye that is sensitive to any behaviour or movement which does not belong to the royal family. If the feelers sense any unusual conduct, they bleed a vile thick sludgy tar that blankets the intruder entirely, stringing round them much like your chewing gum. Disgusting. But effective.

The sun gives some light to the kingdom beneath the Whirl but not much, as we are very deep here. However, the inside of Keppel's home manages to remain bright and light and brilliant. I believe that is partly due to the wonder of Keppel's daughter, Lorali, radiating its passages. The windows allow light to leap in. Each wall in the palace is dotted with the fluorescent sweet warmth of glow-worms, illuminatoroids and lampktons. At all times they shine a powerful multi-coloured light. They provide their resources in exchange for protection from becoming food for larger beasts and for being safe inside palace walls. That is, of course, when Marcia isn't grazing (she pinches them off the wall and gobbles them down as easily as a human would eat a crisp). But this is rare, and it's still safer than being with the monsters in the depths, who like to play with their food.

Keppel loves jewellery and she and Lorali have large clusters of gold and silver, precious stones and gems, shells and pearls and noodling beads and bolts and chains and towers of *things* that they collect. Oddities that they find and keep. They pour out of every open drawer and trunk, oozing out like candle wax. They love art too, and both their bedrooms are swamped with what they believe to be valuable collectables. They have a unique taste. Their home has a life of its own and with Marcia and the gills it feels as if this palace has a heartbeat.

A heartbeat silenced, now that Lorali has gone.

In the courtyard of Keppel's palace, water thistles, water leeks and curly sea blossom creep over the restored garden furniture and the odd chairs made from neglected driftwood. Barrels from sunken ships clatter playfully over the patio. Every charming slant of every leaf, every swirl of twirling ivy and heart of artichoke has been deliberately placed. It is here that a meeting is taking place and every member of the council is present.

'Thank you for coming,' Keppel begins. She is impatient and although grateful for the council's attendance has one rattling eye on her sea-monkey, Bingo, who is building her pipe. She hasn't slept properly and has no appetite; she is surviving purely on three things: anger, hope and seaweed, which she inhales out of a glass pipe to take the pain away. Her three pet seal dogs are figure-of-eighting around Keppel's tapestry.

'Here, boys! Fetch!' Zar throws them a fish head each and they dart off after them, barking.

Keppel's fix isn't quite ready, so perhaps I should briefly take you round some of the chief council of the Whirl so you feel better acquainted with everybody? These Mer make up the committee that work with Queen Keppel's guidance and support. Shall we say hello? All right then.

Let's start with Myrtle. I do like Myrtle. Few have such a brave and touching story. Her tapestry is a deep emerald and glitters when she moves. She looks so glowing, shimmering about in my bodies.

Myrtle's story reads clear from her tapestry as to how and why she landed here, and how she became Mer. Her patterns say that when she was a human, at just thirty-two, she was diagnosed with one of those wretched terminal illnesses that seem to devour your kind in one mouthful. Given a short time to live, and so fragile is the human, Myrtle refused the treatment and the hospital; she wanted to be remembered *alive*. Strong. Happy. Fierce.

Myrtle was single and childless, with no legacy of her own but being very loved, and she asked, as her final wish, that her sister and best friends make her a raft – a 'sea-bed' as she called it – and sail her out to sea. She wanted to go *that* way. Myrtle was sure that whatever I had to offer would be less dull than wilting away in a clinical hospital bed. She was right there.

Her friends, I can still see their faces, did as she asked, covered her bed in letters and photographs, dressed Myrtle in her favourite dress and accessorised her in kisses and tears. Playing her favourite songs from the beach, leaving just Myrtle, her books, some wine and the stars. And I was there too, of course.

She fell softly into my waves. She was drowsy from the wine and dreamily let me take her in. She hadn't even made it a few metres before a cluster of sent-for turtles saved her life. She was carried to her new home on a turtle's back. With a new name, Myrtle: for love of the turtle. She sits here now, thick red hair crowding over her chest and hips, shoulders speckled in turtle-egg-like freckles, her eyes as brilliant as the ripples of a river.

They don't all have stories like Myrtle. But I wanted to demonstrate the types of beings that get salvaged. The fighters. That one there, Sienna, with the maroon hair, was once a talented poet. As a human she drowned on an unfortunate boat trip. The Mer warmed to her intelligence and pitied her bad luck. Still, Sienna is an odd beast. Salvaged at just twenty-one, she remains angry at the human world and the Walkers. And for that, her tapestry is silver, smoky and ashy. It's lizard-like in texture but moves softly like chain mail, which matches her personality – always on the defence, always ready for battle. Her eyebrows are white, as are her eyelashes, and she has filed her teeth and nails to spiky fangs. She somehow pulls it off; they suit her very much. Don't let them put you off. She is a remarkable work of art to look at and to be in company with. That's if you can get close to her from the swarm of protective sea serpents that follow her every move. But once you do, her loyalty and love has no boundaries.

Then we have Carmine, the sea-punk, with ratty pink hair. Carmine is fun and giggly and light-hearted but dipsy and incapable of making any decisions herself. She has a warm, gold, bright heart, but her history is dark. She was salvaged because of the brutal and premature end to her human life, which the Mer don't speak of, but of which Carmine's tapestry cries. It is covered in the raiding fingerprints of men; no matter how positive she tries to be, these textures and patterns still persist. Violence, terror, screams and dark cracks tear through her skin. Her resolution was a painful day for the Whirl. However, over time, new, beautiful colours and shapes are beginning to emerge. It's a slow grind but it is getting there.

To Keppel's left, the one with the long dark straight hair, is her mate, Zar. In Mer culture it is not necessarily rare for a mermaid to practise monogamy, but Mer have a different culture than you humans; their needs are more basic and their instinct more harnessed, their desires more *focused*. It is normal for Mer to engage in same-sex tessellation and have more than one partner, as, unlike humans, physical contact doesn't lead to reproduction. The only way Mer exist is because of the act of salvaging. The act of tessellation – to tessellate, *sex* – is for pleasure, relief or to demonstrate love. (However I *have* seen it done out of boredom, so don't let them tell you otherwise.)

Down here, beneath, in the world of Mer, the mermaids are boss. The females make the rules. It is clear from Queen Keppel's tapestry that as a human she was never *loved*, never *touched*, never *understood*. But that is the way of salvation. It is a time to be reborn, to shed, to thrive. And her situation, so desperate, was swim or drown. Once Keppel had resolved and blossomed into her tapestry, she took to Zar, and solely

Zar, like a fish to water. Her mate. He is her spine, her heart and father to Lorali. She has only ever wanted to know a love like his.

Just in time, before things get mushy and hideous, Bingo places Keppel's pipe in front of her and she impatiently inhales deeply. Keppel is terrifically beautiful even now when she is tired, worn out and deprived. Circles under eyes. Beautiful in a youthful, striking way that makes her seem quite unrealistic. Her skin is an even, creamy dream, and her hair can rival the length of any sea snake as it winds round her head and washes the floor like a golden spill of syrup. I'm sure you've seen hair in water, but you cannot imagine the way this hair *carries* me; it wears liquid like feathered wings.

Keppel is tall and lean but with womanly curves through her breasts and tapestry. Keppel wears a coral tiara, and cuffs and bangles hug her wrists. She is loved and respected. She is a family woman with verve for life and fun. She is a spirit-lifter so it is unusual to see her spirits now so shallow and dried up.

The council of the Whirl make some eye contact, as Keppel furiously tokes from her bong. Once a little lighter, Keppel elegantly clasps her hands. She is trying to hide her tapestry. She is insecure of it. Her main feature now makes her shudder. The frosty, snaky bleakness crawling up and down it like a rash of sadness. Zar rubs her in comfort and she closes her eyes almost as if to remove herself from the moment.

'Honestly . . .' Zar begins, 'we are so grateful fo—'

Keppel interrupts him with a glance. Although Keppel loves Zar, she cannot look weak in front of her council. Her devotion to Zar is already a talking point and she can't have the council thinking that he carries the trident.

Keppel focuses and speaks. 'I do not believe my daughter has died down here. I have not smelt her blood. However, I do know she has left the waters. I can feel it.' Keppel inhales deeply once again, and tries not to cry. 'The Walkers, we've never had to worry about them before but things are different now; you've seen the equipment they charge down here with.'

'Yes, but they've never reached the Whirl,' Carmine adds. 'It's too far; their organs won't allow it.'

'I don't trust them.'

Opal plucks up the confidence to speak. 'I've spoken to the Ablegares.' She sits like she wants legs purely so that she can have the pleasure of crossing them.

'Speaking of mistrust . . .' Sienna lisps through her fangs.

Opal ignores Sienna's jab. 'I've got them scouring the waters and they've headed f—'

'What was their prediction?' Keppel interrupts, leaning back in her chair. 'Because I will just rain on them forever if they do not deliver. I'm sick and tired of relying on a bunch of mindless schoolboy rascals to get a job done.'

'They . . . they . . . Otto . . .' Opal is nervous. She doesn't want to put any sour ideas into the council's heads. Lorali could be fine; Keppel is right: they haven't smelt her blood. No news is good news. But she can't *not* pass on information. That is her job. 'He thinks . . . Otto has said . . . He wasn't sure . . . He thinks that she may be being held captive . . . in a tank.'

'Captive!' Zar roars. 'In a tank?'

'No.' Keppel reaches for her weed. 'Not my girl.'

'*They* don't care who they patch from, Zar. The whole of the Whirl stinks of blood thanks to them. They've already kidnapped so many Mer. Not just Netta! They are greedy. They are cold. They are murderers. They don't respect us. Don't trust a Walker.'

Opal glances at her nails, which are decorated with flamingo wings. She has never seen a real flamingo. She continues once Sienna's bold statement receives no response. 'Otto did say that patching can't have happened or he would know about it, and that whoever was dealing in the skin would come to him first. He knows the black market; they are as locked down as the mafia!'

'What is the mafia?' a voice murmurs and Opal bats the comment away and tries to continue. 'The handbag dealers, the leather shoemakers, the pursemakers . . .' Opal stops there. She knows that her knowledge of the Walkers sometimes irritates the Mer. Has perhaps pegged her as a traitor to her species. Which she can't be or she would have been mauled. Often her contract to both breeds takes its toll. Makes her seem two-faced. 'And he's heard nothing,' she continues. This makes Keppel loosen. Opal takes another breath. 'I wonder . . . I mean . . . I know it's far-fetched but do you think perhaps that she might have surfaced?'

The council is immediately silenced. Heads lower. This is the reaction to the truth. It isn't likely but it isn't impossible.

'Why would she surface?' Sienna rages. 'She has no memory of human life so why would she go? She has no calling there. She knows no different. She is happy.'

Opal looks at her whales. She is already ready to leave.

89

Zar drops his head into his hands. Keppel grasps the back of his neck tightly and clings on to stop herself from crying. Then, pulling the gang of tears crowding in her eyes back, she says, 'She *was* happy. Before her resolution.'

Lorali

LOOSE LIPS SINK SHIPS

I know his face. Or his face knows mine. A familiarity of this Walker. His eyes remind me of my tapestry. The colours folding and swishing. Painting all the time. CHANGING. CHANGING. CHANGING.

'Your mother's worried sick,' he says. His words make me forget how to breathe. Kill my ears.

'My . . . How do you . . . I don't understand.' I forget how to stand next. Down. Floor. Smash. Heat. That boy. Rory's friend. A Walker. *Flynn*. He gets me a chair. Picks me up. Sits me down. *Thank you*. Bruise already on my leg. Purple. Green. Shine. Ouch. Sting. Throb.

'It's OK.' Rory puts a hand on my shoulder. Everything burns.

'It's true,' the old man says. He begins to scratch his head. Almost irritated. 'Your *resolution*.' His words pour into my ears like new ice. Cracking. Squeezing into my eardrums. *Bang. Bang. Bang.*

'Granddad, explain yourself,' Flynn instructs, managing to remain calm.

Rory is interested. He comforts me but I know he is interested. I can feel his curiosity. His senses are wrapping round the old man the way a monster does a whale.

The old man is upset. Flustered. He does not feel safe even though this is his home. I can tell. Do Walkers ever feel truly safe? 'Your mother has left messages all over the forest. On the trunks. I don't know. I don't want to say. I should never have said . . . Loose lips sink ships. I shouldn't . . .' He begins to get angry with himself. He is restless. He keeps his eyes to the ground and charges about. He is stressed. He paces away from me. I hear his feet on the ground.

I feel so big. Like I take up every corner of the room. My eyes search for space like an animal. If I was back in the Whirl I could swim. They couldn't box me in like this. There aren't corners there like in this vast new world. In the oceans there is space for me to be. I want to leave. I only surfaced so that I could find him. Begin again. But now I –

And that's when I see the drawings. All over the wall. Hundreds and hundreds of circles. I recognise them. Every one. But I can't place them. I can hear Rory and Flynn trying to calm Iris down but it is too late. He is already upset. But I have seen the circles on the wall.

Rory's voice sobers me. 'Iris, stop that. Iris?'

Iris. That is his name. Of course. Iris. The rainbow. The seer. The vision. *Iris.*

'I know who you are,' I suddenly say. My own voice sounds loud enough to bring the lighthouse down.

'You do?' Iris relaxes a little. His shoulders sink. He is surprised. It is him. I am certain. I keep thinking of Carmine.

A Mer. From the council. From the Whirl . . . She is the one who let me colour in his circles. She said they were her circles. But I could colour them. He left us things. From the Walker world. Newspapers, toys, ornaments. Presents. Mostly for Carmine. He would write things. And draw his circles.

'Lorali . . . it's OK, we don't have . . .' Rory's words peter out. Flynn watches and says nothing.

'You drew circles on the trees. I used to see your circles. I remember them now. Hundreds and hundreds. Engraved into every trunk.' The old man's face lets go of itself and changes into a shy smile. He is excited. But he stays calm.

'And you used to colour them in,' he replies.

I did. With Carmine or by myself with the sea pens and the feathered sea quills in the petrified forest. I was a youngling then. I miss Carmine.

'Petrified *what*?' Rory says. He is protective. I can smell his intentions, protection, but it comes across as intrusive. Bossy.

'Forest,' I bark back. I had never heard my own tone like that out of water. It is loud.

'Have you never been?' Flynn asks Rory. 'You know, when the tide goes down it appears. The little bay island type thing? It's like a burnt forest or something and you can walk through it. We used to go all the time, didn't we, Granddad?' Flynn picks at the walls, brick, paper. 'Granddad?'

But his granddad is gazing through the window, out to sea, miles away.

THE SEA

THE PETRIFIED FOREST

Queen Keppel has been visiting the petrified forest. A state of in-between. A purgatory, if you like. As all Mer have crossed from human life at some point, the petrified forest acts as a gateway to their past, as little of it as they can remember, to wonder and reflect, to gather thoughts and emotions. It works in this spectacularly magical way because it is shared by both Walkers and Mer. When the tide is low the forest rises to the surface, like an island studded with hundreds of blackened trees, reached by Walkers by the rug of the sand I leave when I go away. I watch from a distance. Dogs and children play hide-and-seek around the stark claws, clamber the wrists and fingers of these skeletal trunks, and engrave their names into the dead skin of the wood. But when the water is balanced, I return and the forest's usual state is low and deep and here it flourishes: every naked spike of every tree flowers and blossoms in the wildest shades of green. It blooms immediately, like the change from winter to summer in an English garden in one swift move. The floor, rich with seagrass and nettles and various exotic plants – sea quills, mammoth water lilies, sea snails and worms. It is a tranquil private paradise that I am very proud of. This was Lorali's favourite place; she would relax in the green shrubbery for hours on end, playing with the fishes and seahorses. Her only escape from her mother's kingdom. Carmine would show her the circles that Iris had drawn and together they would colour them with the rainbow oils they found in the scum of my roof. Lorali didn't know those oils were pollution. Dregs of spoilt poison from the petrol and fuel used to drive engines across my skin. At least *they* found a use for it.

Now Keppel haunts the petrified forest, curling through the precious maze of wildwood as though it were some labyrinth, hoping to find her daughter or some sign from the Walker world that she is safe, but the only imprints she sees are the scores her daughter made when she was young. Now they bear the scars of Keppel's own clawing, spreading, desperate fingertips, as though she believes Lorali will be wound around the roots, hiding somewhere beneath the bark. Her head hangs low in loss and longing. Letting me carry her.

Opal is singing the chorus to a Walker song when her whales groan. She has just taken off her make-up and she tuts as she makes her way towards the entrance to her apartment.

The angry locking tusks of narwhals, who are *far* more aggressive than her own pod of whales, shoot shadows across her front garden and give away who her visitor was.

'Shit.' Opal wraps her hair into a scraggy knot on top of

her head, rehearses a fake smile and takes a deep breath. She has no coverage over her chest but she thinks that is a good thing when it comes to Queen Keppel, who prefers the bare naturalism of Opal, as rare as it is.

'Your Majesty,' Opal says, beaming, her own whales already greeting the army of narwhals. 'Good to see you.'

'Don't lie. No, it isn't.' Keppel rolls her eyes and swims into Opal's home. 'Lying is a Walker trait. Stop doing it.'

Opal unties her hair, hoping it will cover her nipples, and follows the queen inside. She isn't going to stand uncomfortably before Keppel for no reason.

'What can I do for you?' Opal is cringing at the vast amount of Walker paraphernalia on display. Anything she could find: old broken radios, odd shoes, kettles, photographs of strangers. She can feel Keppel raiding it with her eyes.

'You'll be the first mermaid to *grow* legs of your own one of these days, Opal.'

Opal replies with a short knowing smile.

The queen bites her lip. 'Nobody knows I am here.'

'I won't say.'

'I know you won't.' Keppel shifts, holding her nerve, and composes herself.

'Are you all right?'

'I want you to go up. I want you to go up and go to the government or whichever Walker it is up there that you need to speak with.'

'Keppel, you are tired. You should get some sleep.'

'I want you to tell them about us. I want you to do whatever you can to inform every Walker walking this earth that we exist and that we are strong and that we are prepared to fight for the return of our princess.'

Opal knows it is a brave move to try to tell the queen what to do but the extremity of Keppel's solution troubles her. 'Have you discussed this with the council? Shouldn't we wait and see what the Ablegares come back with?'

'Not those clowns again. I want you to say whatever you need to say, Opal. I want *everybody* looking for my girl – everybody on land *and* sea.'

'Keppel! This is madness. We can't do that; they will close in on us! We are outnumbered and in the dark down here. We just about manage to live alongside the mammals and monsters, and the pirates and the fishermen – we can't risk it. It will be the end for us all. I really think you should sleep on it.'

Keppel fights tears. She clenches her jaw, on the brink. 'I lost my mother, Opal. I'm not losing Lorali too.'

Opal, hands on hips, finds her strength. It tugs from the desperation of Keppel and, of course, the chance to go up. *Up*. Finally. This could work in her favour. 'Tell me what to do.'

RORY

BREAKFAST

Iris gets a headache shortly after that conversation. He has to take his vitamins and then have a sleep but he doesn't want to. He wrestles with Flynn to stay awake; he has so much he wants to say. He keeps saying, 'I've waited so long. I've waited. I've waited.'

Flynn reassures us that Iris will be much more helpful once he has rested. That poor old bloke doesn't know his arse from his elbow. How does *he* know that Lorali's mother's worried?

I look at Lorali. She is shivering on the chair. Her eyes . . . bewildered and broken. I start to panic. *Does she hate it here? Does she want to leave?* I don't think I really want her leaving. I want her to feel looked after and special and happy and . . . safe and . . . I don't know . . . *important*, I guess. She looks uncomfortable and tired and, well . . . sad. I want to ask her all the questions that are going round my head. *Why did you come here? Why were you on the beach yesterday naked? Alone? Who are you? Are you running away? Are you in trouble? What do you want?*

My phone starts to ring. It's Elvis. I ignore it.

Flynn scratches his head. 'I've just got a missed call from Elvis.'

'Yeah me too.' I bite my nail quickly. A rough edge catches on a worn throw draped across the back of a chair. A balloon of tension rises in my chest.

'Do you guys want some breakfast?' Flynn offers and we can't refuse. Whilst Iris sleeps, his dreamy snores churning through the house, Flynn starts on scrambled eggs and mugs of tea. There is one main room in the lighthouse, which is the kitchen and living area in one. The kitchen is bare brick with lots of screws and nails driven into the cement to hang stuff from. Some worn blackened utensils, some bits of odd sentimental clutter like pictures and notes and little ornaments. They've got one of those mad old cast-iron stove things, so it's boiling hot at all times. Hanging over the stove are bunches of dried chillies, herbs and garlic cloves. All the pots and pans are ancient-looking, hanging in a medieval hammock arrangement from the ceiling, shabby and charcoaled from years of use. Nothing is packaged in Iris's home. Everything is in brown paper bags or glass jars. Rice. Oats. Coffee. Sugar. It's like stepping back in time.

I watch Flynn take half a wedge of bread out of the bread bin, which looks as dry and heavy as a boot, but then he drips some water from the tap onto it and whacks it in the oven.

'What did you do that for?' I ask him, stirring my third sugar into my tea.

'It revives stale bread; a bit of water brings moisture back into the loaf. Little trick I learnt off Granddad.'

'Water revitalises everything,' Lorali adds. 'Everyone knows that.'

Oh *do* they now? I watch her watching everything.

'Are you all right?' I ask her gently and she nods and smiles.

'I'm really good. Are you?'

'You weren't scared, were you . . . by what Iris said?'

'Scared?' She shakes her head. 'No, you couldn't be scared of Iris. Iris is the rainbow. The eye. The light in the sky.' What *the* . . .? I am baffled.

'The eye?' I ask her.

My brain is straining. And my phone keeps ringing. *Go away, Elvis.* I'll ring him later. My battery is still low and like an absolute dickhead I didn't bring a charger with me, and Flynn has one of them retro Nokias from about the 1800s. Well, when he remembers it. At least his battery doesn't die every five minutes though.

My phone buzzes again: Elvis. *Again.* Probably calling me to ask if I've seen the size of Marie from the Odeon box office's tits or to see if I'm up for helping him refill the teddy-bear machine at the arcade for a zero-split of his wages. AGAIN. I ignore it. Then I see Flynn check his phone.

'El.' He shows his phone screen to me. 'Shall I get it?'

I don't want to tell Flynn what to do but we both know that Elvis is a petrol can meeting a flame. And we can't be bothered for that to go off right now. Flynn says nothing and instead of answering, takes the warmed bread from out of the oven in silence. Then Lorali screams, and her clay mug shatters on the floor into tiny shards of chalky splinter.

'It's hot!' she screams.

'Yeah, it's tea.' I laugh but she isn't laughing and Flynn looks at me in the same way I look at him. We are wondering the exact same thing. Who *is* she?

THE SEA

MAKING AN IMPRESSION

From the east she entered. The river is grey, slimy and groggy. Horrendous to swim in. Loud. Dirty. Ripe bacteria. Full of the decay of London life. Walker possessions. It stinks of grot. It is important to Opal that she looks the part if she is going to get what she wants, and she can't have the innards of the River Thames spoiling her tapestry, hair and make-up, so her whales, like a raft, float her up river. Blowing seawater on her tapestry from their blowholes.

It doesn't take long for Walkers to appear, double-taking whilst out on boats of their own, fishing, walking, lunching, but she is going so fast they can't stop and ask or catch up with her, only reach for their phones. Call the police. The ambulance. A friend. The paper. Or try to describe the vision in 140 characters or less.

Drunk or dreaming? Think I've just seen a mermaid going down the River Thames. Anyone else? A few hashtags would set that tweet alight.

And it begins to get real as she enters the city of London. Her whales neatly tucked beneath her, she praises them by patting their heads, rewarding them with squirms of fish flesh as an incentive to keep going. She gulps. Nervous now. She sees it all – the industrial oversized bridges, the bleak grey and brown buildings, the washed-out people, the ear-splitting noise of machinery and sirens and traffic: deafening, roaring, screaming, angry. Not natural.

Opal is frightened. Was this a bad move? The others in the Whirl will feel betrayed. Backstabbed. But she couldn't refuse Queen Keppel – she's the queen! And then people begin to call out to her, passing boats get close and then there are police boats and ambulances with their disturbing shattering sirens tailing her. The whales are becoming distracted. She feeds them more fish. 'It's OK, boys, keep going, almost there.' She needs to get to the very heart of London. The Houses of Parliament. She wants to see the Prime Minister. That is what she wants. And then she will stop.

Her hair: three jelly-sculpted wet steeples stand tall and remain so, all painted gold. Gold jewellery all about her neck. She is fierce. A warrior. A creature.

The bridges and embankments are stuffed with people now, crammed like tinned sardines up to the barriers. Watching. Snapping. The news has already gone viral. But is it real? She has to make it so.

'OK, boys.' She strokes their backs. 'Slow, slow. You can slow now; you've done me proud.' One by one, as instructed and rehearsed, they flee from beneath Opal, just as the police boat catches up with her, the sirens and the spinning light making everything blue, red, violet, blue, red, violet. The last whale flips her up with its tail, making a dramatic splash that flutters through the air like a whip.

The police officers gawp at her. Shock. Fear. Amazement. Bewilderment. And then, with her frosted pink-glossed lips and bleached white teeth she says, 'I'd like to see the Prime Minister please. It's urgent and please say you have bottled water on this boat. One of you is going to have to keep my tail wet; I can't very well see the Prime Minister all dehydrated.'

Lorali

THE ATTIC

Iris is awake. I am glad. We were all waiting for him to wake again so that he can tell me all he knows. I don't know if I want everything about me exposed. But I don't know what I do want either. I am floating. Purposeless. The reason I surfaced now seems so far away. Secondary. Insignificant almost.

His big body creaks. He potters about and Flynn makes him this hot black gloop. In a mug. That must have been the same poison water that I drank. Only it smells stronger. Potent. Foul. And even though it is fire-hot he sips it normally. It makes me wince. Seems to hurt my tongue even more simply watching it. White smoke drifts from the mug. Though it does not seem to scorch him.

He asks Flynn to bring down his stepladder. Flynn seems unsure about it, but does it all the same. I think Iris is perhaps royalty. And Flynn his slave. And Rory . . . what is he? I don't know.

'What do you want me to get for you, Granddad?' Flynn

asks softly. He goes over to the trapdoor in the ceiling with a long pokey stick. With a hook on the end.

'Nothing. *I'm* going up.'

'No, no, Granddad. Your back. You can't. Remember what happened the last time?' Flynn nudges him.

'Shush up, you. Come on, get the ladder down for me.' Iris stands. Slow. He ambles over to the ladder, which flashes out with a surprising creak. Flynn stands back to make way. Iris looks at me, and puts his hand out as if we are going dancing. He says, 'Up we go, little Lorali.'

Rory follows behind with Flynn.

I am used to ladders. We have them in the Whirl. Ones we retrieved from fallen ships. Ones we made. We used our arms to clatter up them for exercise. Well, Zar did, and some of the other males who had to keep strong. To fight. To hunt. I could never be bothered. But I have this new weight now. Without the water to carry me. I have to get used to my new shape. To understand the absolute density of my bones. My legs. How they hang paralysed. Seem to seize up.

I hear Rory miss a rung on the ladder. *Slip.* I spring back too but my hands catch the wood. I peer down to him. 'You OK?'

'Yeah.' He smiles and goes pink.

This is the top of Iris's lighthouse. I like the rooms. They call it an attic. It smells of the saltiness of the sea. Of home. In the looming, curving arcs are green bumpy spots. I can almost imagine barnacles growing out of the walls. Starfish smooshed into the plaster. Carmine would love to see it here. To know more of her old friend.

I think of the Whirl. But I don't miss it.

Iris begins rifling through some trunks. We had trunks at home too. Iris is rearranging boxes. Shuffling about. I feel cold again, and wrap my arms round myself. My temperature changes so much in this world.

'Your mother is Keppel, the queen, making you . . .' Iris flicks through maps that he has drawn. Page after page of scribbled designs and lettering. That only he can read. I can't read them, anyway. But suddenly I understand. The word. Massive. Pressing against my teeth. Forcing my tongue down with its weight.

'Princess,' I add. *Boom*. My mother. My mother. My heart. My heart. My home.

The room breaks.

Rory's eyes widen.

I was mermaid. I *was* mermaid. A mermaid. I was stupid to think I could pass as Walker.

'Wait. Wait a sec . . .' Rory butts in, looking at Iris. 'Is she a . . . Lorali –' he closes his eyes for clarity – 'are you a princess?'

I feel shy now. Like I have done something wrong.

'Of course she bloody is,' Iris screeches. 'Why do you think the cliffs are falling down?'

'Sorry. Sorry, I – cliffs? Are they to do with you too? How? How do you know all of this, Iris? Flynn?' Rory doesn't mean any harm. I enjoy him and his clumsiness. His ignorance. It is refreshing. 'Princess of . . . *where*?'

Iris fluffs about. Takes out a pair of old shaky glasses. Wears them on his face. I have seen plenty of glasses. They always come down to the Whirl from careless Walkers. Opal sat a few of us down once. Showed us how to wear them. The water tilted. Everything became bigger. Magnified.

Iris starts again, ignoring Rory, his eyes scowling over his sheets. 'Your grandmother, your mother's mother . . . She was . . . yes, here . . . Netta?'

Flynn and Rory both look to me for my reaction. My jaw clenches. I feel my family's pain relived in my newly warmed heart. I say, 'Yes, my grandma was Netta.'

Iris considers this. 'Her story is powerful. Very powerful.'

'Do you want to stop?' Rory asks me gently, and Iris pauses. 'No. No. Not at all.'

'OK. Just say if it gets . . . you know, too much,' Rory says to reassure me.

'Your mother, Keppel, your grandmother, Netta . . . but . . . something was . . . different . . . wasn't it? About you. You're different. I just don't know how.' Iris leafs through his pages and doodles.

I look down. At my two legs. I don't even know how they became part of me. How my brain instinctively knew how to use them. I feel outside of myself. Like my mind knows more than me; perhaps there is something it's not telling me. It feels as though everyone knows more than I do. Vulnerable now. Panic – and then –

'Do you know who you are?' Iris inspects me over the rims of his glasses. He knows. Remember. He knows Carmine. Remember. I can speak. I am safe. Aren't I? 'Do you want me to explain?'

'Yes, please.' Tumble. Out. Mouth. Words. Be still.

'How do you know all this?' Flynn asks Iris, not impatiently, proud almost. 'About Lorali?'

Iris's heart is wilting like the sea moss. 'I have a friend. Carmine. She tells me everything. She tells me everything that happens.'

'In the petrified forest,' I say softly. 'You have those symbols.'

'Yes, we have our own language. It's a bit silly.' Iris blushes and mops his brow.

'No it isn't,' I tell him.

Flynn hides a coy smile. 'So that's why you're always down there.' Finally a big question for him has been answered.

'Yes . . . well.' He looks into his papery, worn hands. 'I'm going to tell you what I know from the trees in the forest and from my friends in the underworld.'

I nod. Instinct. Safe.

'*Underworld?*' Rory shakes his head.

'Where to begin?' Iris breathes like his lungs are full of water; they sound thick and full. He splutters into a dirty old rag from his sleeve. 'Excuse me, this dreadful cough won't go away.' He puts the rag up his sleeve once again. 'The beginning, I think, is probably the best place to start, don't you, little one?'

THE SEA

NETTA

I was there on that fateful day, and I take my share of responsibility. My waters have been known to drive men mad. Its vastness, its foreverness, its boundless greatness.

He was a drunk so that didn't help, and the fish wised up to his laziness pretty quickly. They mocked his negligence and played on his worthlessness. What an insult he was to my oceans. He was slow. He was a pathetic lump and he was nasty. There wasn't a day that went by when he didn't blame his wife for something.

It began with burning his dinner and shrinking his clothes, but then these accusations became far-fetched, extreme, bizarre. Things that were out of her control, out of anybody's control. He blamed her for the lack of fish in my water, which was why they had hungry bellies and empty purses. The hunger added pressure to their relationship. The man accused her of conjuring up the bad weather, the grey skies . . . *they were her fault too*. Oh, and if he was sick it was her mistake; if the tea was too bitter, hers too. If there was a hole in the boat, it was her wronging. She was to blame for everything. In his mind she was an *omen*. Bad luck. Which was bringing their marriage down. However kind and intelligent and beautiful she was, for a Walker anyway, and despite his behaviour, she remained devoted: greeting him when he got in from the cold. His wife knew he was a tired old drunk but she loved him still. She suggested she could find work in the town somewhere. She had skills: she could cook, she could sew, she could count and write. But the husband was too far gone by now. His ideas and designs too black and too . . . mean.

Her suggestion knocked his pride and angered him. He took it personally. Through gritted teeth he said, 'You think you're so much better than me, don't you? Why don't you just leave me? You only want to work so you can meet a new husband and leave me behind to rot.' He said other things, wicked things. And that day when he went fishing, he locked her inside the house so she could not escape. She could not walk, she could not tend to the garden, she could not see the sky.

That evening, when he returned after a cold day of fruitless fishing, he was empty-handed again but his head was full of alcohol. He woke his wife and he said, 'You've done enough damage to us. I won't let you do any more.' And he drunkenly wrapped her in a sheet of fishing net and threw her screaming into his boat, sailing her to the deepest part of me that he could reach. He swigged from his bottle before kissing her for the last time and threw her out of his boat and into my arms. He watched her fall until he could no longer see her. I made sure to reflect his face in my waters, to mirror his expression, in the hope that it might sober him, change his mind. That's all I am permitted to do. But there was nothing left.

RORY

NETTA

Lorali sheds big heavy tears. I find myself staring at her fingernails. They are so new and white and thin like fishbone. Why is she crying? I want to speak up. I want to tell Iris that we are not buying this crap. I don't see what this made-up fairy tale has to do with Lorali. It was a mistake bringing her here.

'I think we should stop now, Iris,' I suggest. Her tears are making me feel ill.

'Don't stop. Please,' she urges Iris, and he speaks again.

Iris considers me and then clears his throat. 'Lorali, your grandmother Netta was the *first* mermaid. Did you know that?' Iris speaks in a deep gravelly voice, like this is a secret. I am too shocked to even find a voice. 'That's why you are royal.'

'Mermaid? Wait – what? So mermaids . . . they exist?' Flynn asks, interrupting, finding a voice for me, which he rarely does. 'How does somebody *become* a mermaid?'

Mermaids? WAIT. WAIT. Are we actually *doing* this? Is this it now? *Please.* I open my mouth to laugh at Iris and maybe even call him a liar but I catch my words. I don't believe what I'm hearing but I don't want to upset Lorali.

Iris stares at me coldly and his pupils deepen; I feel like they go on forever without an ending. I gulp.

He turns back to Lorali. 'Let me finish about your grandmother, Netta . . . Little did the fisherman know that *that* night his wife was saved by hundreds of tiny blue and yellow fishes, fishes that kissed her on the mouth just like he had done, but this time for *real*. With each kiss blowing cool fresh air into her lungs, Netta was created.'

WHAT? Yeah right. What a load of bull. I can't help myself from saying, 'OK, yeah, so mermaids exist. OK, and to become a mermaid all you need to do is dive in the sea and wait for Nemo and whass'is name, *Flounder*, to swim by and begin blowing air into your lungs and that's it? OK. We are not five, thanks very much. Come on, Lorali.'

Iris shakes his head at me.

Lorali doesn't move. 'It's true,' she says. 'It's all true, Rory. You can leave if you like but I'm staying here.'

I give Flynn a *you're not actually serious* look but he seems settled. I am the outcast. I dump myself back down. They all look at me. I'm guessing I have to play along. 'So *fish* turn people into mermaids?'

'Ah, Rory, not any more – Mer now hunt fish. Netta reigned for many, many years. Sadly she died. Things have changed, what with the technology and advances of humans: the environment down there is not healthy, and Mer cannot survive on the greens alone. And so fish and Mer are no longer the friends they once were. I mean, they live side by side, like human and cow but . . . their flesh is hunted. Mer have power.'

'How do you know all this?' Lorali wonders aloud.

'My dear Carmine. We tell each other everything.' Iris's voice breaks into ruins and the authenticity of his rasping voice makes me second-guess myself.

THE SEA

NETTA

This is my favourite part of the story. Weeks later, the husband
of Netta was sailing, drunk, when something pulled on his line.
A big fish. Almost too good to eat; a fish that would feed him
for months. The shocking pink-silver colour and the weight
pulled at him. He had it! He'd got it! He lifted it higher and
higher, up and up into the boat. Sweat beads trickled down
his head and into his eyes, and he panted his deadly alcohol
breath as the pull nearly broke his back in two. The fish rose
up and it made the man laugh with greed; he licked his lips at
the sheer size and weight of it. It was coming tail first. It was
wonderful, the tail: a work of art. He'd never seen anything
like it, *ever*. It was better than anything he'd ever seen worn
by a woman. Nature can be so *generous*. He pulled, more and
more, until he'd got the fish by the fan of the tail – an unusual
fluke. Then he saw the hips, the nipples, the breasts, the arms
and the face he knew so well. The lips he had silenced, the
face of the woman he had loved and then accused, and her

eyes, dissecting him, mirroring him like the belly of the milky moon. It was all too much and collapsed his fragile heart to nothing more than miserable, wispy, soupy scum. Weak. He was so afraid he couldn't speak or even begin to mouth the words of terror that he felt. He begged, clasping his palms, tears streaming down his sorry cheeks. The boat beneath him started to rock violently. He wailed now and reached his arms out for balance and forgiveness but instead, this creature spat a salty wash at him and capsized his boat.

She was strong and although he was stronger no muscle can contend with rage of the brain. He struggled at first before allowing his body to fold into the ice-cold fierce water. I was *cold* that day, I made sure of it, and I snaked into his eardrum and my thaw freezed his warmth from the inside out. The fishes rushed to nibble on this banquet, devouring him slowly to shreds. Netta swam back into my blue and down to my Whirl.

Lorali

NETTA

'Netta. Drowned by the net. That's why she got that name.'

Iris spirals his story to an end. '. . . and that was your grandmother, Lorali. What a powerful woman.' Iris wipes his nose and mouth with the rag.

I wish I could touch her again. Netta. Hear her laugh.

My grandmother and I would roam the Whirl together. She used to tell me that I was *special* and *different* and *treasured* and that I wasn't just *any* baby. I was a baby that belonged to magic. She would stroke my face. Plait my hair. Wink at me whilst Mother disciplined me. *It's OK, little one*, she would smile. *It will all be* OK. Dancing her fingers on my palm she would walk her hands up my arms with her fingertips. Her nails like broken shell creeping up my neck, and then tickling me until we both laughed. Our joy rang through the ocean's passages.

Suddenly I feel like the floor has fallen through, leaving me midair, and I look round to see Rory and Flynn staring at me like I am harmful. Disgusting. I don't like their expressions.

Iris nudges me. 'The boys are just shocked. You're a mermaid and that's a lot to take in. They'll get over it. Flynn, please pass me that blue book, the snakeskin one.' He flicks through the pages. 'I've made this diagram. It's a family tree. There's your name.'

'Is that how my name appears written down?'

'Yes, my dear. Do you not like it?'

'It's beautiful.'

'Yes, well, the boys, once they've got their tongues back, will teach you how to read, I'm sure, then you can look over all of these articles. Of course, they only show life on land; they won't say anything about your family, because nobody knows. Nobody believed. Everybody thought I was crazy.'

'I still reckon you're pretty crazy, Granddad.' Flynn laughs but it isn't nasty.

'You're probably right. I like it that way. I get around town twice as quick as everybody else; they all make a nice big space for a madman to get his errands done. All right, where were we? Ah yes . . . and you . . . you're different from the others. You're special.'

'Wait . . . wait . . .' Rory suddenly says. 'This is all too fast.'

Iris chuckles. 'Well, try catching up!'

I watch Rory. The way the information from Iris washes over him like the tide. Or maybe he is drowning in it all but trying to stay afloat.

'I'm sorry, Rory. I should never have brought you into this. I'm sorry if this isn't what you wanted to hear. Or if you think I'm too strange.'

Rory shakes his head, his cheeks reddening in a blush, and he looks up at me to say, 'I think you're amazing.'

118

My heart. Bash. Bash. Thump. Ouch. Nice. Nice. Moving down. Inside. Belly. Flipping. Darting.

'So mermaids, Granddad, are made from a Mer saving a human being? So we could become mermen, for example?' Flynn asks.

Iris nods. 'If they like you, yes. When a person drowns – accidently or deliberately – they let off a strange aura . . . Think of it like when bacon is cooking and you are in bed and the smell wakes you . . . It does that same thing for a Mer. Sends them a message. The Mer now have a choice. They can feel the pull of a person – are they strong? Full of heart? Powerful? Magnetic? Do they deserve another chance? What will they bring to the Whirl? There is a lot to consider; once they salvage a person they are completely responsible for them. When somebody is salvaged, lifted through into their new life, their life can begin again; their saver becomes the parent. Their mentor, their . . . guide.'

'So . . . Lorali has been here before? As a human? Like Netta?' Rory asks.

Agh. No. No. Too close. Not now. Not ready. Words too loud. Room too small. Out. Out. But I want to hear from Iris. His take on it. On me. I have no memory at all of myself.

Iris looks upset but I don't know why. 'This is the bit that gets me every time. I should tell you that once a human is salvaged, to the best of my knowledge, they have no direct memory of what their life was like as a human. Their only reflection or portal to their past is through their *tapestry* – tail, if you like – the scrapbook to their soul. The tapestry does the work, like photographs or a diary, bearing the scars every day.

119

Little clues and messages can be found in the tapestry but it is very abstract and unclear. It is about interpretation really but mostly it is a new beginning. They are Mer now.'

'So Lorali wouldn't even remember if she had been here before?' Rory suggests. He cares for me. I can see this now. I feel a rush of unexplainable warmth towards him.

'Not unless it shows up on her tapestry, if something, you know, *came* up. Did it, Lorali? Did something show on your resolution?'

And at that I burst into a sea of uncontrollable tears.

THE SEA

THE DAY THE WORLD
TURNED UPSIDE DOWN

'My name is Opal Zeal. I am of the Mer species. This is not a hoax. You may have many questions, which I will do my best to answer in due course.

'It is my dream that Walkers and Mer can co-exist and live in peace and harmony. I hope we can unite and respect one another. I wish that budding relationship to blossom with a big ask: we need your help. One of our kind is missing. Her name is Lorali, though she may not be using that name. She is sixteen years of age with fair skin; her hair will be unusually light as the spectrum of colours in the ocean is heightened and can create more – no offence – developed tones. Her eyes are most probably purple. It is thought she may have been in or around the Sussex coast. Any information on her well-being will be greatly appreciated, and, of course, if anybody knows where Lorali is and can return her to us, there will be a handsome reward.'

I have to laugh. 'Heightened' colours. Whatever next.

I am there. In a tank with her. Keeping her tapestry hydrated. Perky. Even though I know of the consequence. The tsunami that will follow an act such as this. I watch the cameras pan down her tail, zooming in on the seamless shift between her midriff, hips and where the tail begins. Those high-quality lenses are crawling up every scale, every pattern, line, shape and shade. The Prime Minister splutters something breathy and sweaty into the microphone after Opal has finished. The cameras are twitching, snapping, snatching, blinding Opal. People call her name. Ask about the 'purple' eyes. The colours of *me*. Where has she come from? Nobody has ever seen anything like this before. This is breaking history. Or is it just breaking?

Opal takes the Harlequin Suite at London's Dorchester Hotel for 'as long as she needs', where she is promised that everything will be taken care of. She lies, smiling, in a free-standing bathtub filled with specially sourced natural seawater – *more work for me* – and faces a television, learning about chat shows. Opal orders room service. A cheeseburger. Fries. A Caesar salad and a 'whatever wine you do'.

THE FASCINATOR

The fierce girl's online destination

THE TAIL EVERYBODY IS TALKING ABOUT . . .

Here at *The Fascinator* we just cannot get enough of mermaid spokeswoman Opal Zeal, and here is why. The mythical beauty quite literally washed up onto a London riverbank and has already become a viral sensation and celebrity. Opal is the first ever correspondent between life on land and the extraordinary marine Mer life that is now flooding our television and Internet screens. That girl can WERK!

Lo and behold, already haters be hating. Politicians and Hater-ade drinkers are screw-facing Miss Opal Zeal, damning our girl as a fraud and a freak. Meanwhile, we think she is the coolest girl on the block — or should we say rock? With a sun-kissed body and abs to die for we scream ALL ABOARD THE OPAL DIET! We ain't never eating a battered haddock again. Damn. She is easily the sexiest merwoman we've seen (not that we've seen any others!). With her washed-out green grunge hair wrap, pierced nose chain and jawline that could slice sushi (hilare! LOLS!), Opal is fast becoming a genuine style icon. So reach for Grandymama's sewing machine and stitch yourself a sequined tail pronto, b*****s! If only they had the Internet underwater so that this girl could see how much of an impression her fashion has made on our readers. Other than her stunningly attractive features and bang-on-the-nail style, all we know about Opal is that she is smart, exotic and unusual and that she wants world peace. Who knows . . . maybe she could be the next Miss World with those principles? If co-existence means slumber parties and wardrobe raids at Opal's house — baby-crab-cake, bring it ON!

Opal is also pleading with 'Walkers' as she calls us (OMG TOO cute) to help her find missing member of the Mer clan, Lorali. Appaz there is a reward — hopefully it's getting to chill with Opal babe. So keep an eye on the prize.

All hail Opal Zeal!

MERMAID AND MERMEN APPRECIATION TRIBE – aka 'MAMAT'

YO!!!!!!!!!!!!!!!!!! WE R THE MERMAID AND MERMAN APPRECIATION TRIBE STARTED BY MerBaby3000 AND SexSeaOpal. WE EXIST BECUZ WE **LOVE** MERMAIDS AND EVRYTHG ABT AND 2 DO WITH THEM AND ALRDY HVE THOUSANDS OF HITS SO THERZ OBVS A BIG INTEREST. OBVS. AND OMG. OMG. OMG. DYIN. WE HVE JST SEEN A LIVE SPEECH FROM ACTUAL REAL-LIFE MERMAID OPAL ZEAL HERSELF AND WE ARE LITERALLY ACTUALLY DYIN! OMG! RIGHT, SO TO ALL THM HATERZ THAT BE GIVIN US AND R USERS GRIEF. KMT. FFS. FGS. HA. HA. HA. HA. WSE LAUGHING NOW? DCK HDZ! ROFL!

THE SITE CONTAINS EVERYTHING U NEED 2 NO ABOUT MERMAIDS AS WELL AS UPDATES AND COMMENTARY ON THIS AMAZING AND EXCITING TIME! STICK WIV US 4EVA AND WE WILL STICK WIV U! IF U DIG MERMAIDS 2, U CN FOLLOW US, CLICK THE LIKE BUTTON, BABY, AND SEND US A MESSAGE. ADD UR NAME 2 THE FORUM IF YOU WANT TO JOIN OUR CHAT ROOM.

MerBaby3000: Jst Wantd 2 sy, thnx u guyz 4 all the lov3 and support with MAMAT. I know that there is guna be a LOT of exctment cuz of Opal's TV appearance today and this site is most probs gonna totes pop off! But I will neva eva 4get that u lot r the originals. Leave a comment or reply below. Plz fllw me on Twits and I'll fllw u bk asap. As always its difficult to reply to everybdy bt will do my best as u guyz are so worth it.

SexSeaOpal: Awwww, bbz, u r 2 much. Luv u bk. Opal wud b so proud of us rite now. I jst no it.

HASTINGS GAZETTE

1 September

MERMAID DROWNS OUT MYTH!

A real-life mermaid arrived in London yesterday, travelling up the River Thames from the sea to the Houses of Parliament. Witnesses reported seeing 'a strange-looking female riding whale-back'. Others said the sight was 'overwhelming', 'magnificent' and 'distressing'. At first assumed to be a hoax, Ms Zeal, age unknown, met with the Prime Minister before appearing live on television. In a statement she reported a second mermaid missing. Princess Lorali, a mermaid of the royal family, is thought to have fled to the Sussex coast from her underwater home. Zeal states that the royal Mer family will offer a reward for the safe return of the lost princess.

HASTINGS REACH

1 September

'MERMAID' BODY IDENTIFIED AS HOAX

Since the live television appearance of mermaid envoy and peacemaker Opal Zeal, offering a reward for missing Mer princess Lorali, police have been inundated with prank calls and false mermaid sightings.

A strange figure was discovered on Hastings beach by metal detector Samuel Hodgkins yesterday evening. The body was alleged to be mermaid, but upon further investigation was revealed to be an assemblage of leather scraps, human hair and the stuffed carcasses of a monkey, a pig and a house cat.

Hastings Police have urged time-wasters to rethink their actions and have restated their priority – the safety of the Hastings residents and community.

MERMAID AND MERMEN APPRECIATION TRIBE – aka 'MAMAT'

LottieMermaidWorld: Sooooooo many of you have been asking about my secret steps for mermaid transformation since seeing the WONDERFULLY INSPIRING OPAL ZEAL ON TV! YIKES! I have done loads of research on this cos I want a tail sooooooooo bad but my mum says I have to finish my exams first. Whatta b****. But fair play. Cos obvs once I become a mermaid I will NOT be doin any lame-o exams. So I've decided to share it here. The transformation works overnight so you have to be sure to follow the steps exactly rite or else your tail will end up drying out and that will look so shit and you will look like a rite plum standing next to Opal! And plus you mite die.

1. Run a lukewarm bath.

2. Pour in 2 KILOS of sea salt, which sounds like a lot I no but remember soon you will be livin in seawater forevs so get used to it.

3. Get in the bath, naked, obvs or just a bra will do I guess.

4. Press your thighs, calves and ankles together really close and don't move, get comfy, you will be like this for a long time.

5. Repeat this chant over and over until you fall asleep: 'Into this salt bath I have laid, Wake me once you make me mermaid.'

Once you wake up you will obvs be well shocked because you will have a tail so it's best to call somebody you trust and get them to arrange some transport to take you to the nearest sea or whatevs. Good luck.

MermaidFanGirl_1: OMG! OMG! OMG! OMG! OH MY GOD **@LottieMermaidWorld** this is SOOOOOO KEWL! FANKKKKS for sharing! I heard to turn mermaid you had to walk in the sea or that you were meant to wear a really tight pair of jeans in the rain but this one seems much more realistic! BRB! FANKS SO MUCH. LOVE YOU.

MerBaby3000: Thanx 2 **@LottieMermaidWorld** 4 stps 2 mermaid trnsfrmtn. If nebdy does try it out and it wrks cn u let us no asap? I no it will be hard as u will b livin in the sea by then bt if u culd gt smbdy 2 leave us a mssage on the MAMAT forum b great 2 c if it wrkd or nt. Thx. MerBaby. X

CoralCaroline: TBH this sounds like a LOAD of BULLCRAP. AS IF LYING IN A BATH OF SALT WILL TURN YOU INTO A MERMAID! **@LottieMermaidWorld** you are full of absolute horseshit, where did you get this utter crap from? You r such a fraudster. Don't you know you HAVE to be BORN a mermaid to BECOME a mermaid you absolute knob-jockey lying b****.

SexSeaOpal: EEERRRRR . . . SCUSE me **@CoralCaroline** WHT MKES U FINK WE TOLE8 URE RUDENESS ON HERE? **@LottieMermaidWorld** is nly tryn 2 help. We're all in the sme boat ☺

LottieMermaidWorld: Thanks for sticking up for me **@SexSeaOpal**. Nice user name! Good luck to anybody who tries it and yes **@MerBaby3000** of course I will let you know if it works cos I am gunna try it. That will prove if it really works or not! Wish me luck.

SexSeaOpal: OMG! U R SO BRAVE! Lemme no how it goes babe x

MerBaby3000: AHHHHHH! GD LCK BABE!

OpalsBFF: SOOOOOOO jealous of **@LottieMermaidWorld** rite now. DYIN! Good luck!

Say hi to Opal Zeal 4 me! URE so lucky you're gunna get to meet her. Wish I cud!

MermaidFanGirl_1: GOOD LUCK! X YOU WILL BE AMAZING! X

CoralCaroline: YOU ARE A DICK.

RORY

HIDEAWAY

Mermaids. Vampires. Zombies. Fairies. Santa. The Easter Bunny. Too weird. Too much. Now I know why she acts the way she does about everything from cake to pissing on the bathroom floor. I don't want to make her feel like a *freak*. I just want to be normal with her. Granted, I've never been a mermaid but I know how it is to feel forgotten. I can identify with that. We are in the antique shop now, full of Iris's bric-a-brac, tat and crap. Dust sits everywhere in piles, thick, like it was all once alive and is now dead, like roadkill. I want her to feel safe. Not like some project of Iris's.

I watch her curiosity. The way she wriggles her toes, eyeing her legs as she clangs about the shop, bumping into things, learning her balance, her confidence growing. Her feet might be cold but she doesn't seem to feel the bitter moisture of the lighthouse like I do.

'What's this?' she asks.

'That's an old iron. To make your clothes straight.'

'Why would you want your clothes straight?' she asks innocently. *Good point*. I HATE ironing.

'To look smart, I guess. That's an old one. They used to heat them up, the heat with the weight of the metal crushes all the creases out of your clothes.'

'I want some clothes,' she mutters.

She's right. She needs some. I'll have to go shopping at some point. Lucky I've got that birthday money. I watch her beauty. I want to know if she has surfaced for someone in particular. Why has she come back? I feel jealous. Jealous of something I know nothing about. I feel ashamed. Like Netta's husband, the jealous fisherman. But I can't help myself.

'So, your tail . . . I mean, your *tapestry* . . . Did it show you anything . . .? You know, about your past . . . or?'

'No memories came to me. Not as a human. Colours and shapes, yes, but I couldn't work them out.' She rummages through the trunks of clothes and material, tying things in her hair and round her neck, each colour bringing out new bits of her. I stay quiet, hoping that she will talk more, and she does. 'Some Mer get really into the tapestries. They think they are their destiny or fate.' She swallows, her eyes at the window, not at me. 'Others show off about them. Others think they are nothing but colours and patterns. They think the resolution is random and has nothing to do with your human life. A tapestry is a tail but it is so much more. Some Mer spend their whole lives trying to make their tapestries perfect and beautiful because a tapestry never lies. You can say you're happy but your tapestry might speak otherwise.'

'Like those rings with a stone that changes colour to match your mood?' Flynn offers. He is sorting through a box of material.

'Yes, probably. Like that.'

'And what did you think of your tapestry?'

My phone rings again. It's Elvis. I put it back in my pocket. I know I should speak to him but he will be in a funny mood if he knows Flynn and I are hanging out without him. He hates being left out of anything. I want to keep a lid on Lorali and what I have found out. Elvis proper loves drama and I don't need that right now. Maybe he would know exactly what to do but right now it feels calm and contained. That is what I need.

'OK, don't laugh,' she says for the fifth time. She is giggling herself though. And that is making me laugh. My back is against the wall outside the bathroom. Flynn and Iris are pottering around downstairs deciding what to make us for dinner. *How has time got so lost?* It's one of those days that seems to fold itself away into a tiny envelope and post itself to nowhere. Guilt begins to ache in the pit of my belly like a bug. Mum. College. How disappointed she will be when she realises I haven't shown up. Surely this is a better life experience than anything I could learn in a classroom . . . but it doesn't numb the fear. I can hear Lorali changing, the sound of material against her hair and skin. I'm not sure how I'll feel about seeing her in some ancient scraggy white dress from Iris's trunk of clothes. I bet some crusty old nan died in it and I'll have to tell her that she looks nice when really she –

'I'm ready . . .'

I breathe hard and turn round.

My face smiles at everything in front of me. The long white dress fits her just right, proper elegant. Graceful. Special. She looks like . . . well . . . weddingy.

'You look all right,' I say. What an idiot. *All right?* Mum looks *all right*, not Lorali. Too late to say anything else now, I follow her downstairs.

Flynn is frying up this well thick ham to have with mashed potatoes, peas and mustard. This is the kind of food that Iris likes to eat. I think Lorali is confused by her senses but I think everything is confusing her, so it is kind of hard to tell. The rich smoky smell is flooding the lighthouse as the sun drops and the moon begins to shine, giving the lighthouse a UFO igloo glow. Mum *and* Elvis are calling now. I think I should probably call them back soon, just so they don't worry. Candles and lamps are lit and the house becomes warm again. A safe haven where we relax.

'Ham?' Lorali keeps saying it over and over. She is in a good mood and is jittery and giggly. 'The word sounds funny on my tongue.' She beams and Iris laughs too. This is the happiest I've seen him. His eyes are always watery. Eyes that make you look back on yourself. We eat the ham. It is dry and thick and chewy and fatty but it's OK. I keep an eye on Lorali to make sure she doesn't accidently eat the mustard. After the tea thing I don't dare risk her palate with that.

'I want to hear more of Iris's instrument, the wooden one that sits on his shoulder.' Lorali smiles. 'It just sounded so wonderful.'

Flynn and I crack up with laughter at this.

'Is she for real?' Flynn picks at his ham fat, scrounging for extra meat.

'What was that thing? The sawing stick with the hair?'

Iris smiles proudly. 'You mean the violin?'

Lorali shrugs. She is comfortable. 'Yes. That's it. Can you do it again?'

Flynn splatters his mouthful of food out onto the table, choking.

'Of course I can! Everybody usually hates my playing!'

'*Hates?*' Lorali sounds shocked. 'But it was absolutely wonderfully amazing!' She beams and Flynn doubles over into proper belly laughing and I am trying not to laugh, but it just takes over and I can't hold it down.

'So you are a music lover, Lorali. What's your favourite?' Iris asks and then begins to hum various songs from his imagination.

'I don't have a favourite,' she says sweetly. I could die.

'Music – what do you like best?'

'I only know the whales and the dolphins. And we sing. The humfish . . . they make music. Sometimes my father, Zar, he plays the water bells and . . . well . . . there's lots of things to make music with but I don't know what you mean by . . . *best?*'

WHAT THE . . . It is really only hitting me now how alien and surreal everything is. Every sentence is a new finding, something more wild, more extreme, more eccentric. More. And more. And more. We all crack up with laughter, the only way to end the oddity of everything.

Iris drops his fork with a mighty clang. 'Flynn!' he shouts. 'HURRY! Get the records!'

RORY

MUSIC

Iris has set up six of his record players all around the kitchen with old crackling vinyl softly spinning its way round and round, the same lost voice playing from each. He reckons this way Lorali will be able to feel the music in a panoramic type of way. Quite clever really. He's got Flynn on the bicycle-powered gramophone . . . that's *proper* old. The music plays when you cycle. It's rusty and hard to turn the pedals but once you get going it can be kind of fun, and it makes you feel like a caveman when you make music, like when men made their own fire and stuff. Iris and Lorali are dancing in the middle of the room; her cheeks are red, and her pupils are giant and round and open. Her long hair is wrapped up in a big knot on top of her head, and wearing the dress she looks like a perfume bottle. My heart is slamming against my chest. She is so in love with *everything* and I have never seen anything like that. So greedy for life. And the records just keep turning and Flynn just keeps pedalling and Lorali just keeps dancing.

* * *

It is two in the morning. Lorali has finally got tired. She half collapses onto the floor, laughing: her chest is rising and falling, her cheeks are shiny and red, her hair is stuck to her head with sweat.

'I haven't danced like that in years!' Iris chuckles, stretching his cranky limbs. 'I feel a heart attack coming on!' he jokes. 'There was once a king who danced himself to death. He danced so hard that he killed himself. What a way to go.'

Lorali laughs as we carry her to the couch. She is like a tiny broken bird. 'I want to go like that.'

Iris belly-laughs. 'I don't think I'm far off. I heard my knees crack like they were maracas.'

Even in her deep tiredness she is still interested, managing to mumble, 'What are maracas?' We laugh. She really does want to know *everything*. She wants to be part of this world and know everything inside and around it.

'I LOVE legs,' she whimpers drowsily. 'Even though they hurt. I love them.'

Iris winks at me; we all laugh *again*.

Flynn brings her water and a blanket. She is all wrapped up on the couch like a prawn in wool. 'I'm so jealous of the sleep she's about to have.'

'Beautiful, sweet, precious music . . .' she murmurs. 'And the . . . what's its name? Oh don't tell me, the *violin* . . . the ham . . . the swimming pool . . . kind and gentle Flynn and this lighthouse.'

'I'm glad you had fun.' My eyes are dreaming on her now. Too much. 'You idiot,' I add, just to make sure I sound matey and not a pervert.

139

She closes her eyes, a huge smile spreading across her face. Every muscle in her face relaxes. Her breathing changes.

I can't help but plan an escape route for us if we need one. Just in case. Should anything happen. We are on the ground floor, so we can run if we need to . . . bread knife under the couch and the door bolted.

Night falls over us like a fog. The quietness of the lighthouse is now deafening. Ghosts of our laughter haunt the air like the waft of a burnt matchstick. Out of the little window I cannot tell where the sea ends or begins. An endless plane of simple still blackness stares back at me, giving away no secrets. Like a sleeping beast, it doesn't flinch or even murmur. Only dreams. Almost convinced me for a moment that it wasn't hiding all that wonder and wilderness. I soak in this moment of promise, where I'm full of hope and anything is possible. Nobody knows we are here, tucked away behind the little shop of forgotten curiosities.

I get myself ready to sleep on the couch opposite and she reaches out to me, her eyes closed, and says, 'You are everything I wanted.'

HASTINGS GAZETTE

2 September

LOCAL SCHOOLGIRL IN MERMAID TAGEDY

Fourteen-year-old Hastings schoolgirl Charlotte Wood was found dead in her family home early this morning. Wood was discovered in an ice-cold saltwater bath and is believed to have died accidently in an attempt to transform herself into a mermaid.

A post-mortem is to follow and police assure us that no family member is suspected of wrongdoing.

Charlotte Wood's mother, Julie, gave a statement: 'Charlotte was a pretty, clever and outgoing girl. She loved people and was particularly fond of social networking. However, Charlotte's death was NOT an accident. She was following a procedure she believed would turn her into a species of Mer. She was obsessed with Mer culture; she wanted to be a mermaid desperately. I plead with other parents and families to reinforce that our children cannot and will not ever become Mer. There are websites where agitators lurk and they are cowards and they are liars. Please look after your children. Please teach them about the dangers of the Internet and the sea in this dark and horrific time. If not for us, for Charlotte.'

The mayor has put a sea ban in place until further notice to prevent any more dangers to the community and so that marine experts can investigate reports of Mer culture. Fishing, bathing and aqua sports have been suspended. Protestors on the beach argue that the ban will have economic consequences for Hastings as a whole, not just those that earn a living from the water.

HASTINGS REACH

2 September

PROTESTORS IN SEA-BAN CHAOS

Uproar has hit Hastings full-force as fishermen and fishmongers struggle with the sea ban. Protestors have been campaigning outside the town hall, while local supermarkets have increased the price of frozen and canned fish. Harbour Master Thomas Beck says, 'We just want things to get back to normal and as quickly as possible. People are losing their livelihoods.'

There is still a severe weather warning in place. The mayor urges people to take extra care when out and about and to check in on relatives and the elderly.

Full story on page 8.

THE SEA

THE DEATH OF
CHARLOTTE WOOD

This tiny town. What madness is spiralling – I can see it all. The parents of young Charlotte Wood want justice. They are angry at the government and at television for broadcasting Opal's appeal, fuelling Mer mania across the UK. Feelings are running high. An online petition against popularisation of Mer culture is growing by the minute, with comments citing 'perverse behaviour' and 'inappropriate activity'. One angry commenter even said, 'Couldn't they find an uglier mermaid to get the message across?'

I will never understand Walkers.

Zar is in the garden trimming back the seagrass and kelp, and he seems to be warped in a trance.

Keppel is with her sea-monkey, Bingo, smoking seaweed. Bubbles are hiccupping around the room, wafting like small sad, lonely thoughts. Her tapestry runs in blues and greys, like the colour of miserable gravestones. A dark crack scores through her scales, splintering as chalky white does through a Walker's hair when distressed.

And then she hears the engines. Just tiny. Miniscule vibrations muttering through me. Far enough away still to not panic, but she has heard right – they are coming. The Walkers. What has she done? Her brain ticking, she starts to panic. She can't have the council find out that it was she who outed them. She only wanted her daughter to come home. She is queen. She can do what she likes surely? But if it comes to it she can always blame this on Opal, right? Where is Opal anyway? How long does it take to talk on TV? Keppel smokes. Long – hard – drags – puff – puff – puff – breathe. Dealing with the council is one thing, but she needs to do something to scare off these hungry explorers.

Queen Keppel calls for council member Sienna and her serpents, who are needed right away. She needs their loyalty. Their cold-bloodedness. If she is going to lock horns with the Walkers, she has to make sure they know who is boss. She means *business*.

THE SEA

SCHOOL

Otto, carrying the sea air with him, buzzes the bell on the gate at St Leonard's Grammar School for Girls. Mer fever is already reaching a crescendo. Time is running out for the Ablegares to find Lorali before anyone else.

A nasal voice scratches back. 'Hello.'

'Hi, there,' Otto says in his most charming chime. 'We're visiting visitors.'

'All right, hello there. Names?'

'Let's not make this about me. What's *your* name?'

'Carol from the front desk,' the voice splutters, as if delivering bad news.

'Well, Carol from the front desk, hello. The pleasure is mine.'

'Are we expecting you?' the voice of Carol spits back.

'Are they expecting us?' Otto confers with his brothers; they shake their heads. 'Do you know what, Carol from the front desk, if I'm totally honest, I don't think you *are* expecting us, no. Call it a *pleasant* surprise.' Otto then looks right into the shiny hole in the buzzer as if it is a keyhole, running his tongue along his snow-white teeth.

'If you won't tell me your name and you've not got an appointment, I'm afraid I can't let you in.'

'Oh, please?' Otto begs. 'We will be very well behaved.'

'Please leave,' Carol warns, 'or I will have school security remove you immediately.'

'Ooooooh! No! Don't!' Otto winces with sarcasm. 'Don't do it to us, Carol.'

'This is your final warning.'

'But, Carol, I thought we were friends.'

'SECURITY!' The buzzer flatlines. Otto coughs, cracks his neck and rings the buzzer again.

'I didn't like that Carol; it was *very* rude. I like manners.

'Luckily for you, *Carol at the front desk*, I've taken pity on you. And I will, even though you've refused, just have to *Bring. The. Fun. To. You*. Put the kettle on for us.' He checks his immaculate nails and says in a light, almost musical, tone, 'Carol, if you're stupid enough to call for help – the police, the caretaker, the husband that won't press you any more, *ANYONE* at all –

'I will *carve* you.' Otto revisits what it feels like to have blood on his hands. 'Oh, and Carol – don't worry. I'm *only* being serious.'

Egor, the largest, stands up against the barbed fence, allowing the nimble boys to climb his body like a staircase in one move. They are up and over the fence completely unscathed. Then Egor with one hand mounts the fence, the barbed wire not even kissing the soles of his shoes. The Ablegares enter through the door to the PE hall, left ajar to let the last of the summer in. The girls should be in their netball skirts, sweaty with competition, sweaty from growing and young blood. Or better still, they'll be in leotards.

Otto takes out his ivory comb and Jasper stubs out his fag on the lawn. It sizzles to death under his boot.

RORY

MORNING GLORY

I am the last to wake. It's late. I can feel it. But I needed the sleep.
Before I open my eyes I panic. It's like my eyelids are masking
reality. I'm meant to be starting college today. Media Studies. I
made a little film to get on the course and everything. I wrote
the script and directed it, all myself. In the film, Flynn and Elvis
play these two gangsters that hold up a casino. They wore pork
pie hats and long beige coats that I picked up from Iris's shop.
They looked quite convincing. Elvis's parents were bare safe
and let us film in the arcade and casino too, really early, before
all the gamboholic nutters arrived to raid the fruit machines. It
was proper good because there aren't any windows in the arcade
to show the time of day. I think they do that deliberately, so
punters get carried away with themselves and get lost in time.
Like now. Lost in time . . . I was so happy when I got into college.
So was Mum. Now . . . it just seems like a diversion.

Flynn is making coffee and Lorali is dangling her head into
the sink, underneath the tap, drinking water and humming.

I think about the chances of Flynn having found her instead of me. Would he have come to me for help? Involved me at all? Would he have left her on the beach? Would Flynn have dressed her in his clothes? Would *I* have let me in if I were him? I rub my eyes. In the new morning light I notice that the sun, for the first time in ages, has properly come out.

I stand from the couch. 'Morning.'

'Good morning, Rory!' Lorali runs to me, her new legs clumsily pounding over, her arms in the air. I've never heard anybody say my name with such happiness. It feels good. She wings her arms round me. 'I missed you!' she laughs.

'No you didn't.' I blush, laughing, brushing her off to not look obsessed with her.

'I did!' She squeezes me in. 'I didn't see you for all those long hours! My eyes were closed. I was somewhere else . . . in my head. Sleeping is so lonely. I wished you were there in my dreams.'

Flynn is trying not to laugh. I can tell he thinks I am a right soppy mug. The way she is behaving like some brilliant Disney princess, with her guard completely down. This isn't far off a Disney film though, is it? And I had always accepted that I was going to be one of those people that nothing extraordinary ever happens to. Nothing that would make me an anything.

'Well –' I pat her shoulder in a friendly way, fluffing my hair, trying to unhinge the grasp she has round my neck – 'I'm here now.'

'And Flynn was sleeping.'

'I was.' Flynn's sense of humour is completely out of the bag now – it is so unlike him to be relaxed with a new person so quickly, but Lorali seems to have that effect on everybody.

'And Iris. He was sleeping too.' She stretches, and I gulp at the curve of her back, the lightness of her ankles as she bounces onto tiptoes. Strands of her hair are wet from the tap. I shake the soft thoughts out of my head.

'He was,' Flynn says, pouring coffee out into clay mugs.

'I enjoyed the weight of the sleeping. It was heavy. Like a stone in my body. I woke only once and that was because I was so entirely thirsty but the tap was there and so were all these strange shadows. Then I went right back to sleep again. Like a stone. In my body. That I had accidently swallowed.' Lorali tilts her head, expecting me to agree.

Flynn breaks the silence. 'Iris has been rummaging up in the attic. He's got loads to show you.' Flynn froths the milk. He is so domestic. He knows I'm meant to be starting college today but he hasn't mentioned it. We both know I know.

'I can't wait to see him on this brand-new WONDERFUL, TERRIFIC, EXCELLENT day.' Lorali opens up her arms and spins around, her toes slapping on the floor of the lighthouse, the dust particles spiralling around her. There are bruises all up and down her legs. Evidence of her clumsiness, her fun, her brand-new skin and muscle. Flynn shakes his head, a big dummy grin across his face, as if to say *What have we got ourselves into?* And I smile back.

Lorali suddenly stops spinning; she has twirled herself into a dizzy frenzy. Her heels seem happy to keep twirling her round but she finds her balance and says, blistering the mood, 'Who was that other boy that came to the window in the night then?'

151

THE SEA

BACK TO SCHOOL

I am in the air, sneaking in through the windows. The girls are in the sports hall, lined up on benches. As young as eleven, some as old as eighteen. It is the first day back after the summer. There is no talk of new haircuts, mischievous secretive piercings or dodgy tattoos, no whispering chatter of which boys and girls they'd snogged. Just apprehensive tension squashing the room.

Otto is pacing the front of the hall. He has found himself a metre stick, which will do nicely as a cane of some sort.

'Why don't I have a cane *all* the time?' Otto asks Egor whilst he parades about, the suspense exciting him. The young girls silently shiver in fear, their hands under their bottoms and their mouths shut. This is all they need. A local girl has just died and now five strange men have galloped into their building.

'We've never considered it before, Captain, but I think it looks dope.' Egor admires Otto. Egor is a fine believer in *it's not what you got, it's what you do with it.*

'Me too. I might get one.' Otto inspects the stick and looks around for approval from some of the girls. 'Or I could keep this one, I suppose. It's just too short and I don't really like the numbers down the side.' He explains himself to a tiny girl with round glasses who thinks it might be a safe moment to gently roam her eye up to the strange man. Her hair is neatly stretched into two plaits, her centre parting like a gutter between two roofs. 'What do you reckon?'

Otto teases the metre stick underneath the young girl's chin, following the ripe little swellings of chub around her face. The girl immediately returns her eyes to her lap. A brave teacher, a round fuzzy thing, attempts to mouth something soothing towards the child, but fails.

'You lot are dull.' Otto clanks his boots as he struts about. 'I never liked school. My brothers hated it even more than me. That's why we burnt it down.'

One girl gasps. A hand clapped over her mouth.

'You're allowed to be shocked. It is quite shocking. You can't imagine what they want to do with little boys that burn big buildings down, can you? Especially schools?'

The girl shakes her head.

Another lets out a splutter of nervous laughter.

Jasper enjoys keeping the girls in line, making sure their attention is up to scratch, even though there is no need for his abusive surveillance. He has recently taken to biting and his teeth are starting to feel soft and loose under his tongue. Keen to feel a clench. Jasper paces the rows of young women, looping the seats, inhaling their cheap perfume, flowery deodorant, toothpaste and hairspray.

Meanwhile, Egor just has to stand. Say nothing and stand. His bulk and height do the talking for him; he reminds some of the older girls of the nightclub doormen they meet on Fridays and Saturdays, the ones they lie to about their ages and star signs.

The teachers shrink. They are invisible to the Ablegares, who are not threatened by their presence whatsoever.

'You.' Otto points to a sixteen year old. She has long hair that is frizzy but pretty. It is bleached blonde and strands of hair have snatched away like slapped wrists, recoiling, where the bleach was on for too long, burning it to a rusty tinge of orange. But it doesn't matter because she has run a Parma-violet purple through the ends and a smatter of deep blue at the sides. A tie-dye impression of me almost. Hair like the sea. I am flattered.

'Come here.'

The girl points at herself. Amongst the sea of faces it is hard to know exactly who he means. This is a real-life spin-the-bottle. A roulette of absolute terror. All the girls look to each other, lots of hands cling to throats with noose-like grasps, and there's an audible shuffle of confusion and bitten lips.

'Yes, you.'

The girl is used to being disciplined for her appearance. She is often made an example of. The girls are not meant to dye their hair. She does. They are not meant to wear masses of inky blue-black mascara or lashings of dirty kohl round their eyes. She does. They are not meant to have their skirt up above their knees, their nails painted. She does, and yes she does paint them, black, and then she bites them furiously.

154

The girl pads up towards Otto, her tanned, shaved thighs strong and juddering gently as she excuses herself to her peers. They whisper. Her sleeves are rag-ended and her cuffs drag over her hands. She has a wry, smug look about her. She is clearly rebellious. Adventurous. Swamped in youth. She likes being chosen. Some of her friends giggle and snigger. 'Shut up,' she giggles back. Otto is handsome to their eyes, you can tell.

When she reaches Otto she stands in front of him and attempts to put her hands on her hips – all that practising she has done in the mirror of how she will one day stand on the red carpet forgotten. A waste of time. She is vulnerable and cowers as Otto creeps forward.

'She's a spice,' Egor throws across the room.

'Indeed.' Otto sniffs her out. 'She is *nice*.'

The girl gulps.

The teachers flinch.

The other girls wince.

Some are jealous.

Jasper bites his lip.

Egor crosses his arms.

Oska rolls a cigarette.

Momo sucks his cheeks in.

'But she is not *fish*.' Otto teases his metre stick around the girl, as if fiddling a bit of pork fat with a fork. 'But you do look so very much like her.' Otto pauses.

'I am looking for a girl!' Otto's voice bellows through the high ceiling of the hall. 'She is this girl's age, this girl's height, she's as pretty as this girl but she won't wear make-up. She is slimmer than this girl – a-few-less-chippy-wippies-and-cider-after-school slimmer – and her hair . . .' Otto breathes in the girl's hair, then takes a knife from the back of his slacks. The girl takes in the size of the blade and begins to wriggle from Otto's grasp. The rows of students squeal and begin to shriek and cry. Otto brings his arm round and slices off the girl's hair into a blunt bob.

'That's one less girl with long hair that I need to watch out for.'

He pushes the girl to the ground, who with her hand on her heart, gasping for her breath as though she has just had her soul ripped away, shuffles back to her friends who pick her up. Otto clambers up onto the shoulders of Egor, like a child that wants to get a better view at a carnival, and leaves, shouting, 'You see our girl . . . you see her *anywhere* . . . you come find me!' The door opens, letting the breeze in, which comes in the form of a mini hurricane, picking up the dead purple hair from the floor, making it dance.

And even after all of that, the girl, streaky mascara pools dribbling down her face, exhausted from even the touch of Otto on her skin, feels her belly full of butterflies. All the girl wants to ask is, 'But how will we know where to find you?'

THE SEA

NAILS LIKE A CHANDELIER

Under the hot electronic breath of lavender mist hissing from an aroma diffuser, Opal admires the manicure that Lucky the technician is applying to her nails. She wants fingers that look identical to the chandelier in the foyer of the hotel. She still hasn't managed a moment to herself. A moment to think. I am there too of course. In the portable bath that the hotel has provided. No ask is too great for Opal Zeal. There are paparazzi outside the hotel and the deliveries have not stopped coming in their oversized square bags and stripy ribboned boxes. Inside decadent beddings of coloured tissue paper sleep personalised jewellery: rings, necklaces, bangles, bracelets, nose studs. And then there are the ridiculously vast amount of bikinis. *Very funny*. Mac, Nars and Clinique make-up, perfume in all its lavish shapes and sizes, like mini women's figures: Chanel No. 5, Christian Dior and her favourite, Prada Candy. The sharp, rich fragrance from the perfume along with the deep creamy aroma of heavy scented candles makes Opal dizzy. Her manicure is making her head rush. She almost feels a nosebleed coming on. But she isn't complaining. She loves the big *everything*. The woody intoxicated scent of richness and decadence and luxury is everywhere, hidden in the waxy leaves of the plants, the loops of the posh towels, the grand marble floor, and the smiles of the overly friendly Walkers. This is exciting. She is admired. Taken seriously. She is now meeting her appointed publicist, a tiny bleach-blond imp type of a boy/man thing named Marco who laughed dramatically at every line she said and kissed her twice on each cheek when they said hello.

'Have you ever tried an espresso Martini?' he lisps, and when Opal shakes her head he looks as though he has been shot to the heart and immediately flounces off to get the waiter's attention.

'I ordered the kale, beetroot and quinoa salad too. This is all on expenses I assume.' He sniffs hard, rubbernecking the lobby and restaurant to see if any celebrities are about. Not that he cares – he is with an A-lister now all right. Wait until his other clients and competitors get wind of this.

'Lucky, is that Louis Vuitton?' He tries making conversation, forcing a hinged grin at the manicurist who in turn looks back at her suitcase on wheels full of nail polishes, and grunts back, 'Elephant and Castle market.'

'Perfect. Just perfect.' Marco beams sarcastically and puts on some hand sanitiser. 'So, Opal, your schedule is looking pretty busy. *Vogue* and *Elle* both want you for the cover, which I mean just does *not* happen overnight so we should nab those whilst we can. You've had lots of endorsement requests too but I really want us to be picky with those before we get ahead of ourselves. I think we should hold out and wait for the right product and partner rather than making you the face of some bottled teenage-girl deodorant. You've got a few interviews here and there. It's a balancing act, sweetheart, making sure you're doing all the high-brow stuff whilst talking politics, and being accessible at the same time. Likeable. Not intimidating. I thought we'd dine at Sketch tonight, then I can show you a timeline.'

A nervous young waitress rattles a tray carrying two cocktails. Her hair is dyed a washed-out powder blue. She can't help staring at Opal.

'Great, just pop them there, thanks. Opal, you are gonna die when you taste this! Cheers!'

Marco raises his Martini to the sky and Opal imitates him as their glasses chink. Smiling. She is thinking, a) this drink smells abhorrent, and, b) do all Walkers wade in such shallow cosmopolitan waters? She hopes so. *This is it.* She exhales in relief, her glossy mouth kissing the lip of the glass.

Marco sips, dramatically gasping. Smacking his lips, he adds, 'I swear you haven't *lived*.'

Lorali

MOTHER

We are up in the attic again. Just like yesterday. The sun is snaking in through the slats in the roof. The lighthouse is drinking up the light. In so many ways it reminds me of home. The way it seems so muted and detached from the rest of Walker life. Like it has fallen off the edge of the world. Like a shipwreck. It is a secret. Back in the Whirl we are all so fearful of being found by the Walkers. Of being outed and exposed.

'The rain has stopped.' I smile. Maybe Mother has let me go after all.

But Iris laughs. 'This is the calm before the storm.'

'You won't write anything on the trunks, will you, Iris? You won't tell Carmine I'm here? I don't want my mother to know I am here.'

'If you don't want me to, I won't. But if Carmine asks me, I cannot lie.'

'How about you don't go down there? In case you see her,' Flynn offers.

'I wouldn't be able to get there anyway. The water is too high. But if you feel up to it, Lorali, perhaps we could go down there together one day.'

Sick. No. I couldn't. My heart. My head. Bang. Crash. Too soon.

'Maybe,' I lie.

Iris ushers us to the piles of newspaper. 'Get comfortable.'

Flynn hands out cushions, which he knew to bring up with him this time. Rory looks impatient, twiddling his thumbs.

'I've done some work on your mother, Lorali.'

I feel even more sick. Stinging. My flesh burning. My hair on fire. Then dry. Ashes. My eyes hurting. The sound of voices too loud. My mood dipping.

'Queen Keppel. Do you know her story, Lorali?'

I don't know what I want to know. What I don't.

'Your mother is beautiful. Striking. She got herself into trouble, from what I know. Did you know this?' Iris asks. He looks serious.

I can smell my own fear. It stinks. It reeks. It is choking me. Filling up the room. I'm not ready to meet my past yet. I stay silent. But my heart screams. I see these new goose pimples prick up on my skin. A bluey marble blotching over my shoulders. My arms. Blonde hairs standing on end. Rory comes close to me. But not too close.

Flynn jumps up. 'I'll get her a blanket.'

Iris continues. 'Your mother didn't marry for love. She was too young to be married. Especially to this repulsive pig of a man. Their story made the papers. I'll show you if you want to see. There is a picture of her.' Iris hands me the soft paper.

161

It is the most fragile thing my hands have felt in this new world. The words mean nothing to me, just strange symbols. Different from Iris's and Carmine's circles. In an order that I don't understand. And all about my mother.

The page falls open and there she is. My mother. Queen Keppel.

I don't recognise her face at first. Even from this old worn picture, I can see she has red colour on her lips. Her eyebrows seem darker and her eyes . . . bigger. She is standing up. With legs. Like me. Like I have now. Long ones. She is tall. Her hair so yellow it is white. Straight as seagrass. Wrapped in a high ponytail. She is wearing these fantastic clothes. My mum. So strange seeing her in clothes. And jewellery. She always did love jewellery. She is real. She has been here before. She doesn't have that look of strength that she has now though.

It suddenly dawns on me what I have done. I am here. I have made it. Look at me, Mother! Look at me. Being a Walker. Making friends.

Iris gently takes the pages from me. 'Let me tell you how it was, before you try to understand what was said here. The papers don't always tell you the truth.'

'I'm used to not being told the truth.' I hand him back the paper and he begins.

THE SEA

THE ARRIVAL OF QUEEN KEPPEL

If only they all had tapestries that read like Myrtle's. Positive. Healthy. Rich. Green. Pure . . . happy, even. But remember, the act of salvage is to save. Nobody who is safe ever needs saving. These Mer, they often seem to have terrible taste in partners.

Keppel's was rich. He was more than twice her age. It was their honeymoon. He was drunk on fizzy bright beer. He never seemed to fill up, this stocky, bronzed, foul-breathed, sour human. His chubby, stubby digits fingered the laminated beach bar menu. His Rolex sparkled in the sunshine. He ordered my guts, everything I had to offer: the fruits of my belly. Slaughtered. Fleshy, fatty, soggy, rubbery rings of squid, deep-fried crisp mounds of whitebait, and oily mackerel, the skin blistered to a char. And heaps upon heaps of shellfish, the clatter of grilled orange claws, clasping, pegged up like miniature gravestones. Arched over his plate, scoffing, to make sure nobody would beat him to the platter beneath him. Occasionally, between snorts, truffling out the tender oysters, he'd look up to check

I was still there, lapping in and out, making waves. And yes, I was. I saw it all. As he chewed rapidly, spitting out the tiny white bones from the small fish, grease splashing onto his big belly and cleavage, the soft grey rug of chest hair coiling round his gold neck chain, she watched him over her small black coffee. Hating every second.

She couldn't eat. She resented him. The 'arrangement' that her family had made. The only thing she loathed more than him was her own father. How she had been sold off by him. Bargained like the dead fish that lay before her after she had clearly proved to not taste of anything to him any more. He had had his fill. And then this. This violent, cowardly, disgusting *husband* of hers. She despised everything about him; he was an embarrassment.

Her arms were laced with jewellery; he had dressed her in opulent stones, which hung from her ears and studded her fingers.

It was a hot day on the beach. He was infuriating her, repelling her. She was trying to quash the memories of his trailing hands smoothing over her obscure tan lines from the designer swimwear he had bought for her. Triangles. His heaving restless thumps on top of her. His muffled grunting breathing in her young ear. She was angry with herself now just as much as she was with him – no, *angrier*.

She stood. Walked towards me. The sea. To swim. He called her name in between stuffing his greedy grease-smeared cheeks. She stepped into me – one foot. A little lighter, a little easier – the next foot. Breathing. Further and further. He called her name. The white sand was a red carpet for this soon-to-be queen to walk on. I was light. Cooling from the hot sun. Sanctuary.

I was her friend. Up to her knees. Her sun oil left her body, balanced on my surface. Its sheen poisoned my purity. I didn't mind. *Come now. Come now. Come now.* Chest. Neck. He called again. I was calling now too, but loud enough for only her to hear. I was too inviting. I offered escape. Freedom. The jewellery was heavy. A weight. Like I said, I was too inviting. I offered escape. Freedom.

RORY

A PERFECT CIRCLE

'No matter what costly heavy jewellery you wear, nothing weighs a person down more than when they no longer put up a fight. When their heart is heavy. She felt she had no other option. She couldn't escape her circumstance. She was a caged animal. She never came up again. Keppel. Lorali, that's your mother,' Iris mutters, his eyes are wet.

'Are you OK?' I ask Lorali quietly. She nods in a short certain reply. I look around; the attic is full of Iris's strange scribbles. I can see the circles now, over and over again. I once heard a rumour that if you can draw a perfect circle it means you're insane. These circles look pretty accurate to me. I clench my jaw. I know Flynn so well, we grew up together, but I am starting to realise I have no idea who Iris is whatsoever. Does Flynn, even?

'So who salvaged Keppel? *Netta?*' Flynn asks. He is getting the hang of this; I feel ten steps behind everybody else. It is all too much, going *way* too fast. Perhaps living with Iris makes it easier to connect with his craziness.

'Keppel was salvaged by Netta, indeed, who recognised a will inside her, a determination. She took pity on this young girl. She knew how it felt to be ground to sand by a man. She salvaged her, she mothered her, she took her in.'

The question is on all of our lips. Tugging like a loose thread on a wool jumper, a flapping edge of wallpaper you can't leave alone. I take a breath, plucking up the confidence.

'So . . . how were you salvaged, Lorali?' I ask her gently. Because if Mer remain the age they were salvaged, how old does that make Lorali? What was her past?

But it is too late; she is already up and scampering down the ladder.

'Did I say something wrong?'

Iris stares at me as though he is to blame, even though we all know it was my doing. But with her gone I can quickly raise something with them both.

'Lorali said she saw someone come to the house last night. I asked her who it was but she didn't know. I didn't want to worry her so I didn't say anything but I think it's time we moved on. I don't want to bring troub—'

'Oh no, no, no!' Iris mutters, pounding his head. 'No, no, no, no!' He starts to pace, groaning and wringing his hands round his throat.

'What's wrong? Iris?'

'Granddad? You OK?' Flynn looks worried. 'Granddad, you're overexcited. Calm down, come on, let me get you a cup of tea.'

'Flynn, wait, does Iris know who it was? Who was it?'

Iris closes his eyes. Covers his face as though his hands are a mask. 'Pirates,' he says.

And Flynn looks at me with hard eyes as if to say *told you so*.

RORY

KEYS

'A boy. Not a man. That's all I can tell you,' she says. She is fiddling with the corner of a flattened worn cushion on the couch. I can feel Iris watching me, wanting to know more.

'Any other details? What clothes was he wearing? What did he look like?'

'It was too dark. I couldn't see.'

'You can't risk staying here, Rory. You cannot trust anybody. Anybody could find you.' Iris is peering into his wooden crate of keys and metal bits. The thick stench of old brass, copper and iron is making my teeth hurt. It smells of blood. Lorali is wrapped in an itchy wool blanket and a certain sadness that she can't give us any more information.

'Why is it such a bad thing that somebody came to the window? I don't understand. There are Walkers everywhere all the time aren't there?' She feels she has let us down. 'If I had known I would have concentrated much more.'

'Even the garage? That's taken too?' Flynn suggests.

'Yes, even the garage. It wouldn't be suitable anyway . . . It's right in the centre of town. It's not discreet.'

'You know she can stay here, don't you, Rory? You both can. It really isn't a problem. We can work it out,' Flynn tells us.

'They can't. They can't!' Iris yelps. 'Not if we have trespassers, lurkers, strangers. We can't trust anybody. They will come straight for me and find her here.'

'How do you know that?' Flynn asks.

'The cliff face fell, like a great big sign. The pirates are here already.'

I look to Flynn, who looks to the ground. He obviously hasn't told his granddad about the boys we saw at The Serpent. And obviously, by the look of things, isn't planning on doing so now either.

'There is a fisherman's hut. Although it was used for fish smoking for a bit.' Iris peers at us over his glasses. His kind eyes want safety for us. I know that.

But how do I know that Iris won't write about us on the trees in the forest? However, the sheer thought of somebody coming to the lighthouse in the night is sending some cruel chill blazing through my bones. Someone knows we are here. Somebody who knows more about us than we know about them. We have to leave.

'We'll take the smokehouse. The hut. It's fine.'

'Rory, are you sure?'

'Course I am.'

'Why don't you talk to your mum? I really think if you explain . . . she won't want you staying in the hut. It's like the bloody house made of sticks in *The Three Little Pigs*!' Flynn tries to stretch a smile but I'm not in the mood.

'But at least it's hidden.' Iris is trying. But I feel turfed out. Like I'm on my own. I know I don't have to be but it's obvious that Iris, for whatever reason, doesn't think it's fine for us to stay here. I don't want to put them out or endanger them either.

Flynn's eyes look clear but in the centre of them is a misty mucky grey, like a swamp. He knows me. Since we were kids. He knows I'm gonna do this my way no matter what he says.

'Please don't worry about us any more; you've been so helpful. I really am grateful. How much do you want for the hut?'

'Nothing!' Iris says, insulted that I even asked. 'Don't be so ridiculous. Flynn, give them some jars of what we have in the cupboard. The ginger biscuits . . . the honey too . . . whatever we've got . . . and blankets. Take what you need. It's cold down there.'

I miss my bed. My room. My normal life. Tea. TV. My music. Pulling the curtains open in the mornings. Mum. *Mum*. I miss my mum. Now that I can step away from it, be out of the house. I am starting to unravel. Mum has been a different person since my dad left. She doesn't wear colour any more. She doesn't wear lipstick or perfume. She doesn't dance barefoot in the kitchen and 'knock up' something to eat just cos. Or do her art. Or her reading. Or her herbal teas. Or the car boot sales. She is sad. I know why keeping Lorali safe means so much to me. I want to be a gentleman, something my dad could never be. I wish I could just go home but I know I can't take Lorali back. If somebody has come to the lighthouse in the night I can't risk bringing trouble right to my front door. Not to my mum.

When I was little, if I used to cry, Mum would get out the photo album and show me photographs of us. Of me and her.

It would calm me down. Pictures of me riding a horse, playing football, me with Flynn and Elvis as kids, eating ice cream at the fair. As she got sicker, she started cutting them up, cutting the heads off pictures of Dad, editing him from every picture. No more Dad, just a gaping hole to spy through. You could replace that gap with whoever you wanted. I often put the faces of wrestlers or football players there instead. To look like I met them instead of just being with my dad. I had got used to my old man being a faceless hole.

And I don't want that to be me.

The sky begins to swirl, and the windows are rattling furiously with the returning wind. I am keen to get moving. We haven't got time to be emotional.

'We should make a move,' I say to everybody but mostly to try to stir Lorali out of whatever daydream she has vanished into.

Iris is gazing out of the long windows. 'Yes, go now. Don't waste any time. Now. Go. Go. Hurry now ... Where's my violin?'

Flynn rolls his eyes at Iris. 'I'll take you down.' Flynn puts his coat on and leads us out.

Iris stops us. Placing a brass key into my hand he says, 'Take care. What a thing to happen to a person. You were chosen. What an experience. Let instinct be your guide. Trust no one.' He pats me roughly on the shoulder. It is the most sense he has ever made.

Then he hugs Lorali, really tucking her in under his arms. 'Lorali, what you did was a great risk but you made it for a reason. You are not like the others. Remember that.'

And then we leave.

Not like the others? What does he mean by that?

The rain is on its way. A blurred lurk of sky above us stirs. Like a black eye. We walk quickly. Lorali still isn't speaking. We go down along the seafront; it is like a ghost town. So strange.

'What's going on?'

Flynn shrugs. 'Weird.'

We continue past all the shut shops. It feels unnatural to be here without the cheap warm smell of greasy donuts and fatty chips, the sugary cloud from cooking popcorn and toffee apples. No screams or laughter from the fair, no creepy arcade music, no shatter of coins. No splash of dropped ice cream on the floor. The festoons unlit. I can't even hear the caw of seagulls.

Further down the beach, even in this threatening weather, stand a cluster of locals. I can't make out why. The fallen cliff, maybe? There is police tape all round the seafront and police officers are ushering people away. I try to move past quickly, with my head down, holding Lorali close, under my jacket. Flynn frowns, as baffled as I am. I can't help but think that this is to do with her.

Then I see the lampposts. All decorated in cards and letters. Bunches of flowers taped on. Photographs of this girl's face. *RIP Charlotte Wood*. I gulp, recognising her from around the New Town.

'Shit,' Flynn mumbles, his hair flipping like grass. 'I've seen her before. What's happened?'

'I don't know. We stay away for a moment and the whole town falls to pieces.'

'Look.' Flynn points.

There's a shrine. More people are standing by it. We mean to keep moving but hesitate long enough to hear a woman in a wolf-themed fleece mutter, 'Fourteen. Fourteen. Poor thing. Can you believe it?'

'No, I can't,' Flynn politely replies and then smiles shortly, rushing after me.

The shrine is covered in mermaid crap. Photographs, books, toys. I gulp at the sight of it all. Makes me realise how young this girl was. I never know why people spend money on the dead. What's the point buying stuff from shops to just dump on a pile of pebbles with other crap that nobody is ever gonna appreciate? Why am I so angry?

And then I see Bev down there. Her braids. But she doesn't see me. She looks like she's crying.

'Why are all those Walkers doing their eye-sneezing by the water?' Lorali asks me.

She doesn't have a clue, does she? Eye-sneezing. She is like a child herself.

'They're called tears.' It is all I can think to say.

'Why are there tears?'

'They are happy tears,' I lie as I watch Charlotte Wood's dad fall to his knees. Petals from the flowers that have ripped off in the wind leap about him.

And then I see the angry protestors. And I see their placards in flashes. Big and bold. Too much to digest in one take.

PERVERSE

WE WANT ANSWERS

SAY NO TO SEA BAN

JUSTICE FOR WOOD

HASTINGS IS IN TROUBLE

MERMAIDS

MERMAIDS

MERMAIDS

For a second – just a second, I swear – I wish I'd never met her. Undo what I started. This is my home. These people are my neighbours, my friends. What am I doing, betraying them like this? I keep my head down. Sick rises. My tongue seems to expand in my throat, strangling me. Taking all the air away. I manage to have a hot flush, even in the wet air. Lorali's eyes are letting tears go with the wind. It's not her fault. She didn't mean to hurt anybody. It's not her fault she's different, special. It is up to me to protect her, but how can I do that here? Under these circumstances? I look to Flynn. 'They know. They all know. They know I've got Lorali. What am I gonna do?'

There is a cluster of tall narrow wooden-slatted shacks painted black. Each has a hook and a rope for nets. Two small doors and a ladder. They look, especially today, like Victorian prisons. And although I walk past them every day, I've never wondered about them. We are out of sight now. I feel sick. I can hear my heart in my ears. Thumping.

From the outside, you couldn't really say if it was a *nice* hut or not, as they all look the same. Tall and wooden and black and unhomely. I am worried about the smell inside. The remains of fish skin and fin. The charcoal stench of old smoke haunting the walls. I put the brass key inside the lock and open the door.

'Is this another shed, like Mr Harley's?' Lorali asks as we go in.

I nod back. Even try a smile. 'Yeah, kind of.' Thankfully no ghastly fish smell blows back at us. The only clue to fish ever having been here is the shower of metal hooks that dangles above us, slightly torture-chamber-ish but mostly easy to ignore: the roof of the hut is very far away from us, the hut being so tall and narrow.

'It's proper old school,' I laugh, trying to see the positive. It isn't *so* bad. It has a toilet and a sink. A deck for a bed . . . possibly. A wall of strange little drawers and shelves.

'Oh, here.' Flynn goes to light the lanterns. 'They used to use fish oil for these.' Flynn shakes his head. 'Don't worry, not any more. They don't use gas lamps any more either. They make people hallucinate. Granddad and I put one on once at the shop and we both had these crazy dreams. I dreamt I was going out with a horse once. Like proper loved her up. We argued all the time about stupid things like whose turn it was to make the tea.'

Awkward.

Light fills the room. The lanterns speak of hope and promise, casting huge, ambitious shadows on the walls, long legs and triangles. Flynn drops the blankets. 'I'll bring you some more; I'll come back later. I'll bring more food. Text me anything else you need.'

'I can't! My phone's out of battery.'

'OK, phone charger then. I'll think of something.' He looks at me. Why does it feel like this is the end? 'Enjoy your new home,' he jokes. 'Let me know when the moving-in party is!'

'Wait!' Lorali leaps up and squeezes his hand. 'Thank you.'

Flynn grins back. I know that face. Wishing he could do more.

Now the place is warming up, the smell of wood and sea air gently filling the hut, I start to feel less paranoid. There she is, enjoying looking in all the little drawers, fiddling with tackle and feathers, rope and string. Oblivious to the world outside. In the dark. I feel just as isolated as she does now. Keeping her safe isn't going to be easy. Nor is trying to let her know everything is going to be OK.

When I really don't think it will be.

THE SEA

AN EYE FOR AN EYE

I've never understood revenge. However, Queen Keppel, in a state of loss, has chosen revenge as her weapon. After sorrow comes anger. As I said, with the Mer, everything is done with the heart and the gut. The mind's opinion always comes last.

Imagination, a cruel disease, is now snacking on the brain of Queen Keppel. It tells her that Lorali *has* been kidnapped. Opal has not returned with news. Those Ablegares *cannot* be relied on. Her little girl has been captured by Walkers and she is angry. Her daughter is not dead. But not at sea. Keppel is in denial at the possibility of surfacing. She cannot conceive of it.

There are many beasts and monsters in my waters. As host to many species I have to endure all beings, no matter their traits, but if there is one thing that I deplore more than any other characteristic it is the dark trait of crookedness.

Sviley is quick, *too quick*, and oversized, *bigger than he needs to be*, this pot-bellied oily serpent. He enjoys nothing more than being instructed and sent on a mission by his mistress, Sienna, to whom he is totally devoted. And once he is let out of his shackles, where he lurks in the dark frozen depths of my gut, he makes up for lost time. Sviley's hair is ropey, his skin greasy and blubbery and an off-white colour. Sneaking and snaking, he roams with a gentle distressing hum. He is dirty too, and wherever he moves he leaves a smoky trail of grotty deposit behind. But that is all in the nature of beasts; I celebrate it. But there is something else about him that makes him rather dastardly.

I didn't know it would be a child.

There are lots of people on the seafront today taking pictures – a camera crew, reporters, mourners for the deceased girl Charlotte and, of course, the angry people with the signs showing their urge to dissect me. Others are where the cliff face crumbled, trying to work out why and how it happened, interviewing each other and just *staring* at it, helpless, like a wedding cake has collapsed. And at me. I was that endless enigma. The one with no answers.

The child is chasing the dog. Dogs' hearing is heightened and sensitive. The vibrations of Keppel, I imagine, have been fidgeting with their nervous systems. The boy – I'd say . . . age seven, maybe eight – strays away from the vast group of people and runs towards the water, further and further away. The dog stops at the water's edge and begins to bark furiously. It is busy, as I said, a lot going on, and the boy isn't a baby, he is at the age a Walker gives a child independence. Nobody is keeping watch, all distracted by the commotion.

'What is it?' the boy nervously asks his dog. He wears dark colours, bottle greens and greys and blues. He is dressed for the sky.

No, he is dressed for me.

Of course he is.

The boy is confused. He looks back at the swamp of people huddled under the cliff, the crowd of questions – his parents are in that swamp somewhere, sticking their oars in no doubt.

The dog barks again and cocks his head. The boy looks out to the water. 'I don't see anything, Smudge.' He pats his dog on the head. 'And stop woofing like that,' he adds quite rightly. 'It's annoying.' The dog, I mean, *Smudge*, barks again. The boy is about to walk away. I'm never one to side with a Walker usually; they pollute me, use me like a dustbin, but I wish this Walker would *walk* away. But he doesn't; just like the dog, he sees it now too.

The drowning hand, bobbing up and down and sucking itself back under, coming up for air and then back down again. The boy panics and calls for his parents amongst the carnival of chaos, but with the wind and me and *all* those people over by the cliff, his voice is like the breath of an insect. They are stupid. Ignorant. Careless. The irony. Arguing about the sea, and right under their noses . . . ah. They know it isn't a safe time. The dog changes his mind now, begins to pull at the child's leg. *That's it, Smudge, take him home. Not today, he's not ready.* But the boy can't forget what he has seen, and jumps in to save the drowning person.

The dog barks loudly now and runs back to the crowd to try to bark some sense into them instead.

I am ice. The boy swims towards the hand, closer and closer. 'I'm coming,' he gasps, and I am so cold. 'Hold on,' he reassures with his small breath. He probably thinks he will win a medal at school for this. A Blue Peter badge, even. The boy is out so far, and I am so deep, he can't stand. I even try to lap him back with flicks of my wave, tilting myself off-axis to scoot him away, which I really shouldn't do. It's not right to mess with destiny. He is a strong swimmer. He wants to make his parents proud. He wants the cameras on him today for a *good* reason: for saving somebody's life. His will is fierce. The little town of Hastings needs something positive to raise the spirits. To bust holes in the clouds and let the sun shine through. It will be him! Him and Smudge on the front of the *Gazette*, arms wrapped round the person he will rescue, smiling greatly. 'MY HERO!'

The closer the child gets, the more violently the hand shakes. It goes under and keeps flapping back up again, teasing, which makes the boy rush. He grunts, 'I've got you.' And wraps his young hopeful grip round the drowning hand. 'I've got you. Hold on. Don't let go. You're all right.'

But it is no drowning hand. This is the fin of Sviley. That's the thing about Sviley; he has a human's hand for a fin and has perfected the mechanics to move it like a human in distress. Panic. Fluster. Flap. Flap. Flap. Flap. And then: *Got you. Hook. Line. Sinker.* The grin on his face after the catch. The boy, right in his palm, can hear the screaming voices of his parents and the bark of Smudge, as he meets the gluey eyes of Sviley. He takes a gasp as his bubbles of hope pop. One by one. Sviley dashes the young child into the air, and circles up, lolling him like a ragdoll, his small spine spinning. Snapped. Right before he is splattered into the insides of Sviley's guts.

I had been certain that the boy would be salvaged. He was a good one. He is just the type of Walker that the Mer take home with them. And they are a Mer down after all.

But if there's one thing other than salvage that Mer partake of, it's revenge. An eye for an eye does not take the pain away. But it helps.

Lorali

BITTERSWEET

I stay quiet. I am sad. I know he is sad. I may be new but I am not stupid. I may be a different species but I have a gauge. A dial. I may not be able to read words and I may struggle with language but I can tell when somebody feels fear. I can taste it. I can smell it. That's how we stay alive in the Whirl.

It won't go away. I know my mother. I have ruined everything for him. I have trampled over his life with my virgin bones. Crushing everything he had. My so-called family and me. We are communicating through violence that impacts everybody.

'I am sorry,' I say.

'Sorry? Why?'

'That I ever came here. That you found me.'

'Don't say that, Lorali. I'm so glad I found you.' He looks shy and uncomfortable. We are cold. He is scared.

'Are we going to be OK?'

'Of course. It's . . . *great* here. I've always wanted to be inside one of these.'

He is so sweet. I know he doesn't mean it. I know he would rather be at his lovely warm house with the cake. And the butter. And the kelp wash.

The fire is crackling. There's a strange smell from our wet clothes steaming in the heat. The fire is *fantastic*. Beautiful. I wish the mood could be happier. I like the air. Even though my lungs hurt. I like the sound of the waves. The hush of them. I like being this side of the water.

'How do you, you know, keep memories . . . from when you were a child? Do your memories show on your tails?' Rory asks me. His head is cocked to the side, his jaw clenched. I can feel his heat. He is trying to keep upbeat.

'*Tapestries*. Yes. If a Mer wants to remember something they leave it on their tapestry. The important things will imprint there anyway. Like a birthmark. If you want to remember something in particular, you have to scratch it in, or scar it.'

'Does it hurt?'

'Not as much as forgetting.'

Rory leans forward. The clothes he wears are like skin. I have words that I can't use. They are hard. Every one is sharp. Ready to kill the moment. Down in the Whirl we can often go days without speaking. If we feel a feeling we show it. We don't say it. Hardly ever. Words are powerful but they are spiky. Big. Strange. I want to tell him what I *saw*. What I *know*. Why I surfaced. If we were Mer he could read me for himself by my tapestry. He wouldn't need to ask questions. He would understand. But he's not. So he can't. We are a different species. I am stupid to think that the physicality of a set of legs is going to change all of that.

But I want to touch.

I take his hand. It's cool.

He turns to me.

I can hear his heart. It is rapid.

In the Whirl, as the dominant sex, the female Mer always instigate. Not that I have ever done so myself. But I am not nervous.

Rory looks confused by my confidence.

I place my fingers in his. Interlocked. A friendship.

I lay his hand on my body. Where my tapestry would be.

He looks at me. He is not sure.

I place his palm open, unpeel every finger.

He is tense.

I show him the way around. Until he finds his way.

Then I let him explore.

THE SEA

COMING

They are. Their toxic engines spurting gunk. Their tanks infecting my purity. The Cavities have heard of the missing princess. They are not leaving empty-handed. Gossip sails fast but not as fast as the *Cetus*. The price for the return of the mermaid? Keppel will rise to the challenge; she will give *everything*.

RORY

THE MORNING AFTER
THE NIGHT BEFORE

I have imagined this morning before. You know. *After*. I thought
I would be in the greasy spoon. With the boys. After I'd walked
the girl home or whatever. Cos I wouldn't have taken Bev out
to eat. No way. I'd go in big. I'd be hungry. Like I am now. Eggs.
Bacon. Sausages. Hash browns. Fried bread. Beans. No black
pudding though. That's gross. Might even get chips. Tea. With
sugar. Lots of it.

It would go like this. I'd say, 'Boys, guess what?' and then
I'd tell them. They'd want to know all the details. And I'd
exaggerate. Biting into my fried bread I'd laugh off their
comebacks with a wink and a slurp of tea, and possibly buy
them both breakfast to celebrate my maturity and how *bossy*
I was.

That I was a man.

But that is the last thing I want to do today.

She wakes as I am putting my coat on. The rain has settled slightly. I can feel it.

'Where are you going?' She yawns and stretches across the sheets, her hair tumbling after her. She winces and covers her eyes as I crack open the door of the hut. I'm not scared of her vulnerability any more because she doesn't seem as fragile to me now. She is stronger than I thought.

I figure it is early enough to risk going out. I have to get a charger for my phone, I can't wait for Flynn, and I am also anxious to find out about what has happened to Hastings since Lorali's arrival. I feel so paranoid. Like the world is watching me under a microscope, laughing at my every move. Like there are eyes everywhere. Flies on the wall. Judging me.

It would be too risky to take Lorali with me. She is safest here, in the inconspicuous hideaway of the smokehouse.

'It's early,' I say. 'Go back to sleep.'

'If it's *so* early, why are you up?'

'I'm going to get you some clothes.'

'Clothes?' Her eyes light up. 'Woman clothes?'

'Nah, baby clothes!' She looks confused – often her humour can be a little off . . . then again, mine isn't *always* on point to be honest. 'Course I'm going to get you some nice *woman*, you know . . . clothes.'

She leaps up. 'Can I come?'

'No.'

'Why not?'

'Because you'll draw too much attention. Look how excited you are! Imagine trying to discreetly take you around the shops, you nutter!'

She laughs. 'Please? What's a nutter? I won't be excited,' she squeals.

'You will.'

'I'll hide it. I'm good at hiding. Remember?'

'Errr, I seem to remember *finding* you!'

'But I've thought about what I would wear for so long. Opal used to bring us pictures of all the girls in magazines, in long dresses and skirts and ball gowns . . . and high heels.'

'No. No. See? Already *way* too excited. High heels! You haven't even managed bare feet yet!'

'I'll wear trainers. I want to wear trainers like you.'

I laugh. 'I'm getting you the basics. Then, soon, we can go together.'

'Promise?'

'I promise. I'll be back soon. Do you want some tea before I go?'

'Yuck, no. All you Walkers ever do is boil up water and drink it. It's so strange.'

'You'd better get your head around that,' I joke. Then I wink at her, which makes me feel a bit like one of them sleazy old men that hang around outside the betting shop, so I nervously pat my pockets to check I have everything, which I know I do, and open the door to leave. She falls back into the heap that we slept on. Our weird little home on the seafront. What some people would pay for a house on the seafront! If Dad could see me now . . .

THE SEA

BUBBLES

With the flames of Diptyque candles melting fudge-like to a syrup, Opal Zeal is clearly in no rush whatsoever to get back to the Whirl. Her presents from PR companies are stacked sky high, in a furious mountain with a hideous bow on top. So materialistic, the Walkers. Designer handbags, clutches and purses from Moshino, Burberry, Saint Laurent, Prada, Mui Mui, Chanel. Sunglasses. She had waited so long to just be under the sun and now she can shield from it. Not that she has seen much of it in drizzly London. Then there was the fan mail. The love letters. The stalkers. The admirers. The haters. But that was to be expected, of course. Now, she is relaxing in the free-standing gold-tapped bathtub of her suite at the Dorchester. She has just cancelled her room service order of a hot chocolate fudge sundae because she has caught sight of a paparazzi shot of herself in a magazine and was surprised by how *voluptuous* her bottom half was in comparison to the Walker models. And the thought of a *thigh gap*?

The phone rings. She likes the phone very much and so when Marco gave her an itinerary for 'phoners' with journalists for the day, she was elated. She can waffle along to magazines, radio stations, blogs and newspapers for as long as they want her. Her opinions are so *important*. She speaks about fashion, art, politics and, of course, life in the Whirl. It doesn't play on her for a moment that she is giving away secrets; they will all come out anyway in her autobiography. Her new frosted Swarovski-crystal-studded nails are twinkling as she admires them next to the feeble, dreary attempt at bubbles in the bath. *Bubbles.* In *my* water. *Bubbles.* How *cheap*. Disgusting. They are already going scummy. Of course they are. Why would you pollute my purity? Livid.

This phone call is not an interview though. It is an emergency. A young boy has been eaten. Alive. In front of an audience of Walkers, by . . . wait for it . . . a sea monster. You know this. Opal is needed urgently for a press conference this afternoon.

Opal stays calm, thanks the messenger and dials immediately for her hair and make-up team.

'Thank you, Kelly, mwah, mwah, you too,' she nibbles into the receiver, giggling. She is getting into this; Marco has taught her well. She glances over to the stack of gifts, the temporary clothes rail that room service has nervously assembled for her. A white rabbit-fur jacket with a matching muff catches her eye. It is *only* rabbit skin and anyway the thing is dead now; it is too late to save its skin. Besides, it will do nicely for the event. As soon as she puts the phone down she lays her head and hair fully into the bathtub, her hair wafting out like smoke, and then guess what she does?

She screams.

THE SEA

DRIFTING

'Build me another, will you, Bingo?' Queen Keppel is buzzing on seaweed; she and Zar haven't spoken in ages. He tends the garden, attends his meetings and hunts. Meanwhile, Keppel inhales the gas of puffer fish. In the evenings she doesn't want to sleep or tessellate or communicate. All she wants to do is cry until she is sick. Zar doesn't have to see her tapestry to know this; their palace shook when she did. Keppel is trapped in a cycle: sobbing until her tongue swells, combing her hair, plaiting it, unpeeling it and doing it all over again.

Zar knows what she has done, that she has ordered Opal Zeal to go public and out them. His partner made that decision and in his opinion it was a bad one. But he won't say so. It would be out of line for him to ask her for reasons.

Marcia whines; somebody has arrived. Keppel leans over her iron balcony and looks at the smashed green-stone tile flooring of the patio gardens. Glimmering. Lorali had helped choose that effect. Keppel usually loves to look down on it.

But now she is too wasted to admire it.

'Carmine? Myrtle?' she calls down airily. 'And to what do I owe the pleasure? Are we due a committee meeting?'

They are not smiling.

'Have you heard the vibrations, Keppel?'

(Hmmm. They should be adding a *Queen* in front of that, shouldn't they?)

'Perhaps. A little current here and there,' Keppel lies. She knows full well that Walkers are already making fast movements towards them.

They know that Sviley was not on his leash, and they know that Opal Zeal has not been seen in the Whirl, and they know that only one of them had a reason to be angry.

'Is there something you want to tell us, Keppel?'

RORY

SHOPPING

It is early.

The air is ripe with bleakness. Muggy.

I knew I'd probably feel weird but not so . . . displaced. Out of my skin. The people of Hastings look like ghosts. There is still a big crowd at the beach. More police. Tape. Cameras. With those professional mics too. Not just the crappy local lot that would turn up to an egg-and-spoon race on the hill. I watch reporters speaking into lenses. Career-hungry runners from the TV channels rushing about in puffer jackets, holding flasks of hot coffee and asking questions. Susan's dad from the offy is there, saying something into a microphone. I am too far away to hear what. But I see some people crying.

It looks like the old town I know but for some reason it feels like I don't know it. Like a station I'm passing through on a fast-moving train.

I look at all the girl shops. They must have grades, like good ones and crap ones. I mean, what about a few months down the line when she's all . . . you know . . . *embedded* and understands everything and knows the difference between crap shops and expensive shops and thinks I'm a cheapskate? But then again, it's just clothes. Surely anything is better than wearing my T-shirts and Iris's antiques.

The shopping centre is packed as the rain has just started again. I see a few girls walk into the closest shop. It is also the biggest, so must be most popular. I've heard of it anyway. I see a couple of girls I recognise, so I duck behind the wall. It occurs to me that I'm only going to continue to see people I know so I might as well just get on with it. The sooner I've got the clothes, the quicker I can get back to Lorali.

The shop is all bright and girly. It smells of plastic and nail-varnish remover and sugary cola-bottle sweets. I trail the rails. It's hard to know what to pick. I scratch my head. Why don't they put all the skirts together and all the tops together? Everything is everywhere! I feel myself getting in a proper fluster. There are a few mannequins dotted about so I just decide to copy one of them. She, this mannequin, looks kind of nice, easy-going, relaxed, but *cool*; I'd talk to her. I step up to the mannequin, stand next to her, look at us in the mirror. Yeah . . . we look –

'Rory!'

It's Bev. Shit. Not now.

'Bev. Hi.'

'What you doing here, stranger?'

'Shopping! What are you doing here more like?' I say awkwardly, trying to be funny, but not being at all.

'I work here.' She flicks the little pass round her neck up at me like some wretched police officer flashing a badge, all smug that she's sixteen and *already* has a job. It's got her photograph on the pass. 'See? So what about you? Wearing girls' clothes these days or do you have a girlfriend now?'

'A girlfriend?' I squeal, sounding like a right dickhead now. 'A girlfriend, nah, nah, nah.' I try styling it out. 'It's research. I'm doing . . . fashion . . . at college.' Big lie.

'*Fashion?*' Bev snarls. 'You?'

'I thought I'd try it – don't look at me like that – anyway, what's the big deal? You've always told me to dress better!'

Embarrassed, she changes the subject. 'Oh my god, did you hear about that boy on the beach? So sad. Crazy times at the moment, right? Can't believe it.'

'Sorry, Bev, I really need to – Boy? On the beach?'

'Yeah, did you not hear? Where have you been? A boy drowned . . . Well, some people are saying he was *eaten alive* by a sea monster . . . Then all this mermaid stuff . . . so mad. That Charlotte Wood girl used to come in here *all* the time.' She waves at a girl across the shop floor that she recognises. 'I personally always believed mermaids existed.'

I think I am about to pass out. I need to get my hands on a newspaper. I can't find out news from Bev. Not here, like this. She will see my reaction. Plus, she's way too smug.

'So, I bet you can't *wait* to get away from this manic town! I was hoping they'd give us the day off here cos of all the *dramas* but no such luck,' she continues. 'So what got you into fashion?'

'Who are you, the bloody police?' I snap.

'Sorry, it's just Elvis never mentioned it.'

'Do you still speak to Elvis?' What's she been speaking to him for?

'Yeah, sometimes we message. Here and there, this and that. He's a good guy to know if you want to get into the clubs and stuff. He sorted me a fake ID too.' She flicks her hair. Her eyelashes are long like a camel's.

I rub my eyes, proper stressed now. 'Can I get that jumper and this stuff?'

'Sure. So is your range a bit . . . *mumsy* then?'

'Mumsy?'

'Frumpy . . . like a bit . . . you know?'

If you mean I don't want to dress Lorali like a tart like you, Bev, then yes, all right, mumsy *please.*

'I'll take it.'

'What size?'

'Normal?'

'Oh, Rory.' Bev places a hand on my chest and giggles. I think about why I kind of used to like her. Her dark skin. Her upturned nose. Her curly hair, her brown eyes, her freckles, her big lips and the way they tasted like sweets all the time. Every single thing about her different from the girl waiting for me in the hut. She scrunches her face up. 'Ror, sizes come in numbers . . . Eight, ten, twelve, fourteen and so on . . .'

Don't *Ror* me.

'What are you?'

'I'm a . . .' and then her voice disappears. I can't hear her any more because I'm sure I see a face I can't quite place, but I know it. It gives me a terrible feeling. Looking at me, peering over the balcony from the floor above, watching me, watching

197

me, boggling at me, before it disappears into the dawdling crowd of window-shoppers.

'Do you want to come over to the tills?'

I follow her and she starts bagging my stuff up. I've annoyed her. I'm not paying her enough attention.

'Do you want to keep the hangers?' she says.

'Yeah. No. No. It's just going on a model for my, erm . . . portfolio. Thanks.' This one outfit isn't going to be enough. 'Can I get some knickers too?'

'*Knickers?*' she snarls. 'Are you designing underwear too?'

'Just in case the . . . erm . . . model doesn't wear knickers,' I say in a rush.

'Surely this *model*, if she's professional, will wear knickers?'

'Best to be safe.'

Lorali

AN OLD FRIEND

I knot the last feather to the others, using the fishing wire to attach them all together. I loop the feathers round the beams. Softly curling. Floating. Feathers belong to the sky. If we ever saw a feather float, we assumed it was bait anyway. That the hunters used. We never trusted them. We were trained to never trust. An unforgiving, harmful species are the Mer. The Walkers are different. Open. Smiling. Positive. Welcoming. Natural. They don't lie like my species. Not to the ones they love.

I can hear footsteps shuffle along the pebbles. Rory must be home. I am hungry. I missed him.

There's a knock at the hut door. We aren't expecting anybody. The door is locked. Only somebody with a key can enter. Only Rory and Flynn have keys. It isn't Rory. It isn't Flynn.

'Hello?' It's a male voice. 'Anybody in there?'

I stay quiet. I'm good at hiding. I must be good at hiding.

'Hi,' says the voice. 'If you're in there, can you let me in? I know who you are. You can trust me.'

Never trust anybody who says that.

I stay completely still. I watch my feathers. Twirling. Gentle. Gentle.

'Rory sent me.' Rory? I creep closer towards the door. 'Do you know Rory? Tall-ish . . . brown hair? Green eyes? Too good-looking for his own good? Wonky teeth that somehow look better than anybody in the world with straight teeth?' the voice jokes. They do have a point. And a sense of humour. And they obviously *know* Rory.

'Why did he send you?' I ask. The words jump out. Big loud words.

'He's in trouble,' the voice says. 'He needs our help.'

Trouble? And so I open the door. Just like how a real Walker would.

RORY

TAILING

'All right, Rory?'

'Just act normal. Look like you're expecting me,' I say through gritted teeth, and Flynn awkwardly pats me on the back as he lets me shove past him. He looks about before closing the door behind us.

'I've been trying to call you.'

'My phone's run out of battery! For the millionth time, Flynn! No bloody thanks to you!' It's not his fault but I'm scared.

'Where's Lorali?'

'At the hut.'

'On her own? You left her?'

'I didn't have a charger, a newspaper. I had to find out what was going on and how much everybody knew about us . . . *her*, I mean. Listen . . . quick . . . I think I'm being followed. Back from the New Town. I couldn't risk walking back to the hut.'

'Followed? Who by?'

'I was in a shop getting clothes for Lorali and I think it's one of those blokes. You know from The Serpent, that night, when they were all there.'

'The pirates?'

'I don't know. I think so?' I am breathless. 'I was being followed. I'm sure of it.'

'But why would he be in a girls' clothes shop?'

'Probably looking for girls. Probably trying to find Lorali.'

'Pirates?' Iris bear-foots it down from the attic, his rickety ladder twanging with every step.

'He's up there all the time now, since he met Lorali,' Flynn whispers to me. He watches his granddad plodding down the ladder and has to stop himself from trying to help him, like a parent with a curious toddler. I notice blood on Iris's neck but I don't mention it. Flynn bites his lip and stares at me. I don't know what I'm meant to say.

Iris frowns at us.

Flynn speaks. 'Pirates, yes. We think.' Flynn looks to me to speak but I don't. The more Iris remains silent, the more Flynn stammers. His mouth won't close. 'W-we've seen them before, in the pub, Rory and me – we saw them. Five, I think, pirates. Not a hundred per cent sure though, Granddad. I'm . . . I'm sorry we didn't tell you, Granddad . . . Sorry.'

'Before? When?' Iris is serious.

'Rory's birthday.' Flynn chews the skin round his thumb.

Iris looks annoyed at Flynn. 'Why didn't you say so?'

'Because I knew you'd go all crazy like this and because anything to do with pirates or the whole sea in general makes you crazy . . . well, *crazier*, and, well . . . because we were in the pub and you don't like me going to the pub.'

'The *law* doesn't like you going to the pub, Flynn, not me. Now, there are levels of secrets. This is too big a secret to sit on. What do they look like, these pirates?' His urgency begins to frighten me. He seems stressed and he begins to pace. I know Iris is protective but this seems extreme. What does he know about pirates anyway? Flynn looks worried.

'Kind of . . . *good*,' I offer. It's true. If it was them from the pub.

'Good?' Iris shakes his head in disagreement. 'There is no such thing as a *good* pirate.'

Lorali

AWAY

'I don't understand . . . why can't Rory just take me himself?'

'He says it's not safe.' We are walking across the rocks and stones. It is near where I first met Rory. Where he showed me that kindness. It doesn't make any sense to me that he wouldn't be here himself. I know he would want to take me. Want me with him at all times.

'Is somebody after him?'

'We are not completely sure but he doesn't want to risk it.'

'And where did he say he will meet us?'

'On the boat.'

'But we aren't going to sail?'

'No. I've told you this.'

'So you won't lift the anchor?'

'No.'

'Who is after him?'

He falters and then he says, 'Pirates.'

'Pirates?'

'Unfortunately. That's why we've got to get you out of Hastings.'

'Why? Why are they after him?'

But his eyes look at me and he doesn't even have to answer. They are after him because of me. I've put him in danger. The first time I am happy, and I ruin it. I bring trouble everywhere I go. I look back towards Hastings. The rolling thunder above it. The little houses. I had always wanted to live in a proper house. With windows and a door. With a knocker. And a letter box. And letters addressed to me. I want normal things too. But I am so far away.

I let him lead me towards the boats and say nothing. The crunch of the stones beneath my feet crackles. The wind batters my ears. His grip is hard.

The closer we get to the water, the sicker I begin to feel. I feel ill. Like I might pass out. Like I might die. Like I might lose oxygen.

'Please . . . I don't think I can . . . Can we please just wait here?' I dig my heels into the stones.

He pulls me towards the water. 'No, somebody might see us . . . *you*, I mean. Somebody might see you.' He pushes me a little harder. 'It's not worth the risk.'

'But I can't. I don't want to go back. I can't. Not there.'

He knows who I am. He must be a friend of Rory's. I can hear the waves rushing. The water spitting. It's angry with me. It's calling me. It's just like how Iris told me. The way it called my mother. The way it tempted her. The way it took her under. The way it beckoned her down. And she was choiceless. But she had a chance. She was salvaged. I won't be salvaged. Once you surface you can't reverse. I don't even know if I can even swim in there any more, let alone breathe. Survive. Down. Down. I feel sick. The rabid waves are licking. Like a fire. My knees are jelly. My legs are loose. I fall. Onto the stones. My skin is young. It bleeds. It hurts. The sharks sniff me. I fear. The beasts sniff me. Hear my heart. He collects me up. The salt seeps into the new pores on my skin.

'Quick. Hurry,' he says. He is impatient but he keeps smiling at me. Reassurance. Every time I think not to trust him, he just smiles. Softly. He reminds me of Rory. There is an essence of familiarity. I can smell Rory on him. 'Think of Rory,' he says. As if I need reminding. But he reads my mind. The thought of Rory. It gives me strength. I pull myself back up. My bones crack. I flop forward. He holds me up. His arms round me. The water. The sea. It laughs at me.

THE SEA

A HOMECOMING

Come, child. Come.
   Don't listen to me, child. Don't trust this one.
   Come on, child. This is your home. Come swim.
   Run. Use your legs. Use your legs. Muscle. Bone. Veins. Nerve.
Blood. Run.

Lorali

THE SEA

You can't have me back, I think to myself. I am human now.
I am Walker.

He carries my weight. My feet dusty from the specks of
sand. My hair blowing in the wind.

I follow him to a boat. It's small. White. With an engine. It
isn't kind to the eye. It wants to be shiny but it looks pretend.
Unsafe. He takes my hand as he leads me up. Inside. His hand
is smooth. I follow him in. My heart is beating. Thud. Thud.
Thud. I duck my head as we step down inside. It smells old.
Lighthouse. Mr Harley's shed. Soil. Earth. The smokehouse. But it
doesn't feel sound. Or strong. Or warm. I can hear the water. It
laps the boat. The sound makes me wince. Makes me gag. I hold
onto the boat. I shift about. Colour has drained out of my cheeks.

'Sit down,' he says.

'How long will Rory be?'

'Not long,' he reassures me. I don't know about time. How
long is long? A day? A year? A moon?

'Can we not wait on the shore? Do we have to wait in here?'

'I think it's best, don't you?'

I don't know what is best any more.

'Here's a blanket.' He throws it to me. 'Wrap yourself up, keep warm.'

Kindness.

I pull the blanket round me. Close.

'I'm going to see if he's coming. Stay here. Keep warm,' he instructs.

I do as he says. I start to settle. Feel less sick. I look about the boat. There is a lot of skin. Animal skin. Bags. Leather. Belts. Walkers are so strange. How they wear other animals' skin. This is exactly the stuff Opal warned us about. The poachers. The hunters. What they would do with our tapestries. How they would patch us. Opal told me that some Mer were kept in glass tanks. Given just enough water to hydrate and food to survive and then they would be stripped. Patch by patch. The new scales would grow back, repairing with saltwater, and then they'd patch those too. It would go on and on until eventually the tapestry no longer grew back. It would dry out and die. And so would the Mer. A tapestry is much more beautiful when skinned alive. Or so they say. They would think nothing to take our skin and wear it . . . well, not *ours*. Not any more. Now I am a Walker I am wanted for nothing from other Walkers. I am not in debt to anybody on this strange, safe planet. I am free. On land. I am free. Thankfully. All that is done. I have no skin to take.

I can't help but think I may have seen this boy before.

Yes. I know. He was the one who came to the window that night.

209

RORY

MY NEW OLD MUM

'You must go back. You must go back and get the girl. She can't be left alone.' Iris is anxious, peering out of the windows.

'I know. I know.' I am itchy. Irritated. I know Iris knows what to do but him just stating the obvious is stressing me out. I look at the crumpled shopping bag of clothes on the floor. All I wanted was to see her try her clothes on. Be happy. Twirling and squealing. The simplest of ideas snatched away from me. 'I can't though, Iris. What if the pirates follow me back?'

'He's right, Granddad. We can't walk along the front in broad daylight now. Not to the hut.'

I crack my knuckles. I think of the old her, her records and cooking and perfume and say, 'There is always *someone* I could ask for help . . .'

Within twenty minutes her red banger is grunting down the hill. I watch her pale, frail self step out of the car. I know how much she hates to drive. I shake my head; with the tablets she isn't meant to drive, or 'operate heavy machinery'. I remember. I'd promised Doctor Ung. But she knows I am desperate. I run out onto the driveway to meet her. Her hair isn't brushed.

'Mum,' I murmur.

'Hello, love. You look a right state, are you –'

I fall into her. Crying. Big hot salty tears that feel the size of fists. I am in her chest. Like a small child. And I can't help it. I just can't. My mum. I tell her everything. *Everything*. From the start.

When I finish she breathes deeply. And so do I. I had rushed. I wanted to get back to Lorali but I needed to explain her to Mum before she met her, but as soon as I finish speaking I realise this was a bad idea. Telling her all of it. She didn't need or want to hear it. Her eyes are scampering for her pills. She is patting her pockets. Trembling. I can tell.

'Are you all right? Mum?' I watch her eyeballing Iris, who is standing apologetically by the shop front like it is all his fault. The *loony* from round town. Even though he probably thinks the same of Mum. He knows she is like a helium balloon caught in the branches of a tree, ready to float away as soon as the wind changes. Flynn, trying his best to keep his cool.

'In the car, Rory. Come on. Now!'

'No, Mum, I can't go home. I understand if you want to go home and if you don't want to help me but I have to go and get Lorali.'

'Nobody said anything about home, Rory. We are going to get this girl of yours. Now jump in.'

I want to cry all over again. 'Mum, it's a big ask. You really don't have to.'

'I know I don't have to but I want to. I *want* to do something. I *need* to do something. I want to get that girl back. I want to bring Lorali home to you. *For* you. I want to see my son happy. *I* want to be happy! I want to be strong!' She leans on the car as if she is about to fall over. The colour instantly swims back to her cheeks. 'Today. Now, OK?' She sniffs, her eyes on mine. 'I want to be strong.'

'If you're sure then –'

'Shut up, Rory, before I change my mind.'

I forgot how bad my mum is at driving. And years of fear of absolutely everything gives her a new sort of jerky rush when behind the wheel. Still, it is better than trying to get back to the smokehouse by foot. The beach is packed again and if I am being tailed, a car is much quicker. I can't see the pirates anyway, so that is a good sign.

Mum pulls up to the smokehouses by the pebble beach with an overenthusiastic swerve.

'Well, I don't know about you, Rory, but that was just *great* for me.' She breathes, giggling almost, slapping the wheel proudly.

'You were brilliant, Mum, thanks.' And it is then I notice the door to our smokehouse is open. No, it couldn't be our one. They all look the same, those little black sea-eaten sheds. But it is.

I panic. 'Why is the door open?' I ask.

'Maybe she has gone looking for you, Ror?'

'No, I dunno. I need to go. OK, now, Mum, you wait here.'

'Absolutely not,' she says and is already out of the car, her slippers padding across the pebbles. 'I have actually had a fight before, you know. A good twenty years ago, but these things are like riding a bike. You never forget.' She is trying to keep my spirits up as the sea shushes in and out. In and out.

Lorali

SAILING

I have been down here alone for a while now. I think I might have fallen asleep but I'm not sure; it's too cold and wet to fall asleep. It's not sound. I am so heavy with anxiety. I can't stop thinking of my grandmother. Netta. I can't wait for Rory to arrive. To make everything better. Has somebody hurt him? I can't lose him. Not now. He is all I have. In fact, I've loved being with him so much that I've forgotten why I even wanted to arrive here in the first place.

Now all I think of is Rory. Us. I shake the image out of my head but before it has completely faded I hear the scrambled churn of bad sound and we begin to lunge forward.

I jolt. Step up. Try to find my balance. I stoop. Fall forward. Ducking my head, I cling to the rails. Try for the stairs. *WHY ARE WE MOVING? WHERE IS RORY?*

The wind is smashing me in the face. The sea air is sticking to me, up my nose. Home. Salty. Blinding. Sting. In my eyes. In my hair. Sucking out my mouth. Clinging to my ears.

Raiding me. There he is.

'Where are we going?' I shout over the engine. He looks round to me.

He frowns. 'Rory said we should meet him there.'

'Meet him where? Who are you?' I don't trust him. Instinct. Sniff sniff. Negative. Sick in throat. The water is spitting. Some of the salty sea specks land on my skin. I hate it touching me. I feel dirty.

'Give it a rest. Go back, lie down, rest, be patient.'

'No, not with all that dead animal skin!'

'It's not *real*.' He looks proud of himself.

'I'm not resting. Not until you tell me where we are going,' I bark back. Off. No. No. Danger. The grey sky is like the darkest, deepest parts of the ocean. Thick.

He looks sincere. Saddened. The roar of the engine is whining. I wish I had the confidence to dive back down into the water. Swim down as far as I possibly can. Let my colours carry me lower and lower and lower. So deep my brain swells. My ears block. Maybe I would drown . . . the idea materialises. Then it would all be over. No.

'Fine. But I don't want to upset you,' he says.

'Upset me, how?'

'It's not good news,' he says. *Good news? What about? What does he mean?*

'Go on . . .' I say. 'Tell me.'

'No, I shouldn't. I promised Rory I wouldn't say. He didn't want me to hurt you. He just wanted me to . . . agh . . . I've said too much already.'

I bite my lip. I wish I could fasten his mouth together. Take his words out on a ribbon and throw it into the water. Pretend it never happened. That he never spoke. 'Continue . . .'

'I really shouldn't.'

'Please . . .'

'Rory wants you gone.'

I die.

Inside. I obliterate. My insides. Spinning. Chewing. Turning. Parts I didn't even know I had ache. Twist. Knot. Choke. A new loss.

'No,' I say. Not Rory. 'No. That's not true.' But my brain niggles. It was last night. It was too much. Too strong. Too soon. He did leave this morning so suddenly. I can't believe I was naive enough to think he needed to buy me clothes. How stupid. I didn't make sense to him. He didn't understand. We are too different species. I was ignorant to think we could ever make sense of one another. Have an understanding. Maybe things here are not the same.

'You've made things too difficult, Lorali. I don't know if you know, but his mum is sick. She has a nervous disposition. She is on medication. She sees somebody about it. A doctor.' The words fall over my head. Each one cuts, even though I don't know what half of them mean. He carries on; he is enjoying seeing me wince. 'A mermaid came on the television. Do you know that? A mermaid, asking *us* to help find you.'

'You're lying.'

'Well then, if I am lying how would I know the name Opal Zeal?'

OPAL. *OPAL?* I haven't heard her name above water. Out loud. Real. Opal. What has happened? Is she in danger? Have they kidnapped her? Because of me? Used her for patching? These Walkers cannot be trusted. Can they? My species were right. And I wronged them. Poor Opal. It is all my fault. I stay quiet. I don't want to give him more information.

'Yeah, see? Everybody is looking for you because *you've* ruined everything. People are dying and it's all your fault. You're dangerous. You might not mean to be, but you are. You don't belong here. You aren't one of us. It's better if you leave, Lorali. For Rory, for everyone. I've come to take you home.'

'This is my home!' I argue back. Real tears are coming now. Weakness. Where is all this water on my face coming from? I sniff. How does he know all this? 'You're lying!'

'I wish I was.'

'Stop it!' I scream. I cover my ears. I wish Rory were here. Just so I could hear the words come from his mouth for myself. Even though they would kill me. My mother always told me that Walkers are *cowards*. That they hide behind words. That they hide behind others. That they are an untrustworthy species because of their language. Where we use our bodies, they use words. But I thought my mother was trying to scare me and to kill my interest in them. Or perhaps I was stupid enough to think Rory wasn't the same as everybody else.

I feel so sick on the water this time. I have never travelled so fast. I fall. Topple. Backwards. Forwards. But I fight back. Through streaking rivers of tears. This boy was acting so peculiar on that walk along the beach. I knew it was bad. I smelt the sadness and anger. He is right. I am a disaster. But Rory had seemed so happy this morning, hadn't he?

'Rory would tell me himself if he felt this way.'

'He couldn't.'

'Why?'

He looks out into the water. 'He has a girlfriend.'

A girlfriend? 'What is . . .' I don't want to look even more foolish. But I have to know, even though I am sure that I already know the answer. 'What is a girlfriend?'

'He's in love. He's with a girl. Her name is Bev. He's been with her for years. Since they were young.'

A girl. In *love*? I feel like a fish, gutted.

'But . . .'

They can have me. The pirates. The scientists. The government. The museums. The poachers. The hunters. The patchers. The news. The papers. The Mer. The Walkers.

I don't want to be anything.

The water can have me.

I wish I had never left.

'I am *so* sorry,' he whispers, and it kills me because his apology seems so genuine so I know it is the truth. And I am sad. I miss my family. I miss the Rory that I thought I knew, and I miss my instinct. My tapestry. My escape. My mistake.

We move forward in silence. Every time I want to ask another question I stop myself from fear of the answer.

218

PART II

THE SEA

A CELEBRATION
TO REMEMBER

The evening before Lorali's resolution, Queen Keppel and Zar threw a party for the kingdom of the Whirl. It is traditional to celebrate the resolution on the eve of the ceremony. It was common knowledge throughout the Whirl that Lorali was different from the others, that she was *special*. Radical. A miracle. It was blurry to Lorali herself how or why she was supposedly special. She just knew that she was constantly surrounded. Guarded. Followed. Not trusted with independence, unlike the others. Treated like the most rare pearl in my oceans. She wasn't allowed to swim to the surface. She wasn't allowed to roam free. And that was, of course, because of the brutal death of the late Queen Netta. Keppel wouldn't risk losing her most beloved princess. Lorali was her legacy. She was all she had. Lorali always asked her mother why she never salvaged anybody other than her. Her mother always said, 'You are my greatest joy and greatest regret. Joy because I love you so, but regret because I love you *too much.*' Having another child would bring her too much worry.

The resolution is important in any Mer life as it marks the moment their tapestry completes. The colours, textures and patterns *resolve* themselves, sculpting the Mer's identity. It is an anxious day. The tapestry reflects and depicts every aspect of the Mer's creation; no scale goes unturned – the colours and shapes speak for themselves.

With the resolution comes more responsibility: it is when a Mer can – if they choose – tessellate, and also salvage when they are ready to commit to parenting themselves. But resolution meant more to Lorali; more important to her than it being a royal resolution was that she would finally be granted some independence.

The party was big. Luxurious. The entire Whirl was bubbling with excitement. Hundreds of Mer gathered outside the palace to greet Lorali and give gifts: water plants and flowers, coral and crystal, objects from the Walker world that they found beautiful – remote controls, barbecue tongs, children's toys, fire alarms, odd shoes, blenders, hairbrushes, batteries.

Water horns, strings and bells bellowed celebratory music and a great feast was served in a cave where the walls were studded with twinkling splints of fool's gold.

The council from the Whirl and a few special guests were invited to dine with Lorali's family. The seafood in the Whirl is much larger and richer than the stuff Walkers can catch. A feast like this took days of preparation. The Mer were already merry from pre-dinner honeysuckle cocktails drunk from oversized leaf flutes. They ate chilled watercress and smacked sea-cucumber jelly soup and sipped from giant seashells. Clams, salty winkles and gargantuan mussels arrived on a bed of tangled rope weeds, summer cress and sweet peas. Sea-cauliflower heads, chickseaweed and soft-shell crab cakes. Fleshy, juicy lobster tail and samphire salad, paper-thin yellowtail sashimi served with wilted water fungi and speckled toadstools, and fresh oysters with harvest limes squeezed on top for acidity – down the throat in one. Steaks of the best flesh from the best beasts carved by the chef herself, who was there of course, serving steamed skinned eels and the stuffed claws of monsters that were basted and turned on a spit heated from the hot-spring baths. Spirals of noodling tentacles studded in sweet gem-like ruby pips of larpbarp fruit. Water leeks and asparagus mousse. Ocean cabbage rolls stuffed with algae, plankton and spices. Little fancy caviar and cod-roe tartines with sea-salt biscuit and foam cream. The fudge was little squares of paradise, made from evaporated sea-cow milk and the sea-level sap from the trees of the petrified forest. Coral, drenched in honey, made for a warming sticky pudding. Lashings of squid ink liquor, chased down with walrus-milk Martinis, which went straight to the head.

Later, more guests were invited to celebrate at the dance. They arrived with coloured hair, painted faces and bodies, jewellery and costumes that they had made or found. They were tattooed and pierced to mark the occasion. The Mer are a very beautiful species, if you enjoy that sort of thing. Zar had the glow-worms, illuminatoroids and lampktons rigged up in the cave especially for the ceremony, and had given them instructions to perform a choreographed display to the beat of the bass-heavy music, sparking the walls in a disco effect. The Mer know how to rejoice, and their uninhibited selves thrive at these occasions. They drank and puffed until the sun began to kiss me.

Lorali looked more beautiful than ever that evening. Her hair was multi-coloured, splattered with the rainbow: turquoise, bright yellow, purple, orange, lime green, royal blue and pink tones. Her long hair was loosely plaited into a webbed cage that trickled all the way down her bare back, the ends falling to her hips. Her shape had begun to swell, as if her body clock was ticking along with nature's calendar and the queen's diary. She was more curved than ever. Fleshy but petite. Still all feminine. Soft. Although Mer rarely use make-up (unlike Walkers, who seem to walk about in disguise every day), that day Lorali's arms and shoulders were peppered in coloured crystal gems that snaked up her neck and throat and were dotted round her hairline. Her brows were full but groomed; her face appeared dewy and fresh. Ready for what the future would hold. And on this day so important to all Mer she missed her grandmother so much. When she looked in the reflection of the cracked glass before her she imagined what her grandmother would have said to her. She almost heard the soft crackle of her gentle voice.

'Shine,' she would have said. 'And you will.'

Lorali did wonder why nobody else seemed to be changing at the rapid pace that she was. And even though both her mother and grandmother had assured Lorali that it was because she was royal, and that it would all become clear once she resolved, she knew that other Mer in the Whirl spoke of her as though they knew more, saying things they would never say to her face.

Everybody tried to steal a moment with Lorali. But she avoided the confrontation. The older Mer drunkenly congratulated her, some with bellies flopping over the lip of their tapestry (walrus milk is very fattening, taking a toll on the appearance). With goggled eyes boggling down her chest as they pulled her close, Lorali would excuse herself and wriggle free of their embraces. She avoided the nattering pecks of the gossiping ones, the scenesters, who licked powdered-starfish lollipops that made them rush. Who dissolved the dried coral candy on their tongue, letting the cracking electric tingle dance on their buds and became all tactile. Touchy. Seductive. Brave and daring with the added courage from a little celebratory buzz, suggesting and assuming how Lorali's tapestry would resolve:

'It will be beautiful, the best we've seen yet.'

'I think white and gold. Pure and innocent.'

'I think it will be the texture of moss. Soft. Natural.'

Of course none of them could predict really.

Then there were the Mer whom Lorali wanted to know but was always kept at a distance from. Like Yurline, with her knotted cables of dreadlocks entwined with rope and bark; she seemed like fun but Queen Keppel never let Lorali roam with her. Or the girl with the flame-orange hair and the heavy chest, who seemed to know *everyone*. Or the male with the long hair in plaits that hung either side of his chest. With the beard. He was always laughing. Or Opal.

Opal was there tonight with an emerald-green sequin band wrapped round her chest. Her hair towers were mossy green, with gold chains looped round them. She wore big lashes, and glitter and shiny gold lipstick. She had a lip stud today. Gold tattoos. Lorali watched her. The way she moved with superiority; the power she absorbed by knowing so much more about the universe than the rest of them. *What had she seen? Where had she been? What were the Walkers like?*

Even I felt young Lorali watching Opal. The tug she felt towards her. Which is why I wasn't surprised when Lorali got the confidence to speak with her that evening.

'Thank you for coming, Opal,' Lorali began, her eyes drinking her up.

'I am honoured to be here.' Opal was very professional and knew to keep smiling at all times.

Perhaps it was the buzzy heat of the walrus milk or the lull of the squid ink, but Lorali had a sudden wave of confidence that she decided to ride.

'What's it like?'

'What's what like?' Opal pretended ignorance but I knew she knew what the young Mer was thinking; she'd have been lying if she said she could not feel her curiosity.

'The surface. Beyond.'

Opal's eyes rummaged the gathering, desperately checking on the queen and her mate before she answered. 'Why are you concerned with the surface, Princess? You have everything you need here. You live in paradise.'

'What if tomorrow isn't . . .'

'Isn't what?'

I could hear both their hearts taking turns to thud.

'What everybody expects?'

'How do you mean?'

'What if . . . I've been thinking things I shouldn't be thinking? Dreaming of things . . .'

'*Have* you been thinking of things you shouldn't be?' Opal already knew the answer to this.

'What if . . . Say I had . . . Say I had been thinking . . .'

'Keep your voice down,' Opal ordered.

Lorali ducked her head, politely smiling as onlookers waved, beckoning her to dance. 'If I *had* been wondering what life was like . . . up there . . . would those thoughts show on my tapestry?'

'It depends how much you think about them.'

Lorali sipped her cocktail; she was tipsy. Opal sensed as much and gave the young princess some insight.

'At my resolution, my tapestry spoke loud. No matter how I tried to tell my mother that I wasn't interested in humans . . . *Walkers* . . . whatever . . . I could only lie to a certain point. My tapestry was covered with what I wanted from life.'

'And what happened to you?'

'I was an outcast for a while. I was bullied. I was . . . Some would slash my tapestry, cut me . . . deface me. They were angry. I shouldn't be telling you this.' Opal took a big glug from her cocktail then took another from a passing waiter's tray. She clenched her ringed fingers round the trunk of the glittered clay tumbler filled with coral sour, her favourite cocktail.

'Go on . . .' Lorali was hooked. My waters were shifting.

'I was made an example of.' Opal sipped, her mouth continuing to smile even though her eyes were shrinking with the painful memories. 'I was an embarrassment to the Whirl. But it didn't curb my fascination . . . not that I didn't feel bad . . .

227

but I just couldn't help my feelings. I collected anything I could to do with humans. I was addicted. Even though it meant I was a freak. I don't want you to have to go through that.'

'But now you're so valuable. Your work is precious to the Whirl.'

'That's only because they need me. I am the only one with enough experience for the job. I was halfway there already; in my mind I was already gone. Ready to give it all up anyway to transform . . . Why unpick the stitches of my tapestry and train somebody else when I had taught myself so much? But I am lucky. I get to do something I love. I get to enjoy both worlds, but it's not easy. I'm not stupid. I'm not supported, and I'm certainly *not* protected. They allow me to do this job because it's high-risk and, yes, although my work is precious it's not *valued*. They all know they could lose me at any moment. I sacrifice myself for the Whirl. I belong to them. They know that.' Opal looked angry. She was angry at everything. 'Now they try to pretend that they never hurt me the way they did. That they never made me feel like a monster. They let me pretend I'm glamorous. But I've seen the way they look at me. When I wear make-up. When I cover up. When I do my nails.'

Lorali admired Opal's nails. They were glittery. Long. Fake.

'They look beautiful,' Lorali said, but she wasn't sure. Were everybody's nails like that on the land?

Opal sank her cocktail. 'I like them.'

'Why don't you *surface*?' Lorali asked. She whispered it. It was one of those words that just didn't get thrown around.

Opal laughed. 'I tried to. They think they saved me from it. They said I never would have made it, not have survived surfacing. Even though my tapestry was full of Walker threads, they said it would kill me. They said they would find a way to make life work for me. And they did. And here I am.'

'You *would* have survived surfacing,' Lorali said bluntly.

Opal's eyes filled. 'Well . . . that doesn't matter any more.'

'You're strong. You're probably one of the only Mer that I think could make a surface. You could go now! You could go today!'

'I wouldn't now. I am in a good position. I've convinced them that I know what I'm doing. And I have my whales.'

The more drunk they became, the more their heart-to-heart was becoming more obvious. They had been speaking privately for too long. Queen Keppel became suspicious and swiftly left the group she'd been speaking to.

'What about you?' Opal quickly muttered. 'You're stronger than you think.'

'I don't think so.' Lorali watched her mother motor over. 'I haven't even had my resolution.'

'And what if you don't like what you see?'

'I'm not ready. I am not even fully grown.'

'How many Mer *grow* anyway, Lorali?' Opal winked. The strong warm fuzz of the cocktails perhaps, maybe that was what made her say it? Or perhaps it was just an inner burn? Something she had to get off her chest?

She left Lorali with the sting and trailed off to meet Keppel.

'Queen Keppel! Are you having a *euphoric* time?' Opal switched on her professional warmth with the perfected persona she always employed: forced white teeth, eye contact, a straight back and both hands wrapping round Keppel's.

229

'Is Lorali all right?' Keppel asked, a drawn-out look of paranoia snatching at her eyes. She isn't one for trusting.

'She's fine.'

'What were you talking about?'

'Her resolution, Your Majesty.'

'What about it?' Keppel tried to look calm. She hadn't managed even a sip of drink all night and her nerves were getting the better of her.

'Only how *ecstatic* she was.' Opal was well trained in reeling off interpreted information as fact: lying.

'Of course. I am sorry, Opal. I am so paranoid for tomorrow. Zar and I have worked so hard on Lorali. I wish I had my mother here; she loved Lorali so. I just don't want to disappoint. Or be disappointed.'

'You won't be, Your Majesty. You have a good girl there. She is happy. She is golden.'

'Thank you, Opal. For everything.'

'My absolute pleasure.' Opal curled her manicured hand round Keppel's rattled wrist. Keppel's cuffs chinked. Opal smiled sincerely. 'You should get some rest,' Opal suggested and Keppel laughed in relief. Her high yellow-blonde ponytail held her glass-like features in place as she glided away, like a swan on ice.

Lorali

A FAIR EXCHANGE

I can hear him. He is trying to flag down a boat. Why is he doing that? In this emptiness. In this stillness. It seems anything is possible. My brain is torturing me. It could be that Rory never loved me, never wanted me the way I wanted him. I was just a novelty. I feel angry. Weak. Small. Sad. And then I hear the clang.

GA-DANG

GA-DANG

GA-DANG

The clang. The knell. No.

GA-DANG

I know it too well. I panic. I know it. It can't be . . . but I smell their smell. That oil. That stench. It is unmistakable. The one we feared. We have been taught this sound. Told to avoid it at all costs. Then here he is. This one. Tracking down the *Cetus*. I am raging. NO! He is calling for the *Cetus*. Why is he doing that? I hear the bell again.

GA-DANG
GA-DANG
GA-DANG

The bell that was wrapped round my – no. No. I have to get out. But I can smell the salt too. The water. I don't even know if I can swim in the sea any more with these legs. It's too vast. Too big. Too forever. We are out too deep. Too far. What would happen to me? And how would I jump? I have never practised a jump before. Gravity. What happens there? And the Cavities . . . they would get me anyway now. I am too close. But what would they want with me when I no longer even have a tapestry? Surely I mean nothing to them . . . Could I be bargained? Swapped? Exchanged? Tortured?

The boat seems too slow.

I have to jump.

I feel sick.

I have to jump.

I have to –

He has got me. A knife to my throat. Traitor! Before I can even think I wrestle but I don't know how to use these limbs to fight. Kick. Kick. I can feel each bone rubbing against the next. Like teeth grinding. Clunk. Grind. Snap. Brittle. Chalk. Rock. Flint.

He drags me up to the deck. I am wriggling. I am wriggling. But my fear of the water is strong now. Even the smell. I am out too deep. In the middle of nowhere. Darkness. Wrapping. Freezing. Teeth chattering. Warping my vision. The *Cetus*. I see it now. I smell his fear. *Be scared, you coward! Be afraid, you tiny soul!* Their boat. Them. The Cavities. The bell, the gap between each ring becomes longer, further apart. Lost its rhythm. It's slowing. It's coming closer.

GA-DANG . . .

GA-DANG . . .

GA-GA-DANG

I can't look up. I can't look up. Netta. Netta. I can't look up. The two boats bob. Engine purring.

'Far out for a boy like you,' one of the Cavities snarls. I wait for more words. I wait for them to settle. Bargain. Argue. I close my eyes. They are sneering. Laughing.

Then I am lifted. Seized.

It is the easiest lift in the world. I'm not heavy. No, not me. I am a fish bone. I am a slice of moon. I am a teardrop. I flop. Like a dress. Fall. Faint. I can't move. Paralysed with fear. Every inch of me feels too human. Too soft. Too weak to . . . find the strength. Tense. Breathe. Find it. Remember why you came.

I fight. Scrap. Scratch. Claw. Dig. Punch. Kick. Scream. Scream. Throat ripping. Bloody. Snag. My nail. Blood. More. My hair. Pulled. Dragged. Snatch. Slash. Slit. Weep. Kick. Kick. Kick. Kick. Kick. Pull. Wrest—

To the ground.

No air.

'Oi! Oi! She's mine! She's mine! You can't just steal her away like that . . . I want to be a pirate! I want to be a pir— I've shown my worth, now give me MY spot!'

'Shut up, boy.'

'Kill him.'

My wails are uncontrollable. I taste iron in my mouth. Blood. Biting my tongue.

'Just be done with him,' a gravelly voice orders. The Cavities. The heartless crew of the *Cetus*, and they are *not* Walkers. They are capable of anything and I don't want him to be dead, this boy, even though he has led me to this. I don't want that to happen. He is still my only chance. My only hope. Clinging by a thread. A Walker. Somebody with a soul. I doubt. I can't even work out if this was planned or not. Did Rory know about this? No. He couldn't have. Was this part of my kidnap?

I am on their boat now. There would be a plan. There is always a plan. But the Cavities of the *Cetus* never bargain with anybody.

It stinks. Rancid. Fish. Blood. My own blood. The floor is sharp. Wet. It is dark. I don't know what is blood and what is seawater. What is dirt. Death. Spit. Too dark. What comes from me? What doesn't? Fluid. My knees. A filthy woman is sitting on my back. My face squashed into the floor. Sweat in my eyes. Seawater in my eyes. Stinging. Red.

He is scared. The boy. I can hear it in his voice. He pretends not to be, but he is. He is an actor, I suppose. He is a fraud. A trickster. He fooled me. He is no friend of Rory's.

He is holding his nerve. 'Oi!' he tries again. 'I want to be . . . you know . . . a part of this. I've shown you I'm good. Now reward me.' The boy's voice wobbles.

'Give him some. We might need him again,' a voice from a Cavity demands.

'I'm not giving him any. He ain't done us anything,' another argues back.

'We have the girl, don't we?'

'I ain't giving him any. We worked hard for that load.'

'Don't make out that it's work, you love it,' another cackles. 'The thrill. When they cry and scream "Oh, don't!" Those pretty little brainless mermaids.'

'Give him some or I'll give him you!'

And then it falls. Through the air. A big sack of I know just what. Skin. Tapestry. Patched tapestry. It lands in my kidknapper's little stolen boat with a slosh. He knows to sail away. He does it quick. He leaves me. He *sold* me. And away he goes. Smaller. Smaller. Smaller. On the choppy waters away. Leaving me. In the blinding empty darkness. My flickering flame of hope blown out.

'Good lad,' sniffles the gravelly voice.

'We know who you are,' the dirty Cavity woman whispers in my ear, her wet crackly breath splatting my eardrum. Her hands are gritty, like sand, her grip clenching. With her nose snuffed into my neck she lets her voice slink up the vertebrae of my spine gently, like sneaking up a ladder. 'We know exactly who you are, pretty little girl,' she sniggers, taking pleasure in holding my body up against her own. She rocks me. Her pelvis shoved into the base of my back. I gag from her smell alone. She wrangles for my breasts with her worming stiff fingers. 'Now let's see if your skeleton is as pretty as your grandmother's.'

THE SEA

STUNTING

The cameras wink, the crowds cry out, 'Opal!' and she waves like a queen herself. She smiles big. Almost forgetting that she was meant to be defending her kind. I am there. Keeping her hydrated. Today her hair – *a masterpiece*, said Kelly, her stylist – represents my waves themselves, in smooth ripples as though the sea (being, yes, me) had *kissed* her on the forehead with *its* blessing. I mean, AS IF! REALLY?

I am just speechless. Absolutely speechless.

The white rabbit-fur coat has been pinned at the back by her stylist and Opal wears twinkles on her lashes. Each one studded with a new jewel. She looks very . . . jovial. Carnival-ready if you ask me. But apparently she is in mourning, remember, here to show her 'deepest' and 'most sincere' 'sympathy' and 'condolences' to the families of those lost – the Woods and the family of the little boy. Not, of course, that it was *anything* to do with *her*.

The cameras flash. The reporters take their notes. Record

her. And it is then, in that moment, that she decides to do something else, something unplanned. Something spontaneous. Her publicist Marco shifts in his chair and coughs.

'In fact,' she breathes, her silhouette warming under the blinks of lenses and artificial light, 'I would very much like to cut my ties with the Mer and the Whirl entirely. I realise that I have been poorly educated and employed by individuals within the Mer elite in order to facilitate sickening and perverse behaviour.'

The journalists gasp. Take notes. Marco smirks.

'They bullied me. They *cut* me. They ridiculed me for my *human* interest. This has been an escape for me. Finally I am no longer a *fish* in a *net*. I am home. I do not wish to ever return.'

The journalists applaud. Idiots.

'I would like to offer my services and knowledge to the government, here on land. I am happy to participate in your research. I would also like to set up a charity to prevent taxidermy and poaching, hunting, patching and selling of Mer tails, skin and hair. I will campaign to make this illegal immediately. And of course –' she smiles down the lens, communicating directly with her human audience through eye contact, a smile she has practised many times – 'world peace. Thank you.'

'Opal? Opal! What about the reward for the missing princess? Who will take care of that?' A reporter shoves a microphone under her chin.

Marco swipes the air with his hands. 'No more questions, thank you.' And Opal, in a tank carried by ushers, leaves the room ablaze, the waft of Prada's Candy streaming after her.

THE SEA

SAVAGE QUALM

The Ablegares, on *Liberty*, are heading for the coast of Savage Qualm. Rory was right to have been suspicious. Pirates had indeed been tailing him.

But what Rory and Flynn do not know is that the Ablegares have *already* paid old man Iris a visit. Yes, remember that walk Flynn, Rory and Lorali took to the smokehouse? Ah, yes . . . they were just a little too late.

Their shadows, like the bent angles of spider webs, climbed towards the lighthouse. The lighthouse is there to keep sailors safe, but what happens when the lighthouse needs saving from sailors?

'Where is the girl?'

No. He did not know where the girl was. What girl?

'Come on, old man. A cliff face falls, a mermaid goes missing and you know nothing about it?'

Otto had laughed, irritated, but laughter all the same.

No. Iris did not know.

'And there was me thinking that mermaids were your "speciality".'

Jasper. That tongue. Tut. Tut. Tut.

No. He did not know where the girl was. Which girl? Who?

'He's telling the truth.'

Oska had added that.

Otto had inspected the lighthouse. He had sniffed about it like a dog in bins. Jasper had wanted to get at the old man. He had held up his knife to his throat. He had been angry. Wild. Untameable. He hadn't hurt anybody in too long. He had wanted to bite the old man's face. Tear a hole into it. Drink his blood. But Jasper shook more than the man. He had been more scared of himself than anybody else was.

'Where's that precious little loser grandson of yours? You know we could kill him, don't you? If he has anything to do with this. You know we could kill you, old man. You know that, don't you?'

Iris would not falter. 'I know you could but I know you won't.'

'What makes you so certain of that then? I wouldn't be too comfortable if I were you. They all say you're mad round here, did you know that? That you've lost the plot. That you're nothing but a senile, sensitive old man with too much time on your hands. I could cut you, old man.'

Iris retorted. His weapon of words, an arrow to the heart. 'Didn't your mother cut you deep enough to demonstrate the repercussions of violence, Jasper Ablegare? That's a very big scar you've got there. From the neck right down the spine, to the base of your back. But you got her back, didn't you, Jasper

Ablegare? And your big brother, Otto, and your twin brother, Oska, have to suffer for that.'

Jasper had gone for Iris. He had bit at his throat. Like a rabid dog. Blood in his teeth from the visionary's flesh.

'*Jasper!*' Otto had screamed, and he, Egor, Oska and Momo had pulled Jasper off the man. The howling vampire that he was. A shark. Iris was precious. They had not long since arrived. This was their first day on the search. There would be time. Iris could still be useful.

Iris had tended to his neck. He would not be afraid. He would clam up.

'*You're WEAK! You're NOTHING! I'll kill you, you OLD WASTE!*' Jasper had cried.

'No you won't,' Iris had said. And he'd been right.

I do apologise. I suppose, thinking about it, that information might have been interesting to you earlier on . . . How *forgetful* of me. It's just . . . I'm so *caught up*. Aren't you?

The Ablegares arrive at Savage Qualm. It was no use in Hastings. They had been to every girls' school and upturned the town. They had made such an impression that locals would wave to them in the street. They had followed the boy back from the New Town to the lighthouse, and the girl wasn't there. They had already visited the old man. They had run out of ideas. They were not going to sit about and let some *philistine* find Lorali and collect the reward that Opal had promised. They had other ideas.

'Ladies!' Otto calls to the Sirens. He has brought treats and presents from the coast of Hastings. Chocolate. Cigarettes.

Shampoo. Fudge. Even a stick of rock. His boots chink as he lands on the pecked rock beneath him. Winking at the Sirens, he lists off their names as though each one has their own spot tailored into his heart. 'My Valentina, my Betty, my Violet, my Ivy, my Dotty, my Audrey, my Cleo . . .'

The Sirens are not best pleased to see the Ablegares. Especially after they have been deserted. They preen their feathers. Attack their scrawny mascaraed eyes with kohl. Shit more oily liquid cloud in front of the boys to show their absolute resentment and that they don't give a sea-monkey's arse that the boys have come to see them.

'Don't be like that,' Otto says as he lays the gifts down.

'It's our home. We can do what the fuck we like.' Valentina licks her lips. Scrunches her crusty sea-whipped hair. Lights one of Otto's fags. Betty adjusts her tits in her fag-ash and red-wine-stained bra. Pulls that black gunk off her eyeball.

'Are you pissed off?'

'*Are we pissed off?* Listen to him. Course we are. We made the effort to come aboard *Liberty* to have a good time with yous and then that nasty fishy fanny mermaid Opal calls and that's it. You leave us. High and dry.'

'It wasn't like that. We had work to do.'

'At least now we know your priorities.'

'It's not like that.' Otto has to plead with the Sirens. Usually he'd never even give them the time of day for speaking out of line to him but he is about to ask them a favour. 'We're sorry.' Otto rubs his head innocently; he knows what he has to do.

Violet snubs him. 'If you ask me, Opal Zeal isn't even

241

that pretty. I don't know what all the fuss is about.'

'Yeah, she's proper sold out,' Ivy adds. 'Rumour has it she ain't even coming *back*!'

'Back-stabbing traitor! Sickens me,' Dotty spits, helping herself to the chocolate.

'It's decent chocolate,' Otto mentions. He knows all about Opal's literal jumping of ship and, yes, I can see there is a bit of an ache in his gut about it all, a sour taste on the tongue; he does like her, but you win some, you –

'I'll be the judge of that.' Betty hacks a cough, and her dirtied hands wrap round the gold foil. She is sucking, melting the chocolate with her mouth and tongue. Her eyes are on Otto. Floating down to his –

Momo shakes his head. 'Give it a rest.'

'You and me need to have words, Giacomo,' Cleo announces, hands on hips. Her pearls rattle.

Momo rolls his eyes.

'Who do you think you are?'

'Who do you think *you* are?' Jasper intervenes. 'Look at you, sitting round in your own shit all day. Filthy.'

'Ladies . . . gentlemen! Please. This was meant to be a pleasant get-together? Let's play nice.' Otto raises his eyebrow at his younger brother and takes Violet and Valentina, scooping his hand up the backs of their leather jackets, allowing them to drop down their shoulders, and biting the straps of their bras.

The girls soften. They haven't eaten in ages. There has been a serious drought of sailors on my waters recently. But that is when Egor sees it. 'Otto. Otto!'

Otto wriggles free from the grip of the Sirens.

242

'Otto! I want to CUDDLE!' one of them screams.

'Bros before hos, Violet. I've told you this before! Egor, what is it?'

'Here comes a small boat. A boy is aboard . . . Could it be . . . Is it him?'

The boat gets closer and closer. The rest of the Ablegares release themselves from the Sirens, stand strong and adjust their appearance, clenching their jaws, their weapons. Who is this young man sailing to the island of dead men? Of rotting flesh and appetite?

And how did he find it?

'BOY!' Oska shouts.

'Hush your gums, brother. I want to see what the yout' has to say,' Otto whispers.

Otto calls towards him, as the little boat comes closer. 'COME!'

His face begins to make sense now. Eyes. Nose. Eyebrows. Mouth. Not the boy that they had followed. A new one. But they recognise him too. Where from?

The boy pulls in, closer now. He brings tiny waves with him. He is tired. Cold. Thirsty. Hungry. Withered. But he stinks of greed. Ambition. But worry too. Yes.

Jasper reaches for his knife. Grips it. Tight.

'Put that down, fam. No shank.'

Jasper looks disappointed; he might cut up one of the Sirens soon if something doesn't happen.

'Young boy, small boat, rocky waters. Tell me how it adds up.' Otto greases his hair back; Egor crosses his arms, in his bouncer stance.

The boy panics and the words unfold. 'I want to be a pirate. Like you.'

They laugh. The Ablegares and the Sirens. They laugh so hard. Right in his face.

'This isn't nursery. *Oh, when I'm older I want to be a unicorn.* What makes you think you can just turn up here and become a pirate, you absolute dickhead,' Oska laughs.

'I got here, didn't I?'

Otto switches. He is serious. The boy is serious.

'Yes, and how did you get here?'

'I followed you. Well, your ship. The waves.'

Jasper is ready to pounce.

The Sirens are hungry.

'It takes a lot of work. It's hours, days, weeks, months of sailing, to be a pirate. Where the water is your spirit. Your parent. Your friend. Your enemy. It's not all pressing piff chicks and jacking innocent people. You have to show your worth. Tell me, why should we, with the reputation that we have to upkeep, make some nobody a pirate?' Otto explains, coming closer to the boy.

'Because of this.' The boy rolls back the blankets on his tiny boat to reveal kilo after kilo of fresh mermaid tail. The flesh he has been given by the Cavities. It is catching the light. Flashing. It is shining. It makes the Sirens' stomachs growl.

The Ablegares try not to gasp. They hold it down. Keep it cool. They pore over the skin – it is the real deal, they can tell from the light, paper-thin touch, like silk or muslin, and the scales themselves are like velvet. When wet, these scales will sparkle like tears. The colours are gold, silver, petrol-blue, purple, turquoise. They are legitimate.

'Easy!' Otto bites his lip, then begins to snigger with joy. 'How did you get all this? You've gone HAM on this. Are you a poacher?'

The boy hasn't thought about this.

'Yes. I hunt and sell.'

'Sweet. Where? Who?'

'Don't worry about that. They are yours. Proof of what's to come. I'll give them to you; you can have them. At a cost . . . but I don't want money.'

'I've heard that one before.' Otto drinks up the vast amount of skin with his eyes.

'I'll swap it all,' the young boy splutters, overexcited by their reaction. 'Right now, exchange it, the lot of it, for a place on your ship. For protection. Safety. Immunity.'

Otto sniffs a rat. 'Immunity? Safety? Protection? Why would you need safety if you're – wait . . . you jacked this, didn't you? This wasn't yours to take?'

'No. No. Course I didn't.'

'Why would you want safety then if you didn't, yout'?'

'I . . . I . . .'

'Makes sense though, there's too much belly here, patched too well. No amateur here, bruv. Somebody had to know what they were doing to trim this. You're out of your depth. Tell us the truth, boy, it's in your interest.'

Jasper steps behind the boy, inhaling the fresh sweat from his back. The boy gets upset. He is panicked. He is shaking. The Sirens watch on. They like this. Fear smells *divine*.

'OK, OK, I stole it. I took it. I took it,' he cries. He closes his eyes. He doesn't know what is going to happen next but he's come this far. A fear like his can be detected miles deep. Hungry serpents and monsters, beasts and creatures, thrash in my belly for a taste of him.

'Incredible. If you can jack this much Mer skin and get away with it then you are working for my boat. Recruited.'

The boy cannot believe it. Neither can Jasper, but he knows there will be consequences.

'Are you serious?' the boy gushes as the Ablegares begin to unload the boat of tapestry. It is heavy. Drying out. 'It's that easy? That's all I had to do?'

The Sirens look disappointed, but at least the boy is handsome. They can eat him one way or another.

'I'm Otto. I'm the captain. That's Egor the tailor, Momo the philosopher and my two twin brothers, Oska . . . who makes the best straights in the world if you wanna bun a zoot later, and Jasper, who will smash your brains up to caviar if you are lying or having us on.'

The boy shakes his head. This is exciting for him. Real. Scary. But exciting.

'And what do you go by?'

'I'm Elvis.'

Lorali

THE DARK BOX

I can't see anything. There's only the sickening feeling of rocking. Backwards. Forwards. My face on the floor. Every time I think I am going to be sick nothing comes. Dry. Burn. Wretch. Gag. I wish I could just chuck my guts up. Everything. My heart. My lungs. I wish I didn't need anything. I wish I could become the water and slip through the cracks in the box I am now in. Or turn to sea salt. Evaporate. Crystalise. Everything feels awkward. My new bones crunch. The dehydration is overwhelming; it's deep thirst. I have a split in my head. Inside my head. With heavy, throbbing pains. I don't know where I am going. I miss Rory. Does he even know what happened to me? That boy who claimed to be his friend, who claimed to care, that liar, that cheat, that he *traded* me? Like I was meat. Cast me off, and not just to anybody. To the *Cetus*. The *CETUS*. Of all the ships in the world, it had to be the one that carries my grandmother's skeleton on the mast. That wears her bones like an accessory. And now they have me. And if that boy could sell me, pass me over the boat the way he did, whilst I screamed and cried and roared and smashed my heavy legs all over the place. Until I tasted the blood from my own feet in my mouth. Then I could not trust him so perhaps Rory does still want me. Does still love me. But I will never know now. I will never find out. Because he will be looking for me whilst I lie, dying in a dark box.

The lid cracks open. Dust from the wood floats in. The light blinds me. Harsh. Too much. I see his teeth first. Black. Gold. His eyes. Green. Toad green. His hands are dirty.

'We've been looking for you,' he grunts. He smells bitter. His beard is mangled. Matted. I want to spit in his face. They killed my grandmother, Netta. They patched her tapestry. They tortured her. They *touched* her. They murdered her. Slowly. In front of my whole family.

And now . . . they are going to do the same with me.

He pulls the lid off completely and I begin to panic and struggle. My body is tired. I am being lifted up to sitting. I try to use my legs to push myself up but they are too new and weak. The Cavity uses his force to hold my wrists. Then he jumps into the box with me. The weight of his knees are on my stomach. I howl. What are they going to do to me? A new set of hands clamp round my eyes and mouth. I cannot see. This new blindness is worse than the darkness of the box. I feel the dirt-caked fingers smudge into my eyelashes. I scream.

'Be quiet and still, little runt, and we will let you out.'

I breathe. Through the nose. Deep, heavy breaths. Be calm. The weight lifts off my stomach.

And then the hands come away and I can see. I see stars from the pinch of my eyes. And I cry. And dribble.

'Don't cry,' says the female voice of a Cavity behind me and a comb begins to run through my hair. 'Don't cry, Princess.'

The Cavity begins to hum. It's unnerving. It sounds sad. I cry. She tries to soothe me and continues to brush my hair, her fingers softly weaving. I've never had my dry hair combed before. Tears fall onto my bruised legs. What is she doing? Why is she showing me kindness? Tenderness? Maybe I could speak to her, see if she will help me escape?

'There, there, sweet baby girl,' she mutters. 'Mummy never meant to let you float away but you were such a naughty, beastly, mucky girl. You never did as Mummy told you, did you?'

I swallow. Hard. Instinct. Stay quiet. Be quiet. Get your strength. Not now.

After minutes she sighs peacefully. 'There we are.' She kisses my shoulder with her dry scabby lips. My hair is braided. 'Now, isn't that better?'

And before I know it I am grabbed by my ankles and wrists and they shut the lid back on me. And cold wet darkness follows.

THE SEA

CARMINE

To add suspense, to keep you on your toes and tails, I'll tell you a story, shall I? Kind of a story. Kind of a secret. How about that?

I know what the circles mean. And the patterns. Iris's little illusions and etchings. The illustrative carvings on the trunks. I know all about those simple shapes. The ones he used to communicate with Carmine. The ones his grandson tried to understand for all those years.

Not that it matters an awful amount in the grand play of things.

And it is play. All of it.

It's not real.

You have to live your life like you're pretending. An actor living a character's life. Otherwise you won't take risks. You won't live.

How did Iris know what he knew?

His knowledge.

Was he *magic*? Was he special?

Iris was once Flynn's age. Let's go back to then. When he was writing and drawing. He would draw me for hours. Taking me in. He would concentrate. He would look up more than he looked down. He would eat his sandwiches out of brown-paper parcels. He would bunk off school to be with me. Always so fascinated. They said he wasn't 'well' anyway. Teachers never paid the poor boy much attention and his father didn't care either. He was just ashamed of his dismal grades and social inadequacy. Pretended Iris wasn't his, that he didn't belong to him as they got ice cream along the promenade. Walking steps ahead. Eyes on the floor. His son just had difficulties. His art was spectacular. His mind even more so.

She was on the outside too. On the other side of the line of what it meant to be accepted. Not the brightest bulb in the box, but she loved to sing and dance and play, and she was pretty. She loved to sit with Iris whilst he did his drawings. Ask what colour he was going to shade each with. He said *no colour*. He did line drawings. When she asked why, he replied, 'Because there's no colour in my eyes.'

He didn't mind her being there. He was shy so even if he wanted her gone he wouldn't have found the strength to say so. Luckily he didn't want her to go anywhere. Their friendship bound them together.

The local boys would pick on Iris. Call him names, say he was dumb, lazy, slow. He couldn't defend himself. They didn't understand why that pretty girl wanted to sit with that 'waste' all day long. They were jealous.

One day the girl said, 'Why do you let them speak to you like that? Call you names? Treat you so badly?'

And he said, 'They can say whatever they like. It doesn't bother me.'

The girl brought Iris some colouring pencils. He said thank you but he didn't use them. He liked the world best in black and white. Simple. Like the circle.

The boys sometimes got angry that Iris didn't react. When they were bored they would throw stones and pebbles from the beach. She would stand up and throw the stones back because Iris didn't want to. Couldn't. Just wanted to draw me. Over and over again.

The boys would eventually get bored and leave. She would turn to him, freckles and eyes and prettiness, and say, 'What have you been drawing then?'

'The sea,' he would answer as normal and then ask, 'Can you draw?'

And she would say, 'No. I prefer colouring.'

'Here you are then.' Iris tore out a sheet of paper from his sketchpad, quickly drew a few circles for her to work with and handed her the pencils. 'You can colour these. That will give you something to do.'

And she was so touched. Happy to be included. She coloured and coloured and coloured until every circle was completely stacked with colour and when she was done he drew double the amount of circles and when she was done he drew double again. And each time she filled the lines with colour. I think she loved them all the more because she was filling in his hand-drawn pencil lines.

And then one day. When the sun was out. And I was calm. He unfolded his sketchpad and he hadn't been drawing me at all, he had drawn her. She was beautiful. It was perfect and she cried half with joy and half with sadness, and then she kissed him.

But the boys were watching.

They had seen.

This would make Iris angry, they thought. This would make the big tall dumb boy retaliate.

They picked her up and took her down to the beach with Iris screaming and charging behind. He was cross now. Angry. Mad and strong. He fought them as best he could. But he was outnumbered. They beat him until his skin was punctured, beaten like bruised fruit, his bones like a dropped jigsaw puzzle, splattered on the ground. He still reached for her, bleeding on the stones and sand grains. Until they tore her clothes off and took turns and he was pinned down, cheek and ear kissing the stones, forced to watch.

At last it was over.

And he ran to her but she didn't want to talk or hold hands or laugh or be close and he tried to understand and make it better but she just wanted to not be near him. Not be near anyone.

And he didn't draw. And she didn't ask what he was drawing any more.

And three days later she threw herself into the sea.

And Iris . . . the scars on his body were healing but his heart was not. He went to the petrified forest and he pleaded with the trees to bring her back to him. To make her safe. To make her happy. To pass on messages that he was sorry that he couldn't do more and that he loved her and missed her but the trees were always numb. His words would ricochet off every trunk.

So he carved the words in with a key or with his penknife. And dreamt and drew circles and the silence swamped him but it was all he knew, that and the violin. And just when he thought he should give up, that he was hopeless . . .

Something very unusual happened. From the carvings a memory was triggered. She remembered a feeling. Iris. His kindness. The way he saw the world. And with the help of the etchings, she trained her mind to remember more and more. They flickered back to her, came in little pieces, like clues. And as rare and as strange as it was for a Mer to remember, Carmine did just that. She remembered.

And one day there was a message left for Iris.

I am here. I remember you. I am safe. I love you too.

RORY

SKY RATS

Gone.

Gone.

Gone.

I cannot believe it.

I stare into the sea for answers. I look to Mum.

'Come on, let's get back in the car. We can get anywhere we want in this banger.' She is trying to be positive but there is something inside me that knows she has *gone*. She isn't here. I left her once and was warned, and then I've gone and done it again and lost her. My organs are thumping. I am bleeding. It feels like my heart is bleeding. Everything is hot. I gulp. Dry throat. Mum grips me tight. 'It's OK. It will be OK. We will find her, I promise.'

'Mum. I . . .' I can't stop shaking my head. 'FUCK!' I scream.

'Oh, Rory.'

She holds me. I wrestle the hug, then she breathes me in, deep. I feel special. Loved. Important. I feel sick that I've had a parent all this time, one that I've shared a home with, that has loved me, fed me, watered me, washed my clothes, taught me everything I know, wanted the best for me, and all I've done is waste my energy on my dad. Wondering why he left. When I couldn't change that. I couldn't make him come home.

'Come on. Ror, come on. Pull it together, son.' She strokes my hair.

'She's gone. I know it. I just know it.'

'We're not giving up yet.'

But the thoughts in my head and my exhaustion are making me delirious. And I can't seem to move out of my mum's close hug. Then I feel warmth. The sun beating down. The sun. Now. Warm on me and Mum. On our skin. I look up. It's orange. Blinding.

And then, out of nowhere, these crows start crowding above me. For the first time in my life I actually want one to crap on me – bird poo brings you good luck, so it might be worth a go. But they get closer, and closer. They are more like eagles . . . vultures . . . and they come even closer and swoop down like they are about to attack me.

'Mum . . . Mum . . . watch out!'

We duck and it's then I notice their actual size and features and *faces* and they aren't eagles or vultures at all.

They are women.

And their claws, as if I am prey, snatch me up. They are cawing. And I feel myself being lifted. They are prising me out of Mum's hands and I am screaming. And then the strangest thing happens: Mum starts to attack them back.

'No you don't!' she growls, slapping the crow women, scratching blood streaks into their faces. She punches and kicks, clawing the birds. She's not even frightened. She doesn't care.

One topples over. She's angry. Wipes her face. Lipstick smears. *Who are they?*

Mum wrestles with me, pulling me back as I start to rise into the sky. I am shouting for her. 'MUM! MUM! MUM!' She grabs my foot. My mum, she holds me. Screaming, still fighting. My trainer in her hand, all at once, falls off.

I hear her cries as the bird woman snatches me away. And all I can think to do is just shout, 'Mum!' I fill my lungs and make my voice louder. 'Mum, I love you!' I shout into the air.

And before I know it I am in the sky and Hastings is tinier and tinier and tinier and tinier and tinier. And then nowhere to be seen.

Lorali

ABOARD THE *CETUS*

I thought I would never make it this far once I surfaced. *If* I surfaced. But I never ever thought this was going to be my destiny. Here. Of all ships. Do I really deserve this? My mind swims back to my resolution. My interest. My thirst. My curiosity for this Walker life.

I remember waking up on the day of my resolution. The water was clear. My hair was coloured. I was ready. A woman now. My mother wrapped me up in her arms. Held me to her chest. I looked at her tapestry. The shades. Soon I would have one like hers. Would it be like hers? I wouldn't have the light coloured slip I was used to. I would form. Change. Resolve into something. I was excited. Nervous too. It feels so long ago now.

Zar met me. He stood proud. Strong. His chest was a landscape of muscle and shape. The body of strength. His long straight dark hair. His beard. He didn't salvage me, but he raised me and he did well.

I remember what he said: 'Whatever happens, no matter what, we love you. We are proud of you. You have made me the happiest father a Merman could wish to be. You will always be our little girl.'

He smelt of blood from hunting whale for my celebratory meal.

I remember feeling sad. I was nervous about the change. Sometimes a resolution can give away so much about a Mer that it plants seeds. Changes the way the Mer is, the way they carry themselves. Although necessary, sometimes the resolution can do more harm than good.

I knew that.

My mother wore a peach netted veil. Her hair was up high, away from her face. She wore nipple jewellery and a body chain that wrapped round her ribs and hips and pierced her stomach. I will never forget that jewellery. How each stone shone. The cut of every ice.

Mer came from all over to watch from the coral balconies. Many were already drinking. A royal resolution was not one to be missed. It was an event. Only the council and my closest were invited to the ceremony.

And then it was time.

I lay on the white rock, where the light comes through in slants. My mother looked sick. Ill. Nervous. But she smiled at me whenever I looked to her for reassurance. Opal Zeal was there too. Her whales clacked, but I think they were grieving for Dad's hunt. I felt sad for them and their sad song.

Then it began. They bound me up. In seaweed. My family and I drank blessed oysters. My mother held my head. They bathed me in the kissed water. This is water from the deepest part of the ocean. It is freezing cold. So cold the top is frozen sleet. Dark blue. It is sacred seawater that has been kissed by all the council members. Then the projections began. It is a show, for all. Of me. Complicated. A concentrated montage of illusions. Shapes. Patterns. They were amazing. Everyone was gasping. I was royal. Yellows, greens, silvers, golds, iridescent illumination, moonshine, purple, cream. The tones were spiralling, winking, twinkling. The public were gasping, clapping. My mother was laughing, in awe, relief. Zar was proud. Tears in his eyes. I was watching too. It captured everything about me. My likes, my dislikes, my wants, my hopes, my thoughts, of independence and music, of food and conversation and movement, and my love of animals. Of Walkers. Of beautiful things. Of innocence. Of my love for the petrified forest. Of purity. These colours and shapes would soon be on my tapestry and I would be complete. Able to salvage. To hunt. To perhaps visit the top of the Whirl even? Not just the forest. To tessellate. To be an individual. Uncaged. Not a pearl trapped inside an oyster shell.

And then suddenly . . . the shadows crept in. Shadows translate as secrets. Images jarring. They didn't stop either. At first the crowd thought this was my personality. I was cheeky. I was blunt. Sometimes I was naughty. I had been known to pull tricks. To dream. To be devious and rub some up the wrong way – but then more shadows came, and more and more. Hatched, spiked lines. Shrinking grooves and shapes that looked like strangling hands. Terrifying. Mer looked away. Couldn't watch. Hands over mouths and eyes and ears. And eventually a tumble of big blotchy red came. A sun of red. Blood. My mother began to cry. It was written on her face.

'I'm sorry,' she said to my father. I was thinking, why is she sorry? Why would she be sorry? He tried to stay strong but then couldn't. He swam away. My mother wanted to go after him. But she couldn't. She had to be present during the resolution as she had salvaged me, otherwise the projections would be incomplete. I remember panicking. *Where had he gone?* I wanted to go after him myself. I would have if I hadn't been wrapped completely, nearly paralysed in seaweed. I remember thinking, *What did they mean?* Opal tried not to look as the other Mer watched intently like they loved it. This was drama. Royal drama. They were glad it wasn't smooth. That it wasn't perfect. Everybody wants to be at the top. The imperfections tickled them. But then more red came. Shadows. And then groaning. A sound. Audible. Then they weren't so happy. They were shocked. Stunned. Scared. Horrified. I remember knowing this was wrong. I had been to lots of resolutions myself. This had never happened before. And then the resolver dipped his head.

'I wanted it to work. I'm sorry, Your Majesty.'

My mother held her stomach and then I understood. A deep purple scar with a silvering line emerged on her abdomen. Right before where her tapestry began.

I was panicking. Wrapped in the seaweed made me helpless. I wanted to swim away to the petrified forest. Anywhere – but everybody was watching and I was trapped.

'Tell me, Mother, tell me!'

But she wouldn't.

261

And we all just had to suffer as my tapestry morphed and it was written right there in the pattern.

My father was a Walker.

I was half Mer and half human.

I was the first child ever to be born in the Whirl.

I was born in change.

I *was* a miracle.

After my mother's salvation, I was cut from her womb.

Zar had acted as my father but he had lied.

Even Netta.

Everybody had lied.

And it was then that, without thinking – I was embarrassed – I wrangled free from the seaweed and off the white rock. The resolver was warning. Threatening. Panicking in fear of my mother's punishment if he got it wrong. Even though it was too late already. 'You still need a tapestry, child!'

But I didn't care.

I swam. AWAY. I wanted to find *him*. My *real* dad. And all I had were the incomplete images on my tapestry. Of the coast. The English coast. England. Where my real father was from.

Up

Up.

Up.

Up.

Up.

Into the centre of the Whirl. And I held my breath. Just how you're not meant to and when I burst through I did not hold my breath any more and then I swam and I swam. Inhaled. I thought about my real father. Who was he? What did he think when his wife and baby had drowned in the sea? My mother hadn't given him a chance. Given me a chance to know him. To even meet him. And then she had lied. Kept me in the dark. Wrapped inside a lie. I breathed. Deep. And I thought I saw the stars above me, the ones I had never been allowed to see, but everything was happening so fast that I didn't have time to look and I breathed new air. *Human air. Walker air.* I had to concentrate on breathing; the air was flooding my lungs. I was dying, I was sure of it. I closed my eyes.

And then I woke.

And I had legs.

And then I saw Rory.

RORY

PREY

They dump me on what seems to be an island. I am just about catching my breath. Then they fly off. Their wings are so big that when they flap they nearly blow my hair off. They are feathered, their wings black, green, orange, grey . . . speckled in places. They have hair. They have women's faces, women's bodies. But then these claws and their wings . . . They are bird women. It is so weird. Eugh. It stinks. Everything smells. I am in an oversized nest, bigger than a double bed, hanging from a tree. It is made of twigs and sticks and net. Feathers. There are odd things in the nest too: a lighter, a pen, an empty Coke can. It is like a bedroom. It smells so bad. Of blood. Of fag ash and coffee breath. Like bedhead. Of sweat. And dirt. Like your sheets after you've had the flu for two weeks and are finally ready to get out of your pit. I don't want to touch anything because it feels so animal, like everything is made up of scent. I look up and see more nests above me, like balconies on a tower block.

Except they are all made inside the branches. Clothing hangs lazily over some, looking like washing, although I doubt any of it has been washed. Grubby knickers, tights, bras, dresses, jackets, men's shirts.

I can hear the sea. We flew over it. I was too afraid to wriggle free. I would have drowned. We were too fast anyway, and the grip of the bird was so tight. I can still see the red rings round my wrists and ankles where they held me.

It is pointless trying to figure out my location. I look beneath me. I am high up. I see rock. Bird shit is splattered all over it like a distressed artist has flicked white paint everywhere. And red too. Blood. *Gross*. So they shit like birds and have periods like women? Or do birds get periods too?

I can hear cawing. Giggling. I'm not sure what is woman and what is bird. I can't see them either.

Then I see the skulls. Heads. Head after head. In piles. Human skulls. Legs. Arms. Bones. And soggy entrails on the floor just all *there*. I feel sick. Repulsed. Then I see this heap, like a mountain of *stuff* from lost sailors and amateurs on the sea: glasses, wallets, shoes, walking sticks, maps, hats, clothing, bags . . . Items collected from what must be the victims.

And then I notice a little makeshift kitchen. Made from wood and crates. A little table, chairs, cupboards, a sink of some sort. It is covered in empty bottles. Beer, wine, vodka, whisky, gin. Fag butts. Ashtrays. Biscuit wrappers. Knives. Rotten, rancid fruit – pineapples, oranges. Maggots. Fruit flies buzzing about. Strange-haired rat-like creatures sneaking in and out of the cabinets. Scavenging.

I have to get out. I can't stay here.

Then I hear voices.

I flip onto my back. Could I escape?

AGH, why don't I know how to climb a tree? Of all the stupid stuff I did as a kid, *why* wasn't tree climbing part of it? Shit.

'Where is he?' a voice says below. 'Be a doll and bring him down for me, would you?'

Him is me.

I breathe hard. I am out of options.

I can hear a woman's gruff voice, flirting, giggling. She wants something before she hands me over.

I peer over the nest. It's *that* pirate. The same one. The one from The Serpent, the one from the shopping centre, the one who followed me back to the lighthouse.

My heart begins to thud.

Bang.

Bang.

Bang.

I instinctively start climbing the trunk of the tree. It is a crispy old tree, covered in sap and more of that grimy, nasty bird shit and it keeps crumbling off in my hands like dried-up toothpaste. I try to carry my weight but I am so tired. Shit. And I have no shoes. I try again. Come on, legs, work.

And then I hear another voice. One I recognise. One I know well. It can't be. Not a chance. I peer over the nest again.

Elvis.

What? What is *he* doing here?

And before I know it, one of the birds has me in her grasp and is winging me to the ground.

* * *

'We know you lost her.' The pirates circle me. My wrists are wrapped in rope. They are sore from where the bird women snatched me.

'Lost who?' I shake my head. I'm still pretending I don't know who they mean. I know it means they might hurt me, torture me, even, but I can't fall into this. I'd sooner die than give them any information about Lorali.

'Oh, give it up. You had the girl.'

'Why do you think I'd know anything anyway?' I am hot. Getting sunburnt. Thirsty. Tired. Agitated. 'You lot need to get off my back. Let me go. I don't know who you mean, and why do you care anyway? I'm glad she got away, *whoever* she is, so she didn't meet the likes of you!'

One of the other pirates, a mad-looking one, lunges for me.

'Jasper! No shank! No jook!' the ringleader instructs. This *Jasper* skulks away. Pissed.

Elvis. Why is he here? My own friend. Standing there. Now. He looks different. *Older*. Like a clone of himself. I think it's cos he is scared; I've only ever seen him scared once like that before and that was when a man driving a truck nearly ran him over on his bike and yelled in his face to watch where he was going. That was minor in comparison.

'Elvis . . . please? What's going on?' I plead with him.

Elvis sheepishly looks to the floor.

'Oh . . . so you two know each other? I see. Friends?' The pirate giggles.

I panic. Elvis is a prisoner too, isn't he? Just not tied up. On some weird agreement, knowing Elvis. Just like him to find some way to hustle his way out of wearing ropes. He has probably come looking for me. He is probably undercover and I've just baited him up. *Shit.* Now the pirates know we are friends. I have to keep quiet.

'No, we aren't.' Elvis lets the words fall out. 'We aren't friends at all.'

Why is he lying? Does he have a plan? Good work, El. If he could just give me a signal, a sign. Let me know everything is OK. I don't even care why he is here now. I just want to understand that we are in on this together. Hatch a plan. Make an escape and get away from these maniacs.

'You two clearly have some peculiar bromance going on. Do you need a room?'

'They can use mine!' one of the bird women jokes, salivating at the thought; she obviously doesn't get much young blood.

I try to get Elvis's attention, but he isn't biting. 'Elvis?' I say. Loud. Clear.

'Wait . . . now I know why I recognise you. You two were in the pub. Together. When I first saw you.' The pirate clocks it. We fall silent.

'That's right. Now you boys got beef. Fallen out. Over a *girl* perhaps?'

Elvis looks angry. Upset.

'He *was* my best friend.'

Was? What have I done wrong?

'But then he dropped me.'

WHAT?

'You're clearly vexed.' The pirate touches Elvis's shoulders in reassurance. 'Really, I feel for you, bruv, and you can get your

268

revenge, trust me. But only once I've got information from him.'

I am proper baffled. What is going on?

'El, what you on about . . .? I didn't drop you.'

'Yeah you did. I saw you. I saw you and Flynn and Flynn's nutty old granddad that night, dancing and eating, and I saw you with that girl. Hiding her. I watched you. I watched you all that night. Having the best time. Without me. She saw me. That's when I knew you were avoiding me. Keeping a secret from me. You both ignored all my calls. That's NOT what best mates do. She saw me.' So it was him. Elvis. Not the pirates. He is losing it. He isn't acting himself.

'Who is "she"? What girl?' The pirate turns. 'See, Rory? We know you know something.'

I bite down. Elvis. *Man*, whatever his plan is better be good.

'Elvis,' the pirate instructs, 'refresh your ex-best-friend's memory for me, would you? Which girl?'

'HER! THE girl.' Elvis is angry. He is trembling. I didn't know he saw us. I should have answered the phone. I shouldn't have left him out. Ignored him. He is genuinely hurt, isn't he? He isn't the thick-skinned Elvis I always thought of him as.

'Carry on . . .' the pirate says. 'Let it go, get it off your chest.'

'You blanked me every day. I always knew you and Flynn were closer than me, that you'd been mates longer, but it didn't matter what I did, how hard I tried, you and him always liked each other better.'

'Mate, El, that's not true.' I try to struggle free. I need him. He is all I have here. The other pirates watch on. The Sirens crack their necks and lick their lips. They love the drama. Perving on it.

'Then when the girl came it was your little secret and you left me out. You didn't answer the phone; you ignored me. I would have helped you. I would have made it better. I am smart, you know.'

I try to calm him down. 'I know you are. I know you are.'

The pirate nods. 'You are. Very bright.'

Shut up. Stop brown-nosing Elvis!

'Can I please just speak to my mate?' I snap.

'I am NOT your mate!' Elvis screams. He picks up a big stick from the ground and holds it above my head. Is he going to *hit* me? I've never seen him like this. This *charged*. This angry. He is playing up. Just trying to act like the big boy.

'Now, now, not violence. This here is your comrade.' The pirate shushes Elvis, batting down the stick.

Elvis huffs and puffs with rage. It must be the adrenalin. Showing off. Proving himself.

'Where is the girl?' the pirate asks me. 'Where have you put her?'

'I told you. I haven't got her.'

'So where have you hidden her? The last time I saw you, you were buying her clothes, and then you ducked when you saw me.'

I close my eyes. I want to die. I wish none of this had ever happened.

'I haven't seen her since.'

'But you headed back to the lighthouse after your little shopping spree and I thought . . . No . . . he hasn't got her, but then . . .'

'You followed me back!' I am fuming with anger.

'Yes, we did, well spotted. Because we thought you'd have the girl. But alas. We'd already visited the lighthouse.'

I shake my head. I keep replaying Mum's desperate fight for me. Over and over.

'Well, if you haven't got any information for us, and you lost her, or deny you lost her, you're no use to us, are you? You're just an extra mouth to feed.' The pirate pulls a small flick knife from his pocket and starts to play catch with it. 'So we may as well kill you now.' He grins. 'The girls are hungry, aren't you, girls? Come on, all together now . . .' He pours into song: '*Feed the birds, tuppence a bag* . . . Rory, tell me, have you seen *Mary Poppins*? It's my best one. I always wanted a Mary Poppins, didn't you? A lady to come down from the sky to fix everything?'

I say nothing, watching him strut about. I hate him. I hate everybody. I wish I could kill them all.

The pirate chuckles. He is a fucking psychopath. 'That's right.' He slicks back his hair, gaining control again. 'There's something about you I like. So, OK, one more time for luck –' he presents the knife again, close to my face – 'Where's the girl?'

'I've told you,' I whimper. I find the strength to sigh. 'I don't know.' A tear falls and then –

'I do,' Elvis croaks, his face as white as bone. 'I know where she is.'

271

Lorali

LIGHT

'It was our lucky day,' one of them sniggers. 'There we were, following that old crock of shit boat with them sodding amateur Ablegares aboard and then, what are the chances . . . Princess Lorali is getting chauffeur-driven across the ocean by a little boy.' The man laughs. Dirtily.

'It was like being handed a golden platter. Like stealing sweeties from a baby, wasn't it?'

'You should have killed him,' one of the Cavity women mutters. 'Slit his throat right there.'

I have to agree with them now.

'Nah, he was young. He has something, that boy.'

'Let him live with sin. The guilt will kill him. Far more fun.'

'Besides, if I slaughter him now, who would be my messenger? Pass on the beautiful bad news that the *Cetus* Cavities are coming?'

'You're so dirty, Cornway.'

'Half the fun though, innit? The chase.'

'Right, let's get her out.'

'Pity she ain't got her tail no more.'

'Price for newly resolved royal tapestry. My god.'

'Still, better we have her than any of them others. That queen will sacrifice one of them for the return of this one. I wonder what her legs can do . . .'

'Or what's in between 'em, more like.'

They laugh. Dirty. Disgusting. Wretched. Filthy. Snigger. Cackle.

My heart explodes. I am fierce. A monster. Blood rages through my arteries. I feel my premature legs lock. It gives me strength. Adrenalin.

I think of Rory. Whether or not he loves me back, I know I love him.

They open the lid again. A few of them tower over me now. Faces blackened. I can't even tell their sex. Their race. They are drenched in years of oil from the *Cetus*. Thick black sludge. Men and women, I'm sure. But it is difficult to tell the difference. They have long sticky hair, overgrown; they are a new species entirely. Inbred. Unfinished. Terrible.

And before I know it, I am fighting their faces. Ripping, pulling, tearing, biting, kicking, hitting, slapping – and they are laughing at my efforts. Pushing me, elbowing me, humouring me.

And then one of them, a woman I'd guess, something in her arm, a weapon, heavy, lifts her arm high above my head and I am out. Cold.

R O R Y

OLD FRIENDS

I want to kill.

My ears do not accept the information.

For her tapestry? For her tail? He *swapped* her? Lorali. My girl. To the Cavities? The CAVITIES? The ones that took Lorali's grandmother? I can see that the pirates are not best pleased with him either. They are gathering their shit together, getting ready to set sail. They want to find her too. But why? Why can't they all just leave her alone? Let things remain as they were?

Then it dawns on me once more how little I know about this strange girl. About Lorali. Yeah, I know her as a human. Who she is now. That she loves eating raw butter and she loves music. And the stupid glow-in-the-dark stars on my ceiling. But even Iris said that all Mer had been salvaged, that they had history . . . so what is hers? Does she know these boys? Had this pirate fallen for her too once before? Iris said the Mer remain the age they were when salvaged . . . so how old *is* she? And he said that they have minimal memory, if at all, of their time as a human . . . so maybe she doesn't even remember what happened to her? She could be running around making dickheads like me fall for her all over the world and then pissing off. For all I know I am just another mug in the waiting line . . .

I don't know her at all.

Then again . . .

I didn't know Elvis either and we'd been friends since we were kids. Look where that has got me. I don't want to know Elvis at all now.

I am still tied to this post. The pirates stand around me, sorting their stuff, sussing what to do next with me. I guess they don't need me any more. I am useless to them now Elvis has fessed up. I am a waste.

I am fuming. Fuming and shoeless. It is almost laughable.

I kick the stump I am tied to. My skull hits it as I rebound. It feels like blood but I don't care. I can feel Elvis's eyes watching me. He comes close. But not close enough to untie my wrists. Not that I want *anything* from him. I wish I was free just so I could escape him.

'Rory, I'm sorry,' he tries. 'I am. I didn't know how much she meant to you. I was jealous. I thought if I got rid of her then we could all just go back to being friends like before.'

'Don't talk to me,' I snarl.

'But we can get out of this together. Let me help you. These pirates are proper safe. Otto, he's the main one, he's letting me stay with them. He's made me a pirate – *me*! He actually said that I'm recruited. Can you believe it, Ror? How cool is that?' He is trying to convince me to trust him but it is coming across as arrogant self-obsessed shitty bullshit. AGAIN.

275

'Do one, Elvis.'

'Rory, you have a right to be mad, but are we really going to sacrifice years of friendship over some dumb girl? If you just stay quiet I might be able to convince them to make you a pirate too. Otto is *so* safe. You'll get on like a house on fire . . . Look how sick these boys look . . . What a life – sailing, shooting, lighting cannons, finding treasure, getting pissed, getting with exotic women all around the world!' He is trying to joke, but it isn't funny. He is desperate. 'Please, Ror. I can't guarantee that they will spare you the way they've spared me, so let me save you. I mean, it's obvious that I've got what it takes to be a pirate but I just don't know if your skills immediately shine out on a first impression. Come on, mate?'

I don't want him to say another word. I look him dead in the eyes. 'If being kept alive meant one more day spent with you, I'd rather be dead. I don't ever want to see you again,' I spit. 'Ever.'

Elvis's face falls; he prods me in the forehead with his finger. 'Be a dickhead then, Rory. See how far that gets you. You'll regret that mistake.'

The Sirens begin to moan and cry when the pirates take to the ship. They are a right bunch of sluts. I hate them. I wish my mum had killed them. The pirates pretend to miss them already but I can see the loathing in their eyes. They can't wait to leave. It doesn't matter where you come from, if you don't fancy someone back, well . . . you just don't.

Watching Elvis dicking about, *acting* like a pirate, is ridiculous. It is like watching a kid that has been given an empty saucepan and wooden spoon to play with whilst their mum makes dinner and the kid thinks he's the one doing all the hard work. Searching for approval. It sickens me. He is a cheat.

The Sirens are watching me. A couple have already sniffed me out properly and are probably planning what to do with me. I bet they are the kind of cannibals that eat you raw. Just bite into your side or whatever. Shit, why am I torturing myself? I don't want to be eaten alive!

The big pirate, I think Elvis said his name was Egor, the hench one, lifts me and the stump out of the ground, proper de-roots us both, and carries me over his shoulder.

'PUT ME DOWN!' I wail, my veins squeezing out of my neck.

'Quiet,' Egor says. 'Save your energy.'

So I shut up. There is something cinematic about his voice that just makes me clam up. The girls wave goodbye to me, pretending to wipe puppy-dog tears from their eyes, whilst some scratch their arses. Then they run to the ship where the rest of the pirates are already waiting, including Elvis. *Prick.*

Egor carries me aboard. I can't believe it. This is a ship. It looks like an old-fashioned house . . . but it's a boat. But I am so scared. I am breathing hard. My wrists are killing. My arms hurt. My shoulders feel crushed. My neck is wrecked. I am positioned on the main bit of the boat. I don't know what it's called. I'm surprised by how clean and tidy it is. The boat itself is old but it's still so grand and elegant. Regal. Proper . . .

I see them now. These pirates. Otto. Yes. Jasper. He looks nutty. His eyes all wild. Oska. He is smoking. The bearded one . . . OK. And the one who lifted me, Egor. Then there is Elvis, still trying to look cool. Thinking he is some kind of boss, winding a telescope in and out. What a plum. He'll ask for a parrot, a patch and a sodding peg leg in a second. Cringe.

'WAIT!' whimpers a scratchy voice from the island. It's one of the bird women, 'WAIT!' she caws. 'You're not dumping us *yet* again for them ridiculous fishy fannies, are you? Why eat fish when you can eat bird?' Her face peers over the side of the boat.

The other girls join in. 'Where's our payment?' another sniffs. 'I don't think so, Ablegares.' They pout, but with greed in their eyes. 'A deal is a deal. You promised us the boy if we went hunting for you.'

Otto looks irritated. He doesn't have the time for this. Elvis shrugs at me like *told you so*. So smug. I want to rub that face right off him.

'I did?'

'Don't try it, Ablegares. Yes, you did. You said once you'd talked to him, if he didn't know where the girl was, that you'd feed him to us. It's dangerous for us to go to land. We're starving. It's not our problem the boy doesn't have the girl. We brought him back unharmed, didn't we? We made a deal.'

'A promise is a promise; I appreciate you risking your lives for me, ladies, and bringing back the boy.' Otto sighs deeply. Surely he could just sail off? Then again the women do have claws and wings. 'You kept your side of the bargain, now I'll keep mine.' Otto looks me up and down.

I am weak. I'm not strong. I am tired. I am ill. Feed me to them. I want it to be over now anyway.

'Brothers.' Otto combs his hair into place. 'Give the birds the boy.'

I start to tremble. The Sirens begin to jump up and down, overexcited, with their craggy teeth and panda dark-circled eyes. I wait to be thrown overboard. The bird women lick their teeth. Crack their necks. And then two of the Ablegares in one quick move grab Elvis. He screams, panicking, and drops his try-hard amateur telescope; it rolls to the floor and towards my feet.

'*WAIT, WHAT ARE YOU DOING?*' he screams. '*YOU'RE CONFUSED. I'VE BEEN RECRUITED, REMEMBER? I'M A PIRATE!*'

I am shocked. I couldn't help him even if I wanted to. His wail. The noise that is coming out of his throat. It hurts my chest. It is young. He is just a boy. We grew up together.

He struggles. He tries a gentler approach: '*Please, please, please, I'm a pirate, remember? You said I could be a pirate? I'll do anything!*' he cries and then yells for me – '*RORY! Rory! Please don't let them, don't, don't. I'M SORRY. I only wanted to mean something. I just wanted to mean something. I'm sorry. I'll give you anything. I'm sorry!*' He tries to fight their grip. But the pirates are too skilled at this. It's like getting rid of a spider from the bath for them. Easy-peasy.

Elvis screams on, his voice breaking. I try not to care. No one who cared for me could hurt me this bad. The women can't wait to have him. As he falls into their feathered embrace his mouth is wide open, ripping out, '*MUM! MUM! DAD! DAD! MUM!*'

And they begin unpeeling his clothes, running their fingers through his hair, sniffing him, inhaling his jeans like dogs. I can't watch.

'Should have been a better friend, you little rat!' Otto spits on the ground next to Elvis and then with a fist in the sky he cries, 'Let's bounce!' and the ship's anchor comes up, and we are away. I can't believe it. I hear Elvis's screams as we make our way across the water whilst Otto sings 'Feed the Birds'.

Lorali

HUNG UP TO DRY

My grandmother. Netta. Her skeleton still hangs from the front of the *Cetus*. It is a beautiful skeleton. The tapestry bones. Like a fish tail. But more beautiful. I try to imagine her. Alive. With flesh. Working organs. Blood. Hair. Her eyes. How kind she was. How my mother loved her. How they respected her. I think of how she salvaged my own mother.

How would she have reacted when she realised she had salvaged a pregnant woman?

That I was a tiny organism inside of her? The same size as a prawn.

She probably never thought I'd make it.

But I did.

I wonder how her face looked when she saw me for the first time. The miracle that I was. I was against the odds. Did she decide to lie to me too? To hold the truth back?

When she was caught. In a net. The whole of the Whirl went silent. Drowned into quiet. Mer laid flowers at the palace. We were all in mourning. The Cavities hurt her. She was beautiful and her tapestry would be lucrative. They patched her for eleven months. Tiny. Tiny. Tiny bits of scale at a time. It was torture. They hung her from the front of the mast of the *Cetus*. Like a warning. They wanted us to watch her suffering. Bleeding.

She would scream at the Mer not to watch. By watching we were giving them what they wanted. When she wasn't screaming she was pretending she was strong. That she could take the patching, even though we all knew the horror stories of the blinding, excruciating pain.

That's probably why I wasn't allowed up to see the stars. My mother didn't want me to see my grandmother roaring and crying and pleading and screaming for her life.

That's probably why I was so precious to them.

They constantly sprayed her with saltwater fresh from the sea. So she didn't dry out. So she continued to grow more skin on her tapestry. So her body thought she was underwater. Safe in the Whirl. Her own body betrayed her. They would wait for the scales to heal and then attack and cut again, and when it was all cut away they would wait and start again. Even though it was dark in colour and dry, it was still beautiful. Unlike anything any Walker from anywhere in the world had seen before. They would still sell it. Poachers, Walkers. They would all pay. My grandmother cried, begging the Mer not to see her like this any more. She didn't want their support. She believed it only encouraged the Cavities to keep her alive. To taunt and provoke them, allowing them to catch more Mer, using her slow death as bait. The Mer obeyed. And so the Cavities tied a bell round Netta's neck. So we would hear her clanging when she sailed past on the front of the *Cetus*. A knell. If we couldn't see her we would have to hear her. A near-dead mermaid on the front of a deadly ship. So she tried not to move. She tried to be silent, always. My grandmother. So we wouldn't have to hear. But the pirates on board would shake her. Dance with her. Ridicule her. Harass her. Humiliate her. Abuse her.

The bell would *ring* and *ring* and *ring*.

GA-DANG

GA-DANG

GA-DANG

I would see my mother being sick every time she heard the clang. It hurt anyway but it hurt more that such a strong and valiant Mer was being put through this level of torture.

Then one day. On the eleventh month. When it became too much. My mother, she went up. With her bow and her arrow. Even though she was not meant to. Even though it was dangerous and she was risking her life. And she shot my grandmother right in the chest. Right in the heart. Just like she had practised on the clay crabs. She says she remembers her mother's eyes seeing her blonde hair. Happy to see her daughter but happier still that it was over.

The birds pecked those eyes out.

And now they cut her down. Her skeleton. It collapses to the floor beside me, where I am face down. Tied up.

Grandmother. *Grandmother*. My heart.

They drag me up. I am bloody. Bruised. Pale. Veiny.

They haul me up the mast. They are sniggering. Laughing. My hair in the wind. The height is great. The sea. My home.

Spitting at me. The Cavities. Their dirty hands on my skin. Leaving marks.

My ending will be the same as my grandmother's. My next thought is my mother. Then, my father, Zar. I don't want them to see me like this. Where Grandmother Netta was. Dying. Ending the same way my mother began. Dying.

With legs.

RORY

FREEDOM

Oska unties me. My wrists crack. They are already scabbing, and the salt in the sea air is making them smart.

'You must be hungry,' Otto says. They lead me down into the boat. Underneath. It is like a museum. Rich fabrics, silk, velvet, gold threads. A mantelpiece covered in ornaments. Works of art on every wall in big gold frames. Swords and armour on the wall. It smells of posh scented candles. Rich people. There is a platter of food. Food I wouldn't normally touch with a ten-foot pole as it isn't really to my taste. But I am starving and it looks proper inviting. Mussels. Crab. Lobster. Squid. Prawn. Oyster. This is hundreds of pounds' worth of fresh seafood, all mounded up. Something about the way the feast is spread out makes me dubious of the boys. It is too fancy, too impressive. The carved lemon, the little bowls of warm water to clean your fingers. Curly parsley. They are gentlemen. They are proud.

* * *

The Ablegares sit around me.

Vodka is poured. They are treating me like a guest. They take their time. They look in my eyes when I speak. They don't interrupt.

'Drink,' Otto orders. 'Please.'

I sip the vodka. It is clean. Like ice. Freezing cold. It quenches my sore throat. Then I knock back the rest. It eases the pain. The bearded pirate, Momo, tops me up, winking at me. Like mates. I thank him instinctively.

'Call me Momo,' he adds after smacking his lips.

'We are too hungry, too tired to talk. Let's fill our bellies,' Otto announces, and we eat. Occasionally Momo casts me a signal of how to crack open a shell, split a prawn, get at the fleshiest parts.

I shake off the guilt. I can't be stubborn with these villains. I need my strength. There is nothing else to do. It is them against me. And I am glad not to have to talk anyway.

I feel better after the food; it was nourishing. Tasty. And the environment feels fine for now. The alcohol has gone right to my head. I am dozy and as relaxed as I'll ever be.

'Now you sleep,' Egor instructs, but not too bossy, and leads me to the bunks. They are as pristine as the boys. Neatly made individual beds, militarily clean and straight and pressed.

I won't be able to sleep. Too much has happened. I am stressed. Anxious. Angry. Worried.

'I can't sleep, Egor.'

'Yes, you can.'

'I can't. I can't. What about Lorali?' The words hazily topple out of my mouth. I don't want them knowing I still care for her, because they could use that against me. I can't show weakness. But I am just too tired and don't even care any more. Maybe it is too late to pretend.

Egor lifts me into a top bunk and sleep comes surprisingly easy with the low hushing of the boat rocking, a full belly and the swashiness of the vodka in my brain and veins effortlessly tying me down. *I am so tired. I am so tired.* Egor peels open the sheets. He pulls my blood-stained, ripped T-shirt off. I try to pull it back, try to fight it, but I can't. He wriggles my jeans off. They are rank. The sheets are so clean. Like a hotel.

Egor takes a brown bottle of something, a liquid, and I try to push it away. He shushes me, like I am a child. He dips it onto cotton and lightly dabs it on my wrists.

'This should heal them. It's magic, this stuff.' He grins. He looks kind for a second.

It hurts and I wince. It smells of swimming pools. I think of Lorali swimming in Mr Harley's pond. I could almost laugh. I'm so delirious but it feels good to know my hands are cleaned up. One less thing to worry about.

I dream . . .

It's familiar. But I can't place it. No. Of course I can. It's my . . . my house. But from when I was small. Things are done differently. The couch is the same but brand new, back before it was soiled from the stains of life. The pattern not faded. The mug rings on the arm gone. The carpet is fluffy. The TV is different. Old. Things have moved around.

My old living room. It even smells like how it did. These were my toys. One of my old shoes is there too. A half-drunk cup of orange squash. The radio babbles. I want to call out for my mum.

And then he comes out. From the kitchen. With a big smile on his face and a beer in his hand. My dad.

'Dad!' I shout. I run over to him. Like I am a small child again. I don't know why I do. I want to hold him. Touch his face. Squeeze his beer gut. Breathe in his sweatshirt that smelt of engines and wood and dust and warmth. He looks exactly how I remember him. Blue eyes. A naturally tanned face. White inside the crow's-feet wrinkles branching out from his eyes. A big cheeky grin. Straight teeth. I grab him. Under his arms. How I used to do when I was small. My head dipping into his stomach. Then he would pat my back softly, try to calm me down. 'All right. All right, kid, I'm home now.' He would pretend he didn't care that I was *this* excited to see him. Like it didn't make him want to giggle and cry at the same time. That none of it mattered to him.

I want him to react like that now . . .

. . . but he doesn't.

He doesn't even acknowledge me.

I hug tighter. Clinging.

Has he not even noticed me? Recognised me? *Felt* me?

'Dad? Dad, it's me, Rory.'

He looks right through me. With his cold beer he walks towards the couch, dumps himself down, turns the TV on and checks the football scores. Sips his beer some more. I can see it is cold. The beer. See his fingerprints leave marks on the glass. And he is warm. Even the way he sits, the way he was. It is him. For real.

I am angry with him. But happy to see him too. I miss him. I climb on top of him. 'Dad. Dad. Dad. Dad.' My knees are on him now. He doesn't flinch. He looks through me still. Eyes on the TV. He burps. He blows the burp away. I don't exist to him. I don't understand. I shake him. I shake him some more. He is like one of them soldiers at Buckingham Palace. Not reacting. Not even flinching.

I sit next to him. Try to remain calm. I watch the football scores too. I feel Dad's hand next to mine. His rough, worn worker's skin. His bitten nails. His faded, paint-sodden jeans.

'Dad,' I say softly. 'Dad. I know you can't hear me but I hate you for leaving. I hate it that you have another family with another person. Kids. I always wanted a little sister. I hate it that you don't love Mum any more or love me. That you hurt Mum the way you did. That you embarrassed her like that. That you left without even saying where you were going and that you never came home. But guess what? Mum's strong now. She doesn't need you and neither do I.'

My dad sips his beer. Ignoring every word I say.

I get angrier. 'It's not that I'm a child. I'm not a baby. I don't need you to hold my hand or need your shoulders to climb on. It's just not that hard, is it, really, to say *goodbye*?'

His dull eyes fade into the TV. He sips the beer again. And when I can, I say, 'Maybe for you it is but for me, it isn't. Bye, Dad.'

THE SEA

SLEEPING WORLD
ROLLING ON

Liberty flattens me with the weight of her, like an iron across satin bed linen. I let her crush me. We know our strengths well here. The sun is here because Keppel can feel her daughter in my waters. Opal Zeal is making a TV appearance. She is going to talk about the weather change. Opal's stylist has just presented her with a new sequinned brassiere, with shoulder pads. She loves it and it makes the presentation easier to act.

Deep in my abdomen, under the Whirl, Queen Keppel is shooting clay crabs. She is drunk from the walrus milk. She is biting her lips. Her jewellery rattles every time she shoots an arrow. Bingo is waiting patiently. Zar is hunting whale. Lorali's favourite meal. Keppel has told him she is to return home soon. Her daughter is on water. She can sense it. She is coming home. She could be right, but nobody, of course, can go up to search for Lorali themselves because of the fear of being caught by Walkers. Opal's disappearance is raising further questions. They cannot relax. The council of the Whirl are not happy either. They do not feel safe. Keppel awaits trial. For betraying and not consulting the council before sending Opal up, she is facing being demoted as queen.

Lorali clings to the mast of the *Cetus*. Charging across my salty bodies. She is not afraid. She is strong. She has love in her heart.

The knell rings round her neck. They are coming.

Liberty lets the moonlight guide her. She doesn't have to look far, only follow the plume of black tar smoke that the *Cetus* leaves in its wake.

Otto is combing his hair.

Momo and Oska are smoking, manning the ship.

Jasper is snoring. Face down in his chair. Drunk.

And Egor is sewing. He only has the night to tailor a new suit. The rags the boy showed up in just will not do. Not any more.

Lorali

ON A DREAM

The move to the motion of the ocean. The knell round my neck is on my side and keeping still. I close my eyes. I go down. Remember. My home. Marcia would recognise my ripples and already have the palace open for me. The seal pups would chase me past the gate and into the hall. We'd have been roaming in the petrified forest, playing games, watching the grumpy sad little seahorses bob by. Sometimes we would be on turtle backs, lolling about in the slithers of light, chewing on sea cucumbers or plankton. Marcia would never let me swim up the stairs; she always had to take me herself, letting me climb atop her head. I'd feed her shrimp to say thank you but I think she would have done it even if I hadn't given her anything at all.

Mother would be in her parlour painting old worn bits of metal found in the bottom of the Whirl, or just rocks and stones that she liked. Bingo would often be her subject, posing for her or fetching her refreshments. Zar would be hunting, or playing the bells with his band.

Opal would make visits throughout the day and she would bring her whales. I felt sorry for them because we ate whale regularly but Opal's pod were working whales, trained to protect and communicate. I knew they were smart. I did worry that they might be upset by us. But they never showed it. Opal would have news for us, good and bad. She always looked so cool and she would bring me special gifts or tell me stuff that the Walkers were into. Some of it was hard to imagine – a cinema, an aeroplane, the *Internet*, which was difficult to understand. She would give me bits of Walker make-up but I never dared to use it. Mother wouldn't like that. Opal was like a porthole, a chink in the rock, someone I could talk to.

And my time with Carmine in the forest, reading the notes that Iris had scrawled, editing it accordingly, keeping her own messages, meant for her only. Private.

Myrtle would often visit too, with fishcakes. She would tell me stories. Mostly about the sky. The planets. The stars. The giraffe and how its head is nearly as tall as the sky. After she left I would stand in the rectangular funnel of light that shone through the palace the whole way down. If you angled your head properly at the right time you could see the sun. Or at least its reflection. A teensy glow. Like a broken shell. They say Walkers know more about space than they do about the oceans. I feel like I don't know anything at all.

RORY

REFINEMENT

'RORY! RORY! WAKE!'

In the clean sheets I forget where I am. That sleep felt as though it clutched me close for days. My name. This ship. These sheets.

'Get up, washed and dressed,' Egor says. 'We have a big day.'

'Where are my clothes?' I ask, rubbing my eyes. I feel like a blind mouse. In the new morning I feel stronger but more doubtful. This must be what death row is like. Inevitable. Just living it out. These pirates, not long ago, gave one of my best mates to a bunch of shrieking bird women. How do I even know I'm safe? Still, he is bigger than me. There are more of them than me. And we are at sea.

'Wash first.'

I clamber out of the bunk. The room still smells *posh*. Of polish. And shiny stuff. All the boys must be up already. I can't hear anything or even feel the rockiness of the boat.

Egor shows me to the bathroom. It's white and gold.

Frothing bubbles tower out of a bath. The room smells warm. Like a wood fire. Like a Christmas tree pine. My body craves it.

'You lot bathe in this?' I joke. Egor can make you feel relaxed with his dozy, lumbering stroll.

'Every day, mate.'

'Gosh, it's the life, ain't it?'

'Sure is, cuz.' He laughs without irony. 'Step in. Here's a robe.'

A robe? Why are they being so nice?

'Right, first you need shampoo – that's lemon and coriander in the glass one with the stopper – then conditioner. The silver creamy-looking one, that's almond. It's proper dope. Don't be afraid to go *in* on that bad boy.'

'Right.' I laugh. 'I don't think I need conditioner. I never use it at home.'

'Trust me. Use it.'

'OK. I normally just use body wash. Like . . . for everything,' I explain as if I'm confessing bad habits to a beautician at a parlour.

'None of that here. Dries the skin out. Already in the bath are alpine and frankincense drops. That's to keep you grounded, so you don't lose your head – smells like church, right? Use the oat bran to scrub the sea salt off your skin, and then the mitt with the camomile, almond and aloe essence to moisturise. Soak, my man. Let me know when you're done.'

I hide myself in the bath. I want every part of me covered. I imagine what it must be like to have a life completely immersed in water. Everything so weightless and soft. I hold my breath and go under. See how long I can last. Drowning out everything. Only hearing my heart. Time slips away.

'Rory? Rory! You all done?'

Agh! 'Yeah! Sorry!' I have lost track of time. I scramble out clumsily.

'Chill. You're bless. No rush, boss. I'll wait for you out here.'

Egor leads me to another room. A dressing room, he calls it. It is a large purple room with plants and candles. Rap music patters from the speakers. 'Right. Fresh unders. You boxers or briefs?'

'Boxers.'

Egor presents me with a freshly starched set. They are so ironed they could crack.

I panic. 'Oh no, I don't need new ones!'

'What *is* you? We wear new ones every day, boy. You don't get this bossy wearing other people's groin sweat! Jeez! Whack these on.'

Egor ushers me behind a changing screen. I have seen these before in the antique shops in Hastings but never used one for real.

'Don't –'

'Look? No. I wouldn't dare. Man's not a chief. Take the talc, it's lavender and vanilla. But it's not too sweet. You'll see.'

''K, I'm done,' I say, revealing my scrawny, skinny no-hairs-on-chest pasty self. The talcum powder isn't doing me any favours.

'You look flossy, brother.'

I don't. But I almost believe him.

Egor slathers his hands in cream.

'What's this?'

'This is sun cream. Factor fifty.'

'I'm not that pale!'

'Our skin is precious, brother. Look at mine, so dark and I *still* wear factor fifty. Come here.' I go over like a child that wants a parent to see to a cut hand. I think of Mum. I bat tears away. I can't do anything about my circumstance right now. 'Every day,' he tells me. 'All over.' His hands are big and firm. They are not tender and gentle but there is a kindness there. He wants me to feel good.

'OK, now sit. Look at these nails.' He tuts. 'You're worse than Oska. Come.' Egor unravels a leather tool wallet and draws from it lots of little spikes and files. He begins filing. White powdery bone instantly makes new dust.

'How you gonna neglect your cuticles like this, bruv, and expect anyone to take you for real? After all the hard work your hands do for you all day, every day, and no love there. You're on a madness, ain't you?'

'Sorry,' I sniff. 'I never noticed. I didn't even know what a cuticle was.'

Egor shakes his head. He begins to scoop out the dirt from the underside of my nails.

'What you been doing? Climbing trees?'

'Actually, yeah.' I laugh and then so does he. He is quick. But effective. His brows furrow, a cheeky smile on his face. Sometimes he raps along gently to the music.

I feel sick about having to put my old mash-up clothes back on. I am so clean now.

'Where are my clothes?' I ask.

'Oh . . . OK . . .' Egor smiles even broader. 'Man's been busy.'

And then he steps up, so light-footed for his size, and unveils a rail. On it are pressed trousers, a shirt, a vest. Underneath the rail sit boots. Shining. Polished. Laces. Leather.

'I don't know what to say!' I almost whisper.

'Them clothes can't hear you, fool! Get them on!'

Egor helps to dress me. Like the way a tailor does. An extra help and a hand here and there.

'This is a granddad shirt.' He brushes my shoulders. 'You see where there's no collar and a top button? Fits you like a glove.'

'Where's it from?' I admire the material, looking for a label.

'I made it, bruv.'

HE IS SO COOL.

'Let's hope these babies fit. Step in, I've cut some slack round the waist in case we need to adjust, but I think it's a good 'un.'

The trousers slide on like skin.

'Oh, Egor, they are wicked.' I am desperate for a mirror. I wish Mum could see me. I wish Lorali could see me. I wish Dad could – 'And I'm not even going to a funeral or a wedding or *anything* – this is just for a normal day?'

'Just for a normal day, although we don't get those much round here. Sit.'

I do.

'See, this is why I'm glad we got you and not that Elvis kid; see the yellow heads on that boy?' Egor laughs. 'I was thinking, *What me gonna do with dat?*' I crack up with laughter. 'You get what I'm saying.'

'Oil.' He combs it through my hair and makes a slick side parting. It smells like dark fruits. 'You got that smell? Good, huh? From my home town.'

He reaches for the buzzer. I gulp. I haven't had a shaved head since I was a kid, and even then I looked like a convict.

'Wait –'

'Cuz, you nearly died yesterday. Worse, nearly yammed up by some crazo chicks. What's a little trim and fade gonna change?'

I nod and he buzzes away. My hair falls to the floor.

A little ointment on the neck and wrists and I am ready to meet the mirror.

I look like a *boss*. As Egor would say. That is all.

'Easy,' Otto says as we reach the deck. I feel like a fraud in front of him, an imposter. I prepare myself, in case he laughs at me and makes me feel stupid for playing dress-up. But he doesn't. He grins, as though I've always looked like this, like him.

HASTINGS REACH

5 September

LOCAL BOY RIPPED FROM MOTHER'S ARMS BY 'BIRD WOMAN'

Another Hastings teenager has been reported as missing. Rory Francis, 16, was last seen by his mother, Cheryl Francis, as they stood together on Hastings beach. Mrs Francis said that her son was physically 'torn' out of her arms by a 'bird woman', which she said appeared 'from out of nowhere'. This alleged event follows the disappearance of Francis's friend, sixteen-year-old casino worker, Elvis Caine. The two cases are thought to be linked although there were no eyewitnesses to the disappearance of Caine. Online reaction has signalled that the disappearances are not coincidental but 'organised' and are following a pattern.

HASTINGS GAZETTE

5 September

'BIRD WOMEN STOLE MY SON' CLAIMS LOCAL WOMAN

Victim of depression and Hastings local, Cheryl Francis, 41, has reported her son, Rory Francis, as missing after a 'flock of bird women' swooped down 'from out of nowhere' and snatched him away. Mrs Francis's psychological state is an open secret in the town. Neighbours have described her as 'distant' and 'in a dream-like state'. Others say she is constantly 'off her head' on sleeping tablets and antidepressants.

Mrs Francis said the last she saw of her son was in the grasp of the bird women, 'winging it across the sea' to an unknown location, fighting for his life. Mrs Francis was found by the cliff side, shouting her son's name and holding one of his trainers. Her car was also on the scene, despite her licence having been revoked. There are no eyewitnesses to support Mrs Francis's story.

RORY

SAILING

The sea is massive. My god. The sea is MASSIVE. I had no idea. I'm not even sure where we are now as the sun smashes us in the face like a wrecking ball of fire.

'Do you want me to do anything?' I ask Oska, who is steering the ship. Not that there is anything I *can* do to try to look less useless and keep busy.

'Nope,' he replies, fag in mouth, eyes wincing at the clear view ahead. 'Just chill, I got it.'

I walk over to the front of the boat. I spread my arms out. Close my eyes. For a moment I can almost pretend I am in a different life. That I am strong. Fearless. Indestructible. Fierce. Not afraid. Not hurt by Elvis or missing Mum or worried for Lorali. But I am none of those things. I am terrified. The water occasionally spits me in the face with a spritz of ice-cold sea. But it feels good. In the heat and that. Every way you look there is nothing. For miles. Just blue. Blue. Blue. Blue. Every shade of blue you could ever imagine. Without the disruption of pylons or cranes or wires or the sound of sirens. Just emptiness, but everything at the same time. It is a lot to take in. I wonder why these pirates took me with them? Why they didn't leave me to rot with Elvis? Was I useful? A bargaining tool? A device? Or maybe . . . was it so far-fetched to think that maybe they might like me?

And then, out of nowhere, next to me, but below in the water, rises the body of something huge. Just the back – must be a whale; I've never seen a whale in real life. But it keeps going. The size of it! No, can't be a whale. Too long. Too grey. Too scaly . . . It is still moving, gliding past, never-ending.

I gasp. Stumble back. 'What . . . what was that?' I shout to Oska.

'What?'

'That great huge mammoth thingy that just swam by. It looks like a . . . giant . . . sea . . . lizard!'

'Oh!' He laughs. 'That's a slizard.'

'Huh?' The wind is stealing his words.

'It means we don't know the name of it but it's this hench *sea lizard* thing that swims around here. HUGE! And it eats men! Oh all the great brave souls are lost to the belly of the slizard!'

'Slizard. Got it. And it eats . . . men, you say?' I gulp. A slizard. I do not want to be meeting one of those.

'I'm having you on, you fool.'

'Oh! Phew!' I laugh awkwardly.

Oska cracks up too. 'Ha ha! Proper got you, didn't I? A slizard!'

My laughing slows. 'So if it's not a slizard, what is it?'

'I don't actually know.' Oska sighs and that just makes us laugh harder. Together. Creasing up, tears coming out of our eyes.

I look over at Jasper. He looks at me cold and then back down at the fishes he is scaling. We still haven't said a word to one another since I've joined the ship. There's something about him that gives me the feeling he doesn't like me, so I leave him be.

I feel the weight of an arm thrown around my shoulder. 'Let's not waste time.' Momo smiles. 'Have you ever held a sword before?'

'I beg your pardon?'

'A shank? A blade?'

'Huh? What?'

'A jook? A knife?'

'Er. Only to . . . you know . . . butter toast with.' I sound like a right goon.

'How about a pistol? You ever held a gun?'

I gulp. 'No.'

'Come.'

I follow Momo to the bunker. He opens a door to a room that is, honestly, just filled with guns and explosives.

'I'm gonna show you how to blow stuff up.'

THE SEA

TROUBLED WATERS

Liberty, the old soul, is going at her fastest pace, but there is slim chance she can ever catch up with the *Cetus*. Her sails, although loved dearly, are taking a beating from the remorseless wind. It seems the wind is biased and has decided to back the deadly crew. Shame. *Liberty*'s salt-chewed beams are decaying, rotting, but the boys ride her well still.

Meanwhile, across the way, the *Cetus* are devouring me. Hacking at my surface, raking my guts and spewing darkness back at me. Thick. Heavy. Oil. Regurgitating unnatural dark hateful, harmful spool. A skull-and-crossbones flag drags behind them. Their waste on my tongue. But greed leads them on. Eyes forward or on the girl at the front. Who is mostly naked. In and out of sleep. They have no idea the floating house is on their trail.

RORY

BECOMING A PIRATE

'Oh no, no, no, you don't. I've just dressed the boy. Look how cris
he looks.' The silhouette of Egor in the doorway interrupts us.

'Egor, the boy needs to know how to *fight*,' Momo says
defensively.

'*Fight?* Why?' Egor tuts. You can see he hates the word. He
is a tender person, I realise.

'In case we go into battle.'

'And in that case, *we* can do the fighting.'

'Just some basics. For protection.'

'He knows the basics. He's got the basics. His mind. His
experience. He shouldn't even need to reach for a weapon.
Remember, a weapon is last –'

'*Last* resort. I know, I know. I just wanted to, you know . . .
educate.'

'You mean, behave like a little boy. Go read him one of your
poems instead Momo. Do something productive.'

Momo does as he is told. I've noticed the power Egor has

aboard. Momo sighs deeply as he puts the gun in his hands down. I recognise his embarrassment. I have felt like that a million times before, when you think you are more responsible or cool than you are. Your pride is knocked. Bit by bit I am seeing bits of myself in all of the Ablegares and it kind of feels good to relate.

I help Momo lock up the weapon room; he moans about Egor's authority for a bit, how Egor should be taking advice from him as he is *clearly* the best pirate on board and then he slaps an arm round my back, joking, and tucks me in close, his beard hairs tickling my cheek.

'Oi.' Momo sniggers. 'Shhhh. Don't tell.' And in my top pocket he places a small grenade. 'You never know when this might come in handy.'

My chest ticks with the pressure of the baby bomb by my heart and what I could do with it.

Up on deck I relax. We drink vodka. It's so frozen you can't even taste the alcohol. I don't know where I am in the world or even the time of day.

'Have you ever been in love, Rory?' Momo asks me.

'I, errr . . .'

'Course he has, you moose!' Oska butts in. 'He loves that girl. Lorali. The mermaid.' The colour of my cheeks must speak for me.

'Yeah. I dunno. I can't explain . . . I'm just . . . proper glad she came into my life and to think of her . . . you know . . . suffering, kills me. I just want to be next to her and make sure she's OK. I wish I could make things better. I want to hold her . . . be near her. All the time. Without sounding weird. Does that sound weird?'

Momo grins. 'No, it sounds like *love*.'

'We'll get her back, don't worry,' Oska chips in.

'And when you do . . . what happens then? You lot are obviously looking for her too . . . so . . . what's in it for you?'

'Aww. You are a good kid, Rory,' Egor reassures me, but Jasper sniggers to himself. It's a noise I don't like. It makes me think further about why I've come this far. Maybe I am wrong to think of them as my friends or trust anything they say to me, but it is so difficult when they make me feel so at home. Like one of them.

'Ignore him.' Egor winks at me just in time and then I hear Otto's boots clapping over. 'See that dark spot there in the distance?'

I don't see it. 'Errrr . . . no.'

'Yes, just there ahead, a tiny spot.'

'Really sorry, Otto, I can't see it.'

'Look for the smoke, grey smoke, like a little fire. Can you see it now?'

And suddenly, out of nowhere, as though it was there all the time, the smoke appears and below it a dark, black, almost burnt-looking ship.

'Yes!' I say. 'I see it now. I don't know why I couldn't see it before; it's like it appeared out of nowhere.'

Otto shakes his head and laughs. 'I know.' He sniffs, stretching, rubbing his tummy, almost acting disinterested, like it's no biggie. 'That's the *Cetus*. They've got Lorali.'

'What?' I panic. 'There? Well, what do we do?'

'We eat, of course.'

THE SEA

CLOSER

Rory is one of them now. He is fitting in. Nicely, I see. The role suits him. They drink little flat whites and eat silly spiced knots of pastry studded with currants and orange peel. They take vitamins. Evening primrose, omega-3, iron, vitamin C. But the boy, after food, doesn't look so certain any more. He has said too much maybe about the girl. What makes him think he can trust these Ablegares? How is he so certain that they aren't about to use him as a pawn to win back the princess? How does he know they aren't going to leave him high and dry? Just because they have fed him, bathed him, put clothes on his back and given him a bed to sleep in does not mean they are his friends.

RORY

RAGING

The wind is really bad now. I don't want it to knock my great new hairstyle out of place. It's hard to look cool when it's so windy. The vodka from earlier has put me in a bad mood. My nose is also sunburnt from the early sun, even through the factor fifty.

I look around. The Ablegares seem to be doing a pretty good job of looking cool still, so I guess I just have to assume that the same applies for me.

It is annoying me now that I can see where Lorali is but can't get to her. Can't help her. I remember when I used to watch people playing the vending machines at Elvis's arcade. They would put all their money in to win some dumb poxy teddy that probably only cost a quid in the first place. The metal claw would always open up, like a big grasping hand, and it would always, *every time*, drop. Scoop up the head of the teddy bear and then drop it at the last minute. People couldn't understand how they were so close and yet so far in the same moment.

I start to feel proper sick.

THE SEA

A STORM

The whirling, purring wind is smashing now. The young boy, the new recruit, is being sick over the side of *Liberty*. Little undigested raisins are sliding out of his retching throat. Momo has fixed him some ginger but it isn't working. I am too rocky now, no thanks to the howling sky. There is just some weather that seems to be out of Queen Keppel's control, especially when it comes to a flapping little boat in the middle of the ocean. And her excitement of a potential homecoming from her beloved daughter means room for neglect.

We begin to fight. The wind and I. Horns locked. Battling each other with elements. I curve and swamp and chop and foam. It snatches and rips and slaps and sucks. I fold and drop and scoop and leap. It rummages and roars and invades and steals. All the while, little lady *Liberty* trembles and quakes, and her limbs shake, and then she lets me into her home.

I don't want to be there. *I'm sorry, Liberty*, I even whisper in the shushes of my salty swallow as I enter the hold. The undergarments. 'I'll make this as quick as I can.' I try to hold back as she breaks a little more under my weight. The Ablegares are screaming. The boy is inside now. Told to concentrate his vision onto something. *Focus. Don't lie down.*

And the wind still blows and torments. I fight back. The sky crackles. Rain falls. Nasty. But water I can deal with. The sky frowns, whipping up mousse-like clouds. Thunders. I arch. Try to bend. To stop each crash from impacting the boat. They hold on tight to their mother. She tilts. She is going. The wind is stretching. I can't help it. I am eating her. I don't want to taste *Liberty*. I don't want to take her down with her boys. Not today. Not like this. I want this unfolded story to be put to bed properly. I want to see the end. How it will play out. Still the wind forces its weight. Like slamming a door on a loved one over and over again. The weight. The force. The power. I am meant to buckle here. Capsize *Liberty*. Devour her. Squash her like machinery. Until she splinters and the boys all perish. Until the sails rip off. Snatched into the mouth of the whisk. No more Rory. No more Lorali. No more Ablegares. No more *Liberty*. Over. Done.

But I cannot. I cannot let that happen. In all my existence I have never broken the rule.

She doesn't fall. I don't wait on fate. I oppress. I become strict. I reinforce. I strengthen. I shouldn't. I turn myself to ice. *Liberty* slides to safety.

Lorali

THE CAVITIES

After the storm they decide to hang me up again. They want me to be *grateful* to be taken inside, but I am not. I am not grateful to be kept inside a dark box, shuffling and scraping and scratching around. I would be grateful if they let me go. If they killed me.

RORY

A BAD HAIR DAY

I look a mess. In the mirror. I am green. White. My eyes. All veiny and blood-vessely. I look like some drug addict. My mouth tastes like battery acid. I spit again. Brush my teeth again. Spit. Chew the chalky powdery pill that Oska gave me. I am so grateful and surprised to be alive. I have to move with these boys. Where they go, I go; I have no other choice. I have to believe in them. That they are going to help me. Why would they show me this much sympathy if they weren't? Why would they behave normally in front of me, as though I am one of them, if they are planning to backstab me?

Up on deck the boys are fixing *Liberty*. Otto has been crying, it seems. He clearly cares very deeply for his ship. It hurts him to see her falling apart.

He puts on a bright welcoming face when he sees me. 'Ah, there he is! The man of the match! Feeling frowsy?' He puts on a smile.

'Is there anything I can do?' I ask, hoping for a job of any kind – cleaning the toilet, *anything*.

'What can you do?' Otto looks at me like he is inventing a job for me inside his head; he knows I don't know how to fix up a ship.

'I can make tea?' I suggest.

'Tea!' Otto beams. 'What a great idea.'

Egor winks at me as I head to the galley to make the pirates tea. Lorali was right. We do love boiling water.

THE SEA

A SPANNER IN THE WORKS

The knell has stopped clanging. The *Cetus*'s engine has stopped. The motor has jammed. I can't think for the life of me how that happened.

Lorali

THE KNELL

I must have fallen asleep to the jolting rhythm of the bell round my neck, so when the ringing stops it wakes me. Interrupts my peace. I am able to sleep upright. I never knew a *down* before, so it is OK. But my back hurts. My neck from the positioning of the rope. I am cold. I am thirsty. I am hungry. Why have we stopped? The Cavities begin to swear and curse.

'Sumfin's jammed up.'

'We're broke down.'

'Nah, you *don't* say . . .'

Big puffs of black smoke chug out of the ship. Evaporating into the clear sky like blood in water. I watch the patterns dissolve. So their ship isn't quite as unstoppable as they had hoped. *Chink. Clunk.* We are halted. Black smoke. *Chug. Chug.*

'Get down there, Tush,' one orders another, and we wait. Bobbing. I thought I saw the water turn to ice at a point but

it must have been in my dream. It is getting difficult to tell what is real and what isn't now. In this surreal lucid state, this in-between. I am starting to think that I never made it past the surface at all. That I died. That I am dead. That this is what it is like to be dead. That all this is nothing. This is my punishment for attempting to surface.

'It's a large rock.'

'Must have been from that ice.'

'That was odd, weren't it? All that ice?'

'Gone now though. Stop banging on about it.'

'Get the bleedin' rock out then.'

'I can't. Too stiff. Stuck right in.'

'Try again.'

'Turn the engine on. See if it will flip it out.'

'Wait I'm still down he— WAIT!'

Blood. Crying. The engine has taken one of their arms off. Blood. More blood. Crying. Panic. Shouting. Blame.

'AGHHHHHHH!'

'You idiot! Why didn't you move?'

'Why didn't you wait?'

'AGH!'

'Look at him, his arm's off completely! The bone is showing. Get Wallow to help him. Quick!'

'AGHHHH! HELP ME!'

'He's losing a lot of blood!'

'Stick him over there! His blood's everywhere!'

'MY ARM! AGH! I'M DYING!'

'Did you get the arm?'

'No. Shark feed.'

'AGH! QUICK! HELP! HELP ME! SOMETHING, LORD, GOD, CHRISTOPHER, ANYTHING, HELP, THE PAIN, AGH, MY ARM!'

'There's no god for you.'

'You shoulda waited!'

'KILL ME, KILL ME NOW! I CAN'T! I CAN'T TAKE IT! KILL ME! KILL ME NOW!'

'Get over it! It's just an arm!'

'Wallow, something for the pain.'

'Yes. Lot of blood.'

'Stitches.'

'Pass me that drink.'

'AGH! I'M DYING! WALLOW! WALLOW!'

'Shut him up, will you, I'm trying to get out this damn rock!'

And then I see it. A mist. A white smog. Pouring. Drifting. Flooding over the sky. I can hear the Cavities still fighting. The fiasco and drama of the lost limb is sending shivers down my spine. I hate them all. I HATE them all. I want them all to die. Still the mist swamps us. Covering me. The boat. The Cavities are clumsy. They are laughable. Ridiculous. Pathetic. I don't even respect them as villains.

'Have you fixed it, you numpty?'

'Trying, aren't I?'

'Try harder! Fog coming!'

'What is going on today?'

'Must be them Mer. They knows we gotta treat for 'em brewin'!'

'I need a professional! AHHHH! I need a doctor!'

'Wallow is a professional, calm down!'

'I can't see! I can't see!'

Neither can I. I can't see anything except mist. Underneath the distorted cries of the Cavities I can't hear anything other than the rushes of the seawater beneath me, the sea, who in this instance is my only ally. All I have. The sea I know. I am not afraid.

And then out of the fog. The strangest thing. The sound of music. Music I do not know. Music I have not heard. And then coming through the fog, what looks like a house. An old house. An old-timey house like Opal has shown me. But floating. On the water. How strange and unreal. And it's coming closer and closer.

'FIRE! FIRE! FIRE! FIRE!' shout the Cavities and I can hear them leaving the bleeding man and running to the big cannons they talk about. Blindly. I am tied. I cannot move. Only hope. The ship comes closer and closer. The music plays louder. It is happy music. Grand music. Great big grand music. Here it comes and that is when I see people. Strange-looking males. I see them. Poachers, no doubt. Coming for the sound of the knell. I hope they don't have cannons to blow me up too. They must have seen the *Cetus* all broken down and want to steal. Want tapestries. Me. Well, I have nothing for these men. As they get closer. They don't look too bothered. They don't look angry. Or upset. Can't they hear the cannons? Are they not going to fight back? Are they not going to protect themselves, these young new men? And that is when I see him. Not in *those* clothes. His hair! Can it be him? Really?

Rory.

My love.

And that is when he sees me.

THE SEA

BATTLE

I do like the music. It's good to make an entrance. Don't you agree? Jasper and Momo naturally make the jump first, eager for the battle. They launch onto the deck of the *Cetus* with swords upright. Jasper grits his teeth, with eyes that could gut fish. Momo laughs. Like it's a game. The fog, miraculously, soon starts to lift.

They fight with the Cavities; Jasper is quick and brutal, slicing nippy and to the point. His blade sharp. He likes this painful. Light-footed he shifts, left foot, right foot, his sword cutting through the air at speed, whipping, making no mess as he steals the limbs, hair, fingers and organs of the Cavities.

But the Cavities aren't slow. They are deadly and there are lots of them. They set bloodthirsty snakes out on the deck, hypnotised to despise and crave all the Cavities' enemies. They wind straight towards the dancing feet of Momo. Momo, hot-stepping, is a rapid fighter too, but messy. Likes the theatre of battle. Enjoys the sight of blood. Cuts deep. *Weapons as a last resort.*

'This is what I call a *last* resort!' he shouts up to Egor, who has just landed on the *Cetus*. His nimble fingers are best to untie Lorali. Oska with his older brother steers *Liberty* closer. Rory is there too. Losing his breath to his beating heart.

'Lorali!' he shouts. 'LORALI! LORALI! I'm here!'

And she, the girl, bursts into tears. She is free. Her wrists are sore but she doesn't care about that. Hugging Egor as he picks her up, cradling her. She does not know him but anything is better than the arms of the Cavities. Anything. He carries her away, back onto the breast of *Liberty* if he can.

The Cavities send their women first to fight their battle. Minions. Replaceable, they think. Momo is sliced in the chest. A fanged snake is already whipping up his body to suck the blood of the open slit. A flap of skin. He laughs. Another scratch. His blood dots the boards.

'I hate beating women!' Momo coos. 'Why don't you try to brush your hair once in a while?'

This makes the female Cavity cross, and she swipes more. Anarchic grotty growls seem to scream from their wombs. They use carving knives, butcher hackers, nailed planks – anything with a sharp edge. Jasper is picking off the Cavities like he is cutting the heads of flowers; they almost seem to be appearing from nowhere. More blood oozes into the sewage spillage on the deck.

Cannons continue to fire at *Liberty*. She takes blows, big ones. Her body whines. The boy Rory is brave. He is scared but his eyes remain on Lorali, his eyes ushering Egor to move quicker. She is over his shoulder. Her hair flowing like music.

'Oska, go in. Kill the rest. I'll drive Mama,' Otto instructs.

'Yes, boss,' says Oska, his pigtails bouncing as he leaps into the air, fag in mouth. 'Come, we go!' He scales the mast of *Liberty* and, using the sails like vines, swings his way to the top of the *Cetus*. From here he shoots with a pistol. His aim is good.

Egor is close to the edge but one of the Cavities, a big one, wrestles with him, dragging the girl out of his hands and playing with her like a floppy doll. Lorali kicks and punches. Egor headbutts the Cavity woman, cracks her skull and snatches an eye with his nimble fingers.

Egor looks over to Momo. 'What? Still no weapon!' He winks and dashes the eye to one of the squirming snakes who swallows it down. More cannonballs fall and crash, some biting the heart of *Liberty*.

'Rory, you have to jump. You have to get onto the *Cetus*,' Otto says sternly as they watch on.

'I can't. I'm not leaving you.'

'Go.'

'I can't. I can't fight. I'm useless.'

'Who told you you were useless?'

'I'm not like you lot!'

'Us lot! Listen, *we* were told we were useless. Every day by everybody. Jasper, my baby twin brother, he had enough of that one day.' He thinks about crying, that Otto, but he does not. 'He murdered our own mother for calling us useless. That's how strongly we feel about it. You are not useless. Go get your princess!'

'I'm not leaving you, Otto.'

'Do you know why we saved you, Rory?'

'No.'

'You're just good.' Otto smiles. 'You're just a good boy who is going to grow into a good man. And we are not. We are horrible. It's too late for us to be good men, but you, Rory, you have a shot at it. We saw how your snide little weasel of a friend dicked you over, we felt for you, we took you under our wing and nurtured you and, well, actually, in truth I suppose we do also quite like an adventure. We never were ones to leave the party early. So, oh, go on, please, Rory. Make me a bit of a better man by making yourself one. You're so close. It's just a jump. Here, take this!'

Otto gives Rory his sword. The Ablegare crest is on the handle. A carving of a little house, engraved into the metal. It is heavy for Rory but he is honoured.

'If I take this, what will you have?'

Otto puts on his sunglasses and says nothing, steering his ship.

Rory sees the edge, the lip of *Liberty*. And he jumps. Sword in hand. Lorali sees him jump. Gestures him away. Egor is fending off more Cavities now – men too, although it's hard to tell – the entire crew, it seems, who are grappling with him for the girl. He tries to fight them off.

Lorali is screaming his name so hard – 'RORY, RORY!' – her throat scratches.

Rory has never properly held a sword before. It only seems to be getting heavier. It is. He lifts it in the air. Egor shakes his head. 'Don't use it,' he advises. 'Use your head!'

Use your head? Rory really feels he should at least be swinging this heavy blade about a bit rather than just standing here, but then he sees it in the reflection of the sword: a rowing boat. A small cockboat tied on for emergencies. They could sail away in it. Freedom. Escape. He nods at Egor, who winks back, tipping his head. 'You got it!'

Rory makes his way to the boat and climbs in. Not knowing how to lower it properly, he begins to gently cut the strands of the rope with the sword. Gently, gently, gently. Focus. Work. Work. The boat jolts. Sudden. Has he cut too much thread? Sweat trickles out of his forehead. Then it loosens. The boat slides towards me. Egor, grimacing, screaming, takes a punt, bravely throwing Lorali across the air and landing her in the boat. Perfectly. Next to Rory.

He laughs. So does she, but not for long. He still has to slice the ties of the rope.

The remaining Cavities lunge at them. Pulling at the rope. Screaming, wrestling. The ties are thinning now, the stiff salt-drenched rope beginning to untwine. I make it an easy landing. I don't have to.

'Rory!' she cries. 'You did it!'

They hold each other. Hard. But it isn't over yet.

RORY

LITTLE BOAT, I LOVE YOU

I can't believe it. She is in my boat. OK, not *my* boat, but now it is, kind of.

'I'm not a strong swimmer!' I suddenly, inappropriately throw out there. 'So in case I'm nervous, it's, like, not cos of you or anything . . .' It is true; I'm not a strong swimmer, but my chest is squeezing just being close to her.

I let out a deep sigh. 'OK, OK, oars . . . paddles . . . whatever . . .' I am shaking but I find them. 'I can't even unclip them.' I panic. Lorali helps and manages to unhook them straight away, even with sore wrists.

The water is choppy and there isn't even time to think; I just know we have to get away, but I don't know where to or how long we'll have to row for. I am so terrified even the backs of my eyeballs are pulsating. I can still hear the noises around, the grunts and groans and screams and explosions behind us.

'Are you hurt?' I ask her as I begin to paddle.

'No, not really, are you?'

'No. I'm so happy to see you, I really am.'

'Me too. I thought I'd never see you again.'

The clang of swords, of metal and slicing, is still so loud, and the water so heavy, so difficult to paddle in. I look up and see Egor fighting and Momo too, and Oska shooting and, in the madness of it all, Jasper surprisingly looks down to me and screams, 'Rory, don't look back, don't look back! Go far! Go far!' And I nod as it's the first time Jasper has spoken to me, and I paddle harder and faster with this new strength and encouragement and bombs and explosives are *still* happening and I am happy because they are all alive.

But then, it seems from out of nowhere, more of the Cavities suddenly hurtle from the lower deck to *Liberty*, roaring, swords in the air. The Ablegares are too slow to stop them and the attackers begin hacking into the boat, and before I can think I hear Momo shout, 'The grenade! The grenade, Rory! In your pocket!'

I act quick. Too quick. I do it. Find the small grenade in my inside pocket. The one Momo gave me. I gather its weight and pull the detonator, hurtling it at *Liberty*, aiming for the members of the *Cetus*, and as the cold metal hardness leaves my hand I remember Otto.

It's all too quick. The fog. The fire. The cloud. The ash.

Down.

Floating empty pieces.

Sailing.

The shouting stops.

Momo steps on the last of the snakes' skulls. They crack beneath his boot. He nods at me.

The *Cetus* is bobbing.

The Ablegares stand.

I paddle loosely now. Not as fierce.

'Otto!' Momo screams. 'Where is Otto?'

Nothing comes back.

I paddle back a bit closer.

Otto?

Otto?

'He was still on the boat!' Momo screams. 'Did you know he was still on *Liberty*, Rory? Rory? I thought he had got off!'

Lorali

RORY

'Leave him. He's gone!' I shout. 'Row. Row. Row!'

I grab the oars. They are too heavy for me to row alone. I try to turn them as much as I can. We have to get away. 'Rory, row. Come on, row, row. We have to get away!' But he doesn't seem like he can. He is bound. To these, these pirates. I force the oars into his tightened grip and try to close his palms round them.

'I just want to make sure he's OK. Let me just make sure Otto's alive,' he says gently but sternly. His hand holds mine and his touch makes me know this is important to him. I nod. 'Momo. Momo told me to. Momo . . .' he mumbles. But I know Otto is gone.

'Otto!' he shouts. 'Otto!' But it is over. It is clear. The rafters of that sailing house floating. What a beautiful sight she was. Now drifting. Down. In pieces. After the explosion.

One of the boys, the pirates, leaps into the water; he dives down and searches through the broken ship. Under. Down. Watching his head emerge each time makes me swallow. Deep.

Hard. I can taste the sea on my lips. He doesn't look at my Rory once.

Under again. Another breath. It's like we all take a breath with him. Find him. Come on. Find him. So we can leave. So we can escape. So we can go home. So we can go back home to Hastings. He didn't mean to. He didn't mean to hurt anybody.

And then he finds him. *Otto*. Asleep. No. Gone. But it wasn't Rory's fault. He was instructed. He was told what to do. He was trying to help.

And then it happens. Before Rory can even react. Right then. Rory is shot.

He falls backwards out of the little boat. No. No. No. No. He falls into the water before I can catch him. My arms and hands have no choice but to follow in after him. The sea salt hurts my cuts from the rope. But I don't feel. Not really. I shake. Shake. He is silent. His blood already losing itself. Like sand, dancing. Like seaweed, floating.

'Rory! RORY! It's OK. I've got you, I've got you.' I hold him. The boat is tipping with the weight of us. I am flapping. Boiling. Burning. Rage. Love. 'I love you. I love you. I've got you. It's OK. It's all right. I love you. I love you and I won't let you go.'

But he is heavy for me. He doesn't understand. He doesn't come back. He doesn't hear me. His eyes are closed. He looks young in the water. Beautiful. I don't recognise him. In those clothes. That way. That hair. My love. I love you. I love you. I want to fall in too but I don't know if I can swim in there and he's too heavy.

'I don't want to know who my father is! I don't care if I find him any more because I found you! You are all I need!' I cry. Hard. I don't care what they think of me. 'Please don't leave me!'

If only somebody would just help me. I'm shouting. Yelling. Screaming. Not making sense. Talking in another language it seems. My mouth too slow. Or too fast. Talking from the heart. And then before I know it. That one, that big one who untied me, with the hair, he is somehow in the boat too. Only felt the weight changed and before I know it he is holding me and he puts a hand deep down, right into the water, on Rory's neck, two fingers, right on his vein. Where the blood pumps. And he is telling me to let go. He is telling me to let go. That I have to. I don't want to. He calms me down. He says, 'It will be OK. But you have to let him go now.'

'How do you know he is dead? He isn't dead! He might be alive!' His hands are forcing mine to let go of him but I don't want to, I can't. He's my Rory. 'How do you know he is gone? How do you know he isn't alive? Check!' I scream. 'Check again! Check again! Why don't you check again!'

'I know he's dead,' he says. 'Oska never misses a shot.' And then he looks up to Momo who shakes his head in remorse, itching his beard, wondering if the pistol will be aimed at him next.

RORY

OTTO

I don't like seeing the little scabs round her wrists. Little cuts. I'll clean those up for her. Like Egor did for me. Otto won't be dead. He will have found a way. He will have got through the sea. The sea is a breeze to him. *Liberty* won't let him down. She'll have a plan. I just want to check he is OK. Momo didn't know. Momo wanted me to save the day. He didn't mean any harm. Oska was probably only honouring his brother. Nobody wanted to hurt anybody. I know what it's like to fight for love. I don't blame anybody. Even as I realise how vulnerable and fragile I truly am. Just flesh and blood and bone and water. Let's go home now. Let's go home. Back to my mum. She'll be happy to see me and Lorali. Really happy. We could all live together. I'll buy a camera. And we can take photographs of Lorali. And we'll put them in frames. And have them up all round the living room like normal people do. Without the heads cut out.

I am alive. I have never felt more alive. And then for some

reason I'm just not. Not alive at all. And I hear Lorali's screams go from loud to quiet as I fall into the water. Don't scream. Don't scream. It's OK.

THE SEA

SALVATION

The Whirl has never felt a pull like this before. This scent is pure Walker, but why does it feel so true of Mer? Why does the rhythm of Lorali ripple through me the way it does?

Walkers drown all the time. They often die in me but this one is different. A magnetism. A pull. What bravery. What heart. What a good one he was. Such spirit and identity. So pure. So pure that even I warmed up when I felt him fall. His glow. Like the rich sun. And even my beasts leave him for the Mer; they know he is precious, worth saving, and don't dare take a bite of him. He falls into the hunting ground of a Mer, and the empty desperate haunting hole of Lorali within Zar is what draws him close, makes him go that extra mile the moment he decides to do what he does. When he doesn't come home with a whale for Lorali's welcome home dinner, but a young boy instead, one he has decided to salvage. In smart trousers, a white shirt and with a puncture to the chest, his memories already are nothing but foam on my surface.

THE SEA

EPILOGUE

One year later

I am the sea air.

I sift, like a spray of stars.

Time has passed and things have changed.

Let me show you around.

You want to go under first? Very well, let me lead you. Hold your breath, human. Five-four-three-two-one . . .

Mer culture is protected and safe. Opal, from a salt pool in her ground-floor mansion flat in Kensington (very nice actually, Farrow & Ball Elephant's Breath-coloured walls and Conran Shop interiors) kept her promise, and the Whirl is a sanctuary. Still and sound. King Zar sits on his throne at his palace. His strength and kindness weakened the council of the Whirl to grant him the position of king after Keppel's rash, selfish and thoughtless disloyalty to her kind. He is the first merman to hold such a position. This is revolutionary. He flourishes. And does what all good leaders do when facing an obstacle. They lead. Guiding, supporting, diffusing. Gently dissolving the tension. Calming the weather and the spinning Whirl to make it impossible for Walkers to visit. He's a tonic, a rationaliser. Balanced. Leads accordingly. It was about time my waters freshened up. A good leader is a good leader, regardless of their sex.

Keppel tends to the garden. Hunts. Grieves for her daughter still. For her throne still. Collects.

And then there's the boy. Zar's salvation. His first salvation too. So young. But already making waves. Here he is now, playing with the pups. Not long until he will be ready for his resolution. As with every Mer there are triggers for memory, aren't there . . .?

Above water, the town of Hastings has become itself again. The summer is long and warm. The market is full. The cobbled streets are busy and bustling. Whipped ice cream on paper-light cones, cawing gulls and laughing dogs. The crackle of fried fish and the stench of malted-vinegar chips on the dirtied nicotine- and coin-stained fingers of the fairground workers. Salt in the air. The greyness has lifted. Through the keyhole, there she is. Lorali. Fully grown. A Walker. Walking. Running. Her room simple. Just as Rory had it. The windows are open, music playing. She and her adopted mother are singing together, taking turns to do the lead vocal. They will be having dinner together on the patio. It's a nice evening and they've fixed the lawn. They talk as they stir the pots and pans, chinking wine glasses. Iris and Flynn are coming over too. They've brought chocolate mousse for desert. They talk of Rory, whom they miss desperately, but always with laughter and fond memories of their brave boy, who they think of every day. Bound by their love for him. After dinner they walk down to the beach. The sun is lowering in the late-evening pink sky. Although Carmine has been helping him, they still know it's too soon for Rory to write, but they often find themselves at the trunks of the petrified forest. Just in case.

But today is no ordinary day.

There, on the trunk, a new circle has been engraved. Inside, two grooved words, and Lorali, who has been taught to read by Flynn and her adopted mother, says the words from Rory aloud . . .

I REMEMBER.

Acknowledgements

Thank you to the Cathryn Summerhayes and Becky Thomas and all the staff at WME. Especially Siobhan and Antonia for the readings of the initial chapters.

Thank you to Sarah Odedina and Meg Farr for welcoming my glittery boots into the Hot Key Books keyhole.

Thank you to my agents at United Agents: Jodie Hodges, Julian Dickson and Jane Willis for all of their hard work.

A very big thank you to the Hot Key Books team. The talented Jan Bielecki for the beautiful twinkly cover art. Thanks to Sanne Vliegenthart for her amazing creativity, and Jennie Roman for the copy-edit. To the WONDERFUL press and marketing team, Rosi Crawley and Jennifer Green, for their fantastic, hysterical and bravely ambitious ideas (and the framed merman on your wall. One day we WILL eat sushi on his hairy gut!).

Thank you, Jenny Jacoby. My knight in shiny shoes, stripy top and blue frock. You rocked up, slayed all the monsters and made me love my book. You are more than oven gloves.

Thank you to my friends and family for listening to the ideas and letting me be a bit of a hermit with this book. I appreciate that. This is for you. I owe you all a drink. Obviously.

Thanks to my pug, Pig, for being patient when my brain was lost out at sea and all you wanted was a walk in the park.

Thank you to my readers. So glad you came back for more of the madness. I hope you like what you read. See you soon.

Laura Dockrill

Laura Dockrill is a poet and novelist whose wonderfully inventive and creative approach to life is reflected in the rich and vividly imagined worlds she creates. Laura lives in London, and you can follow her on Twitter @LauraDockrill.

HOT
KEY
BOOKS

Thank you for choosing a Hot Key book.

If you want to know more about our authors
and what we publish, you can find us online.

You can start at our website

www.hotkeybooks.com

And you can also find us on:

We hope to see you soon!